MW01230209

MIDNIGHT JONES

PRESENCE UNKNOWN, PARANORMAL INVESTIGATORS #1

BY MAIA STRONG

This is a work of fiction. All the characters and events portrayed in this novel are fictitious. While some of the locations are real and can be found today, others have been renamed and/or relocated for the purposes of this book, and sadly some are no longer with us. #VanishingSeattle

© **2021 by Maia Strong**

All rights reserved, including the right to reproduce this book, or portions thereof, in any form, except in case of brief quotations embodied in critical articles or reviews.

Cover art by Jocelyn Grant

ISBN-13: 978-0-9884004-5-0

*For Madison, Colleen,
and everyone else who has told me
a true ghost story.*

Chapter 1

"NO, MA'AM."

Pause.

"I understand it can be quite upsetting, but I'm afraid I can't help you with that."

Pause.

Ben rolled his eyes behind his rectangular, metal-framed glasses as the woman nattered on over the phone.

"You need to call the UFO Hotline. They'll be more than happy to take your statement, and—"

She interrupted and he covered the mouthpiece of the telephone's handset so she wouldn't hear his exasperated sigh.

"Do you have a pen?" he asked when she stopped for breath. Before she could reply, he rattled off the spaceship spotters' 800 number. It had been months since he'd had to look it up for anyone or even glance at the sticky note on the edge of his computer screen where he'd scrawled the number once upon a time. Enough calls by misguided people like the woman on the other end of the phone line had burned the number into his memory. Why was it that so many people couldn't seem to grasp the difference between "paranormal" and "extra-terrestrial"? It was a question for the ages, and one that was unlikely ever to be solved.

"That's right." Ben repeated the number a little slower so she might actually have a chance of writing it down.

"You call them, and they'll help you out. And keep that number handy. I recommend sticking it to your refrigerator with a magnet"—*with one of those big-eyed aliens on it, probably*—"so it'll be easy to find the next time you see something. Thank you for calling Presence Unknown, Paranormal Investigators." He emphasized the last part and had no doubt the woman didn't notice. "If you ever experience something more earthly in nature, please give us a call."

His reflexively polite smile vanished the moment the handset hit the cradle.

"Another one?" asked Frieda, although the answer was obvious. Seated at the scarred old desk in the corner of the cramped room, she'd easily overheard his half of the conversation and the annoyed tapping of his pen against his leg.

Ben stared at her, eyebrow raised, and chucked the pen he'd been fiddling with into the broken-handled coffee mug that sat next to his monitor.

"Right," she said. "Gods, but people are stupid."

"How did the game go? Is it still on?" asked Ben, not wanting to rehash the same old grievances about the idiots of the world. The thought of the massive number of them was just too damned depressing for a dark, wet October night.

Frieda's expression was enough of an answer, but she filled in the details for him anyway. "Lost it in twelve. Shitty way to start the playoffs, but there's always tomorrow. We just need three out of five. There's plenty of time."

"Since when did you become an optimist?" He quirked a smile at her as if she needed reassurance he was teasing her. She returned the look with a pursed-lipped smirk of her own.

"Ever since we made the playoffs for the first time in far too fucking long. Don't worry. I'll revert to my cynical self by November. Solstice at the latest."

Ben leaned forward, resting his elbows heavily on his desk, his knees hitting the keyboard tray beneath it just like they always did. "So what are you watching now?"

"*Ghost Hunters.* I missed last week's new episode."

He made a disgusted noise somewhere between a grunt and a snort. "Why do you watch that show?"

"Just because you're bitter about that Eastside church hiring them instead of us doesn't mean it isn't a good show. They know their shit."

"I know, I know. It just pisses me off that people in Issaquah would rather hire someone from the other coast than support the local economy by hiring, you know, *locally.*"

"Ben, those guys have serious tech and their own cable television show. We can't match that."

"Don't remind me." He tried not to be jealous, but it was tough.

"So it was a slow summer. We did have that one job the other night, remember."

"I know. Adam and I are taking the data to the client later this week."

"See? And we're only just getting into October. Someone's bound to spot a spook and give us a call any night now. You know how incidents increase the closer we get to Samhain."

"Yeah, but those are just seasonal hauntings." Ben had a love-hate relationship with October, and at present the irritants outweighed the positives inherent in more business. "Single events that we'll end up being unable to debunk or confirm. It's so unsatisfying. We're overdue for a proper haunting. Something we can dig our teeth into and really investigate. That church gig would have been so perfect for us!"

"Oh my gods, let it go. I love you, but seriously. Stop."

The shop's obnoxiously loud doorbell caused them both

to jump. Frieda leapt to her feet. "Must be dinner. I'll get it." She pushed past the velvet curtain, a cut-down remnant of theatrical masking, leaving him in the quiet.

Ben stretched out his long legs, the spring in the old wooden desk chair creaking with the motion, and stood. He stretched up onto his toes and reached overhead until the tips of his fingers brushed the low ceiling. By the time he sat again, Frieda was back with a paper grocery bag that smelled deliciously of peanut sauce, coconut, and spices.

She set the bag on the corner of her desk and unfolded the top, popping the staples that held it shut. "Mmmmm! How much do I love that My Thai delivers?" She started to unpack the bag.

Ben was already fishing silverware out of his desk drawer. "Did you get my *tom kha gai?*"

"Would I fail you?"

"Three stars?"

"Three stars," echoed Frieda, lifting the large, insulated container from the bag.

Ben smiled. "Then hand it over, please."

She used both hands to pass the steamy soup to him and then followed it with a box of white rice.

"Thank you." He popped the lid and took an intoxicating sniff. "Ahh!"

Frieda dug into the bag and pulled out a white carry-out box. "And there's my Swimming Rama, three stars with brown rice. Mmm." She inhaled the spicy peanut scent and sighed happily. "Perfect."

"Is there tea?"

"Oh yeah! Sorry. Here." She passed him one of the two cups of Thai iced tea from the cardboard cup holder and a napkin, and then finally sat down at her desk to eat her supper.

"You know," said Frieda around a mouthful of fried tofu and steamed spinach. "Tonight I'm okay with it being quiet."

"Me too," agreed Ben. He was tired enough that he supposed a slow night wouldn't be so bad. "As long as no more UFO idiots call."

On cue, the phone rang. Ben glared at it, and Frieda, taking pity on him, reached over to his desk and answered it.

"Presence Unknown, Paranormal Investigators. How can I help you?"

Pause.

"Let me give you the UFO Hotline... Yes, it's an 800 number... Do you have a pen?... Yes, I'll wait while you find one." She rolled her eyes at him, and Ben had to cover his mouth to stifle his snickers. She made a face and mouthed, *Fucking flying saucer freaks.*

Ben burst out laughing.

Chapter 2

JOHN LENNON BURST FROM THE SPEAKERS, BEGGING TO be pleased.

Todd reached out and hit the last preset button on the old-fashioned car radio, tuning it to the local alternative station. Smashing Pumpkins came blaring out at him, and he turned down the volume before hitting the third preset button. "That's better," he muttered as U2's "Sunday Bloody Sunday" played. "Now why can't you go for this sort of rock 'n' roll? Not that I have anything against the Beatles, of course," he continued, shifting his classic Volkswagen Beetle into reverse and checking his mirrors. "The Beatles are great. They're just not what I'm in the mood for right now. It's when you feel the need to play the Beach Boys or Paul Anka that I take issue."

Despite having left the car in the garage all day, it was so cold he could see his breath. He shivered and was glad for his leather gloves on the hard-plastic steering wheel. It would be a couple of miles before the engine was warm enough for him to bother turning on the heater.

It was tough to see around the big old trees in the parking strip in the darkness and the heavy drizzle of rain, but there were no telltale headlights in view, so he judged it clear. He backed out of the driveway onto the narrow residential street, again glad he'd chosen to buy this house and not that one on Twenty-third that his ex,

Michael, had been so set on. Fabulous as that house had been, the prospect of backing out onto that big arterial every time he wanted to drive somewhere still gave him the willies. Risk his beloved '63 Beetle—the car that he'd spent so much time, energy, and money restoring—every time he needed to get out of his driveway? No thanks.

Todd much preferred the older house, on a quiet residential street, he'd eventually purchased. He'd needed a new project once he was done restoring his vintage car, and it had provided ample opportunities from rewiring to bring it up to date and up to code, to remodeling the entire upper floor into the perfect master suite.

He shoved the memory aside and went on chatting to the car. "What was up with you yesterday, anyway? Was it Lesley Gore's birthday or something?" It would explain why the oldies station seemed to be playing her stuff every time he'd gotten into his car, which had been a lot; it had been his errand-running day. Of course it didn't explain why the radio kept finding its way back to said oldies station whenever he was out of the car. The only explanation he'd come up with for that phenomenon was the reason he was talking out loud even though there was no one else in the vehicle. At least no one he could see.

His car was haunted.

"Although that one song. What was that? The one about 'Judy's turn to cry'? That was pretty funny. Is it a sequel to 'It's My Party' or something? It sure sounded like it." He chuckled. "Every teenage girl's revenge dream, that song. Although, man, girls sure cried a lot back then, didn't they? I mean, judging from some of those old songs, high school in the 1960s was nothing but parties and tears." An unpleasant realization hit him. "That pretty much defines high school in any decade, doesn't it? It did when I was there. Well, parties, tears,

and cliques, really. Ugh. I wish I'd never thought of that."
He'd hated high school. Bad enough he'd been both a
computer geek and into working on cars—two crowds
that generally didn't mix unless it involved being pantsed
or shoved into a locker or something equally demeaning.
The fact that he had known he was gay well before he'd
hit ninth grade hadn't helped. If only he'd been into
theatre, he might have gotten laid more than once before
going to college. As it was, he knew he was lucky he
hadn't gotten beat up. Being over six feet tall by age
fifteen had helped. So had the street cred he'd earned
from winning friends amongst the rockers and stoners in
his gas engines class.

Home hadn't offered any solace either, not until he
and his mom finally got out and away from his abusive
father. Todd didn't know if the bastard was alive or dead
nowadays. He hoped his father was rotting in a personal
hell somewhere, whichever the case was. His mom might
have forgiven his dad for all the hurt he'd caused, but
Todd wasn't interested in that path.

"Christ," he muttered. How had his mind gotten onto
such a heavy road?

He pushed the past from his thoughts again. Those
days were decades behind him, and he wasn't sorry. His
mom was happily remarried and living with a great guy
in Arizona, and Todd had actually enjoyed his twenty-
fifth high school reunion he'd attended that past
summer. It didn't hurt that he'd done well in the first
Seattle tech boom, and having escaped before the tech
crash, was now the successful owner of an independent
coffeehouse. That looked good in front of old friends and
enemies alike.

Of course, being in charge sometimes meant you had
to do things that no one else had time to get done. Like
tonight. The coffeehouse was nearly out of a few things,
and he'd been unable to make it to the Cash & Carry

before it had closed yesterday. So he was on his way now, armed with a list: stirry sticks, honey packets, napkins, to-go lids made of compostable plastic, whole wheat flour, raw sugar, eggs, milk. Okay, more than just a few things. He'd promised Mona and Shell that he'd have it all waiting for them when they got into work on Tuesday morning, and he would catch hell from both his baker and his business manager if he failed them. Unfortunately, or if he were being honest, *typically*, he'd left it until nearly too late again today. The Cash & Carry closed in less than forty-five minutes. He silently cursed the tied score that had taken the baseball game into extra innings. To add insult to injury, the Mariners had lost it in the twelfth. *That is not the way to start a playoff series,* he thought bitterly. And now, because he hadn't wanted to miss any of the doomed game on TV, he was stuck trying to go from east to west across town while fighting postgame traffic. It was the opposite of smart, but that was what happened when you were a baseball fan in Seattle. Hope sprang eternal, and foolishness was only half a step behind.

To take his mind off his sports-induced idiocy, he continued to talk to the car.

"Or are you just a really big fan of hers? Me, I prefer something a little more edgy. Although, I don't know. Was she considered edgy for her time?" He imagined the sixteen-year-old Lesley Gore had been when her first big hit was released in 1963. "Probably not." Maybe if she'd announced back then that she was a lesbian, she'd have been "edgy", but that revelation had come more than forty years later.

"But on a more serious note," he went on, turning onto the arterial that would take him over the freeway, "we need to talk about the spoons. I didn't mind so much at first. I mean, my everyday flatware isn't anything special. But now you've dipped into the Norwegian silver,

11

and that's not cool. I'd appreciate it if you'd put those spoons back where they belong. Okay?"

He didn't expect an answer, so he was neither disappointed nor surprised when he failed to get one. When it came down to it, he wasn't even sure he was talking to the right ghost. The spoons were disappearing from the house, not the car. Since he'd never had any problem with ghostly shifts of the radio inside the house, there was no real reason to presume this ghost had expanded its territory. He just wasn't ready to consider the possibility that he was being haunted by two completely separate entities. One was plenty, thanks very much. Companionable, even, on nights like this. The idea that an invisible someone was living in his house with him was plain creepy. At least whoever, or whatever, it was seemed to be containing itself to the main floor. If there were any evidence it was hanging out in his bedroom... well, then he would be forced to do something about it.

He conveniently ignored the fact he had no idea what that something might be.

Figuring he'd been driving long enough, he reached out and turned on the heater. Warm air flowed through the vents and he relaxed into it. The drive across the city was tedious, but now that he was warm, it became less disagreeable. He wove his way overland along the sorts of back streets only native Seattleites or people who were lost ever used and arrived at the Ballard branch of the restaurant supply store with ten minutes to spare. Predictably, his car was the only one in the parking lot.

Once inside the store's cavernous fluorescence, he loaded up one of the flat rolling carts with the stuff he needed. It looked a bit small on the big orange pallet and he tried to think of anything else they might be low on.

"Don't be stupid," he muttered. "This is plenty for one trip unless you want to put something in the passenger seat." He loved his restored '63 Beetle dearly, but it wasn't the best vehicle for hauling coffee shop and bakery supplies, and he didn't like loading things into the car proper—especially not things like flour that inevitably left a powdery residue on his leather upholstery. As it was now, the messiest of it would all fit into the luggage compartment with only minimal Tetrising needed, leaving things like lids and stirry sticks to go safely into the backseat.

He also didn't want to take any longer than necessary to load up, what with the rain pouring down outside. At least here there was an overhang in front of the store. He wouldn't have that luxury when unloading at the coffeehouse. He began to think he ought to have grabbed his hooded raincoat instead of his usual leather jacket. He sure as hell should have brought an umbrella. He heaved a small, resigned sigh. Oh well. His hair and jeans would get wet, but at least his Doc Martens would keep his feet dry, and there was a golf umbrella he could use back at the shop.

He wheeled the big cart up to the cash wrap and smiled at the assistant manager, Marco, who currently manned the register. Marco greeted him with a familiar smile and nod. "Hey, Todd, my man. How's it going? You're in late tonight," he said as he scanned each item.

"I'm okay. Damned baseball game went into extra innings," said Todd, his opinion on the outcome obvious in his tone.

"We lost, huh?" Marco was clearly unsurprised.

Todd shrugged. "It's a playoff game and Sweet Lou is not the manager."

"Yeah."

Really, what more was there to say? They'd only made it this far as a wild card team. They *might* make it to the second round of playoffs, but no die-hard fan was going to hold their breath for it. And the World Series? Well, the phrase "pipe dream" came to mind.

Todd paid the bill with his company debit card and took the receipt Marco handed him. "Thanks, dude."

"Next time ask that business manager of yours to run your errands, huh?" Marco said with a grin. "It's always good to see you, but she's way better looking than you, man."

Todd smiled back, familiar with this banter. Marco had been crushing on Shell since the first time Todd had brought her in with him, showing her the ropes of shopping for the coffeehouse. "I'll see what I can do."

"You want a hand out with all this?"

"Marco, it's raining buckets out there. Would I do that to you?"

Marco gave him a grateful smile and nod. "You're all right. Later, man."

"Later."

While Marco locked up the store behind him, Todd loaded up his car as quickly as he could, doing his best to keep the big bags of flour and sugar from getting wet. Mona would rip him a new one if he ruined her supplies before he even got them to her. Occasionally it occurred to him to wonder when he'd started allowing his in-house baker to push him around. Probably it had been the day they'd first met on the playground during recess in the second grade. He smiled at the memory as he slammed the hood shut, ditched the cart under the store's overhang, and got into the car. He turned the key and the radio blared to life along with the engine.

This time it was Brian Wilson, bragging about his little deuce coupe.

He turned the radio off with a decisive click. "What did I *just say* about the Beach Boys? Now you're just being bitchy."

Traffic wasn't any better as he worked his way back across town, but eventually he arrived at the coffeehouse.

He called on the spirit of Doris Day to bring him a parking place in front of the shop. With what seemed to be half the city's population trying to get from the ballpark to their homes, he didn't hold out much hope. To his astonishment, someone was pulling out of a spot only a few steps from the door to Midnight Jones just as he came up to them. "I never should have doubted the power of the mighty Doris Day." He chuckled to himself as he took the spot.

A quick jog around the car brought him to the coffeehouse's door and out of the rain. The bell over the door jingled as he entered, cheerfully oblivious to the dismal weather and Todd's equally dour mood.

Even in the limited light provided by the streetlight across the road, he could tell something wasn't quite right. Shivering as a sudden chill passed through him, he tensed and looked around slowly. At first examination, nothing appeared to be out of place: chairs were upturned on tables just as they were every night at closing time; the framed photos on the walls were undisturbed; the little music stage was empty of all but Willa's second-best amplifier and the old upright piano, its keyboard closed; the bakery case was empty and clean; the condiments counter—

His heartbeat picked up its pace as he crossed the room. Reaching behind the front counter, he flipped the master switch for all the shop's lights. He blinked in the sudden wash of brightness as the whole place was bathed in incandescence.

Relax, Todd thought, taking a deep breath. *Check the dishwasher before you go leaping to any crazy conclusions.* It was ridiculous to think the empty bin that ought to have held spoons was at all sinister. Of course, it didn't help his feelings of unease to note that the bins of forks and knives were fully stocked. A quick look under the front counter and over the big industrial espresso maker deepened his sinking feeling. The little plates for pastries and the various sizes of coffee mugs were all neatly put away where they belonged, as were the assorted accoutrements for the espresso machine itself. Checking the dishwasher in the kitchen was little more than a formality at that point, but he did it anyway.

Empty.

He looked around the kitchen, checked the drawers where Mona kept the baking utensils and other paraphernalia. The only spoons he found were the measuring sort and a couple of industrial-sized ones.

His patience was running thin lately, and with the Mariners losing the game tonight, it was even thinner. He spoke out loud to whatever might be listening, his voice sharp. "Okay. This isn't funny. Messing with me at home is one thing, but you *do not* mess with my *business*. Got it? This. Stops. Here."

"Hey, buddy. Who're you talking to?"

"Gah!" Todd nearly jumped out of his skin. He spun in place to face the voice, his heart racing at break-neck speed. "Shit, Mona! You scared five years off my life!"

"Sorry," she said, peering out from under the hood of her Gore-Tex jacket. "I was walking home from the grocery store and saw your car out front. I figured you were here with supplies and thought you might want some help unloading." Mona lived in the apartment building across the street and a block down. She'd said when she first took the place that she liked the idea of being able to get out of bed and be at work in less than ten minutes. She'd always been one for sleeping as late as she could get away with.

Todd followed her back out into the dining room where she put her two canvas bags of groceries on the front counter. "Thanks," he said. "I could use some help unloading." His heartrate was gradually returning to normal. "I'll get the golf umbrella."

"Good," she called after him as he popped into the shop's tiny office. "They're called 'dry goods' for a reason. I hope you kept them that way when you loaded them into your car."

He emerged with the umbrella as she pushed back her hood to reveal her dark brunette curls, cheerful smile, and mirthful green eyes.

Todd shook his head, sending a light sprinkle of raindrops from his hair to the already damp shoulders of his leather jacket. "That was *once*, years ago, and for bringing it up at all, you get to haul the heavy stuff while I hold the umbrella."

"Pansy."

"Dyke."

They chuckled and went outside where he opened the umbrella under the tiny awning before stepping out into the rain.

"So, who were you talking to, anyway?" asked Mona as she easily lifted a fifty-pound bag of whole wheat flour from the luggage compartment of his car. Years of professional baking had built her upper body strength more than any gym membership. "Your ghostly DJ?"

He grabbed the box of honey packets before closing the hood to protect the remaining items. "I don't know. Presumably." They carried their burdens inside, set them down, and went out for more. "I mean, assuming I'm only being haunted by one spirit, then yes, I was talking to my ghostly DJ. But really?" He shrugged as best he could with a case of napkins balanced on one shoulder and a box of stirry sticks tucked under the arm holding the umbrella.

A couple more trips to the car and they had everything inside. Mona began loading cartons of eggs into the big industrial refrigerator. "I should have told you to get butter."

"Do I need to go shopping again first thing in the

morning?"

"No, but before Wednesday would be good. Sorry to make you go twice in two days."

"No big deal. Maybe I'll ask Shell to go. Marco would thank me."

"But would Shell?"

"Good question. I don't know." He leaned against the big stainless-steel worktable and crossed his arms over his chest. "I'm thinking about one of those delivery services."

"You think it's worth it? I mean, I'm a one-woman kitchen here."

"Maybe. I haven't done the research yet. Who knows? Maybe we'll find you an assistant and you can become a two-person kitchen."

"It would have to be the right person."

"Absolutely."

Mona shifted from eggs to milk, hefting the jugs onto the sturdy shelves. "So tell me why you think the spirit haunting your car is haunting the coffeehouse. I'm here a lot and I haven't noticed anything spooky."

"I don't, necessarily. It's just—" He hesitated. It sounded stupid to say it out loud. He hadn't told anyone about the spoon issue he was having at home. Not even Mona. Now it seemed he should have. It would make this new mystery marginally less ridiculous. "The spoons are missing."

"The spoons? What spoons?" She rose and closed the fridge door.

"The spoons. Out on the condiment station. They're not there. I checked the dishwasher."

"I emptied the dishwasher myself last night when we closed up."

"Were there spoons?"

"Yes. Everything was there. I took *all* the silverware out *and* refilled the napkin holders."

"You didn't have to do that. It's the opening barista's job."

"I know, but I was here, and Lily is scheduled for opening, as usual, so I figured I'd do something nice."

Todd understood what she wasn't saying. Lily was such a giving person that it made people want to do nice things for her in return for the overall goodness she exuded like pheromones into the universe. "So you're sure there were spoons?" He sincerely hoped she would change her answer and at the same time knew it wouldn't happen.

"I just said there were. What's the deal with the spoons?"

"Come back to my place. I'll open some beers and tell you all about it."

Chapter 3

DANNY SKIDDED HIS BIKE TO A STOP IN FRONT OF Midnight Jones and checked his watch. Five minutes until they opened. He supposed he could wait that long. At least the rain had stopped just as he'd left his apartment. The streets were still wet, but the sky was a clear, pale blue that he could only hope wouldn't turn into gray overcast or back to rain. He took off his bike helmet and shivered as the chill midmorning breeze raked his short, deep brown curls. Maybe if he peered through the window and looked pathetic enough, the barista would let him in a little early.

Chaining his bike to the nearby rack, he resettled his courier bag across his body, secured his helmet to his handlebars, and went to look in through the coffeehouse's glass door. To his delight, it was his favorite barista, Lily, behind the counter. He knocked on the glass and waved at her, smiling. She grinned and waved back, mouth forming the words, "One minute." He nodded in understanding. She finished counting the morning till and closed the cash drawer before coming to open the door for him.

"Hi, Danny!" The morning sun lit her face, glinting off the amethyst stud in her right nostril and the many small silver hoops that ran up both of her ears.

"Good morning, sunshine!" he greeted her. "I love your pigtails. Are those skulls on the ponytail holders? Very cute! New boots too, I think. Très chic!"

"Stooping to flattery so I'll let you in early again?"

"It worked last time." He fluttered his eyelashes at her like Bugs Bunny to Elmer Fudd in *What's Opera, Doc?*.

She laughed. "You know I can't resist when you bat those big brown eyes at me. Come on in. It's only three minutes 'til we open anyway."

Danny's horn-rimmed glasses steamed up the moment he entered the warmth of the coffeehouse. He stood still and inhaled the heady scent of fresh baked goods and brewing coffee while they slowly cleared. "Hi, Mona!" he called. "It's Danny!"

"I should hope so," the baker called back from the depths of the kitchen. "If Lily's letting anyone else in early, I'm going to have to tell the boss."

"It's only three minutes," the barista protested.

Mona poked her head around the open doorway. "I was teasing, Lily." She looked over at Danny and the greeting she was about to make was preempted by her snort of laughter. "What in hell are you wearing?"

He turned in place, showing off his new green bike shoes, favorite black bike socks with yellow Kokopellis on them, baggy cut-off cargo pants complete with dangling bits of thread where they were unraveling, fleecy orange biking jacket with reflective stripes, and purple half-fingered gloves. "It's the latest in bike courier chic. Don't you like it?"

"You look like a grunge musician who's been vomited on by Jackson Pollock."

He blew her a kiss. "Love you too."

Mona shook her head, still chuckling, and ducked back into the kitchen.

"You want your usual this morning?" Lily asked as she returned to her post behind the counter.

"Yes, please. And make it extra hot, okay? Like you." He purred at her and leaned on the counter in what could have been a sexy pose had he been sporting a different wardrobe choice that morning.

"If only you meant it." She sighed heavily, playing along. "Have you gotten a new travel mug yet?"

"Not yet."

Lily shook her head, fond but chiding. She ground beans and loaded up two filter cups with the ease of habitual motion. "I'll double cup it for you this time, but you need to get on that."

"I know."

She pumped caramel into a 20-ounce to-go cup. "Where are you off to this morning?"

Danny swung his bag off over his head and plopped it onto the countertop. "Some used bookstore in Ballard."

"Did you get your money changed to Norwegian kroner for the trip?" joked Lily. Ballard was the Norwegian capital of Seattle, with the "Uff da!" stickers and handmade lefse to prove it.

"I thought they used Euros."

"Don't let them hear you say that!"

"Foreign money exchange will have to wait. I've already picked up this rare book to deliver over there, so I'm seriously jonesing for my first cup of coffee." He looked at her with his best sad puppy-dog expression.

"It's coming. Keep your hair on." But it was said with love.

"Please, please, please." He batted his eyelashes once more, and Lily laughed again. "I've been to Madison Park and back already, and it's a hell of a ride up that hill." Maybe the locals didn't mind the hills so much, but Danny was a Midwesterner by birth and upbringing, and he wasn't ashamed to admit it.

"How could I say no to you?" She flipped the switches to pull the four shots of espresso needed for his grande caramel mocha. "Why didn't they just mail it? The book, I mean."

Danny straightened up and spoke with exaggerated dignity. "Because we bike couriers are far faster and more reliable than the US postal service."

"Really?" She gave him a dubious look, glancing up and down his skinny, absurdly garbed figure. "You look super professional and reliable, all right."

He made a dramatic show of being stabbed in the heart. "You wound me, dear lady!"

"And I'm one to talk, right? I know what you're thinking," she scolded playfully.

"Now that you mention it... all that goth black you wear makes you invisible to drivers, no matter how much pink you add. At least I'm easy to see."

"You mean you're hard to miss!" She laughed again, stirring the fresh espresso into the caramel. She followed it with steamed whole milk, making a pretty pattern in the foam.

It was a game they played, all the shameless flirting. Danny knew he wasn't kinky enough for her tastes, and Lily knew she wasn't male enough for his. It made it more fun for both of them. They could say outrageous and ridiculous things to each other that they'd never say to someone they actually wanted to hook up with.

"D'you want a pastry this morning?"

He peered down into the bakery case. "What have you got today?"

Lily pointed to each as she named them. "Lemon ginger muffins. Whole wheat cherry almond scones. Pumpkin muffins with walnuts and without raisins, of course."

"Of course."

"And zucchini bread with chocolate chips."

"No cookies?"

"Cookies are not breakfast foods. Come back after lunch if you want cookies," Mona shouted from the kitchen.

"You have hearing like a bat!" Danny shouted back at her. He returned his attention to the case. "Zucchini bread then, please. Two slices."

"You got it."

While Lily got his bread and rang him up, he secured a lid on his piping hot, double-cupped drink.

"Be careful you don't burn yourself on that," she cautioned.

The doorbell chimed as more customers entered.

"It'll be the perfect drinking temperature by the time I get to Ballard. Thanks, Lily." He dropped a dollar into the tip jar, shouted a farewell to Mona, and headed out with his breakfast. "See you tomorrow!" He smiled in passing at the trio of pre-coffee zombies as he headed out the door.

*

Todd stepped under the small awning and greeted the wiry bike messenger just emerging from the shop. "Hey, Danny. I see you got your breakfast."

"Hey, Todd! What up? How's it going?"

"Okay, thanks." It wasn't a great morning, but customers, even regulars he knew well, didn't need to hear his woes.

"What's with the box?" Danny settled his coffee into the holder secured to his bike frame and took a bite of bread from the paper carry-out bag in his hand.

"Compostable spoons. The real ones went missing. Long story." He shifted the cardboard box from one arm to the other.

"Weird. Okay." With the rest of the bread safely tucked into his satchel and his helmet on his head, Danny mounted his bike. "See you later!" he said, already pedaling off.

"Bike safe!" Todd shouted after him. He watched the young man maneuver his way into traffic, admiring his ability to navigate through the vehicular madness of

Seattle, and then turned and went inside.

"Hey there, boss man!" Lily greeted Todd with her usual cheerful enthusiasm. She handed off the last of the lattes and smiled thanks at the appreciative customer.

Todd took the person's place and set the cardboard box on the counter.

"You're here late today. What gives?"

"Spoons."

"Ah, killer! Thanks!" She pulled it over and opened it up. "You got the good ones too! Way better than the pack of cheap plastic ones Mona picked up on her way in this morning."

"I'm glad you approve. I had to go to Cash & Carry this morning to get them. Grocery stores don't carry compostable flatware in bulk." He'd had to go to Cash & Carry anyway for butter, so at least it hadn't been an *extra* extra trip. He'd dropped the butter off earlier, before the shop opened, and then walked back from his house with the lighter-weight spoons.

She offered a sympathetic frown. "Still no sign of our real spoons, huh?" Since no one was in line for a drink at the moment, she came out from behind the counter, revealing the full glory of her perky-goth outfit. She wore a long-sleeved pink and black striped t-shirt under a frilly black blouse with short, puffy sleeves. Tights that matched the t-shirt's colors led from her studded black shorts to her tall black boots. She looked like a Catholic school girl from the second level of hell.

Todd chuckled to himself. Looks were deceiving. She was probably the kindest human being he'd ever known.

He leaned his back against the corner of the pastry case while she replaced the plastic spoons in the condiment station with the eco-friendly kind. "It's only been since yesterday. I'll consider investing in more 'real' spoons once I know for sure ours aren't just temporarily misplaced." As if one could "misplace" that many at one go.

"That's smart." Lily nodded in support.

A pair of customers entered, and she retook her station behind the counter, ditching the handful of plastic spoons beneath it. Todd stepped out of the way. He shot Lily an inquiring look and pointed to the office. "Is Shell in?"

"Yeah."

"Thanks." He didn't knock on the office door, however. He wasn't looking forward to discussing the possibly ghostly spoon theft with his hyper-skeptical business manager. First, he wanted to check in with Mona. He stuck his head into the kitchen to find her with her back to the door, measuring sugar into the big mixer. He waited for her to turn and see him before saying hello. No point in distracting her while she was operating heavy machinery. Instead, he stood happily soaking in the positive energy she'd imbued into the kitchen over her many hours spent working there.

"Hey there," she greeted him once she spotted him. "Come on in. The kitchen's warm."

He smiled. "It is."

"Thanks for picking up butter, by the way." She frowned in concern. "What's wrong? Where's your latte?"

He sighed wearily. "I didn't even think about it when I came in, that's how distracted I am."

"That's pretty distracted. You want to go get one now?"

He shook his head. "I'll get it before I go talk to Shell."

"Good luck with that conversation." Mona started the mixer going again slowly. She added chunks of butter a little at a time. "She's more than a little curious about the spoon situation. Don't be surprised if she talks about installing a security system."

"Thanks for the warning." He wasn't surprised to hear it. Shell had been on him about getting an alarm system for over a year, and this incident would fuel the flames of her argument. Yes, they needed one. No, he hadn't looked into it yet. He grew annoyed imagining how the conversation might go.

Let it go, he told himself. *You can't win an argument that's only in your head.*

"She thinks it was a prank, you know," Mona added.

"I'm not surprised. That's what a sane person *would* think."

"Unlike you?"

"Unlike me." He came farther into the kitchen and leaned against the wall near the mixer but still out of Mona's way. "When did I become the kind of person who automatically assumes anything slightly weird must be paranormal in nature?"

"When someone started haunting your car?"

"That long ago? Damn. What are you making?"

"Pumpkin scones."

"How seasonal."

"So did you need something, or is this a social call?"

"It's a stalling call," he admitted. "I dawdled as much as I could getting here with the spoons, but it's not enough. I had a crappy night after you left. I don't want to talk to Shell until I'm in a better mood."

"And I cheer you up? That's sweet." She smiled at him. "You can be my assistant for a while. Pass me that bowl."

Todd chuckled and moved to pick up the bowl she'd pointed to.

"Careful. Those are my wet ingredients. Don't spill them."

He carried the bowl of pale orange-brown slurry to her with both hands. "You want me to pour it in?"

"Can you do it right?"

"I make no guarantees."

"Then hand it over, please." She took the bowl from him, and he stepped aside again. She began to pour the mixture in a thin stream into the big, stainless-steel mixing bowl. He peered into the bowl, watching the dough come together under the slowly turning paddle. When it reached whatever magical point Mona was looking for, she turned it off. She scraped off the beater and removed the heavy bowl from the stand.

"Do you need a hand?"

She cocked her head at him, amused. "And they say chivalry is dead. Thank you, but I'm fine." She did this several times every workday. She was plenty strong enough to heft the thing, even as full as it was. "Seriously. Go get yourself a latte."

"You're awfully anxious to get me caffeinated. Not that I disagree with you, but I feel like you have an agenda."

She didn't look at him, instead focusing on turning out the dough onto her floured worktable rather more intently than he thought strictly necessary. "Have you thought about the suggestion I made last night?"

"So, that's it." He crossed his arms over his chest, annoyed that she'd brought it up even though he was the one who'd pressed her for disclosure. "I did. I haven't decided yet."

"Okay." She set the bowl in the enormous sink and, reaching for a bit of flour, dusted up her hands. She dug into the dough, kneading it a few times before cutting it into the proportions she wanted.

"But...?" He knew there was more. He knew *her*.

"But I really think you should look into it. Presence Unknown is a highly reputable paranormal investigations company."

"Shell would have a field day if I even suggested it."

Mona pinned him with a look across the stainless-steel table. "It's not Shell's decision. It's yours."

"That's right. *Mine*," he said pointedly. His irritation edged toward anger.

Mona held up one doughy, floury hand. "Yours. Yes. I get it. I do. But please, think about it?"

"I already thought about it to the point of insomnia, thanks."

Understanding dawned in her green eyes. "Oh. No wonder you're Mr. Grumpypants this morning. I'm sorry," she went on sincerely. "That wasn't what I intended when I brought it up last night."

"I know. I'm sorry too. I *am* grumpy, and I don't want to take it out on you." He uncrossed his arms and took a cleansing breath, doing his best to let go of his irritation. It usually worked, but it had been less effective of late. He took another breath and let it out.

That was better.

"I appreciate it." Mona started forming the many dough blobs into balls, and from balls into flattish disks.

"You know what? I'm going to go get that latte right now."

"Do that. Come back when you're caffeinated enough to be civil."

"Pusher."

"Grouch."

That teasing two-word exchange improved his mood as much as any coffee or deep breathing could. "I'll be back, and you can extol more of Presence Unknown's virtues for me. There'd better be a scone for me later too."

"I promise. Maybe even two."

"I'd rather have one and then grab some lunch if you're up for it."

"You think you can avoid Shell long enough to eat a scone and then sneak out without her spotting you?" Mona took a long, serrated knife and began slicing the dough disks into wedges.

"I can try."

She laughed. "Get your coffee. That's step one."

Chapter 4

IT WAS DRIZZLING BY THE TIME DANNY PULLED UP IN front of his destination. He took a moment to dry his glasses on the little cloth he kept in his jacket pocket and then looked at the store-front properly. The two big front windows were nearly full with displays of old books. Only the top eighteen inches or so were clear to catch the light. Not that there was much light to be caught on an October morning when the windows faced west.

He got a good feeling just looking at the place. The books they'd chosen to put in the window made him smile. It was mostly spooky fiction on one side—*The Halloween Tree*, *Blood and Chocolate*, *Interview with the Vampire*, and stuff like that—and spiritual nonfiction on the other. He recognized several classics of Wiccan lit: Adler's *Drawing Down the Moon* and an old edition of *The Spiral Dance*; the requisite Scott Cunningham and Raymond Buckland titles. He'd grown up with them all on his mom's bookshelf. Fake cobwebs and a variety of plastic spiders enhanced the display.

He took a couple of swallows of his caramel mocha, finally ingesting his first caffeine of the day, and settled the cup back in its holder.

The nearest bike rack was halfway up the block, so he just parked in the inset doorway. He would never have done that in certain neighborhoods in town, but this was Ballard. The worst that might happen was that some jackass would slap a "Free Ballard!" or lutefisk-fish bumper sticker on his bike. Although... He looked at his sturdy, hard-used bicycle and its collection of random and ratty stickers that ranged from Rat City Roller Girls to an old "Eat the Rich" sticker he'd picked up gods-knew-where last spring. "I suppose another one wouldn't hurt."

He took a moment to turn off the GoPro on his helmet and radio in that he was making his first delivery, and then stepped into the shop. He glanced around the cramped space. It was aptly named Hole-in-the-Wall Books. It made even him feel oversized, which was something that hadn't happened since he was in kindergarten—better known as the only year he'd been the tallest kid in class.

Shelves of books stretched from floor to ceiling. Boxes of books were stacked on the floor down several of the aisles. The air inside was dry, and the scent of old paper and dust pervaded the place. The little light shining through the windows and door caught dust motes as thick as a miniature version of the Milky Way. The remaining illumination came from an eclectic selection of track lighting fixtures along the ceiling.

His first urge was to go poking through the shelves. See what sort of literary treasures he might find. Maybe a first edition of Arthur C. Clarke's *2001* lurked in there somewhere. Or maybe he'd find one of Wylly Folk St. John's books. He'd loved her mysteries when he was a kid and it had been years since he'd seen a copy of any of them. He peered at the ends of the shelves, reading section labels, and started to move toward Children's when a voice caught him by surprise.

"Hello."

Danny turned to find a short, curly-haired brunette woman with inquisitive blue eyes looking at him. He hadn't heard her approach, and he hadn't seen her come in. In truth, he hadn't seen the cash register where she stood either. The counter was stacked so high with books that it hadn't struck him as anything more than additional shelving.

"Hi."

"Let me know if I can help you find anything." She smiled, her face wreathed in steam that rose from the enormous coffee mug she held in both hands. "There are maps of the store here on the counter if you need one. Although it's pretty tough to get lost, except in the books themselves. Or if you saw something in the window display that you'd like to take a closer look at, I'm happy to get it for you."

"Thanks. Actually, I have a delivery for a Mr. Benedick Chalfie." He dug into his messenger bag and removed a carefully wrapped bundle.

Her smile widened. "He's been waiting for that. I'll get him for you. Just a moment."

Setting her coffee mug on the counter, she ducked down an aisle and was back in less than a minute. "He'll be right here. Are you sure I can't help you find something while you're waiting? A special printing of an Asimov or a Clarke? Or a childhood favorite? Wylly Folk St. John is tough to get a hold of, but there are other good YA and middle-grade mysteries I could recommend."

He paused and narrowed his eyes, peering at her through thick lenses. She'd pegged exactly the kinds of books he'd been thinking about. It was spooky and a shiver raced down his spine. He shook it off and focused instead on the woman's coffee mug, big as a soup mug, as she took a sip from it. The stick figures on it were just the distraction he needed. He wondered if she'd painted it herself at one of those you-paint pottery places.

"Will he be long?" Danny asked, her mug reminding him that his perfectly cooled mocha was getting colder sitting outside on his bike. He really needed to get off his ass and buy a new insulated travel mug to replace the one that had been stolen last month.

She shrugged. "He shouldn't be."

As if on cue, a tall man with softly curling hair and wire-rimmed glasses emerged from between two rows of shelves.

"Hi. I'm Ben Chalfie. You have a package for me?"

"Yeah. Right here." Danny handed it over and followed it with a digital pad and stylus. "I just need you to sign for it, please."

Chalfie signed the little screen and handed the unit back with a smile.

"Thank you." Danny tucked it away.

"Thank *you*. I've been looking for this book for years. I couldn't believe it when I found a collector in the area who was willing to part with it."

"Come back sometime when you have time to look around," the woman said.

"Yeah. I'd like that. This looks like a cool place." He glanced from her to Chalfie and then back to her. She took another sip from her mug. *Shit!* His coffee! He'd forgotten it again, and it was undoubtedly chillier than he liked by now. "I need to get going. More deliveries." At least the other locations weren't too far from where he was now. His dispatcher was a decent and smart guy when it came to logistics.

The woman nodded. "And your coffee will get cold."

Danny stared at her, dumbfounded. She'd done it again. Said just what he was thinking. Two coincidences like that, one practically on the heels of the other? Was she reading his mind? "How did you know that?"

A smile curled her mouth. "You keep eyeing my coffee mug, and I know the artwork on it isn't that fascinating. You're traveling by bicycle. It's October. It's before noon. It's Seattle. In my mind, that all adds up to a rapidly chilling coffee beverage somewhere outside."

"Oh. Right." He gave a rueful chuckle. "Bye." He turned to go, glad his ridiculous assumption had turned out to be wrong. He felt dumb just for thinking it.

He opened the door.

"Enjoy your breakfast too. I love zucchini bread."

Danny stumbled over the doorjamb but pretended not to hear her, making the hastiest exit he could. Safely outside, he wheeled his bike out of the doorway so he could turn it and climb on.

There, right on the seat, was a new sticker declaring, "Free Ballard!"

He shook his head and muttered, "Of course."

*

Ben looked up from his much-anticipated package and over at Frieda. "You're in an extra wicked mood this morning."

"I am, yes. I'm still annoyed about yesterday's baseball game, and I needed a pick-me-up."

"And you got that from messing with the bike courier?"

"Would you rather I mess with you?" She challenged him with a look.

He matched her stare with his own. "As if you could." She'd often complained that she found him more difficult to read than most people.

Her eyes narrowed. "Dare you to try me."

"You are evil."

She shot him an unapologetic half smile over the top of her coffee mug. "It's part of my charm."

He chuckled and shook his head.

"Come on," she said. "You know I'd never use my minor psychic talents to anyone's detriment."

"Not everyone would consider your psychic talents minor."

"So, are you going to open that or just fondle it?"

Frieda nodded in the direction of the package.

Ben perked up. He really had been hunting for this book for years. It was one of the few remaining missing pieces in his collection, and now it was missing no more. "Right! Is there a box knife behind the counter there?" He set the padded manila envelope on the counter and leaned to look over the other side.

"Here." She pulled one out of the drawer below the cash register. "Don't cut yourself. We all know you have a limited amount of natural grace per day and when you run out, you run out."

"God, I know! Good thing it's still early." He extended the knife blade and cautiously sliced open the envelope, cutting through the bubble wrap lining. Closing the knife, which Frieda promptly took away from him, he slid out the precious book. The unevenly cut pages had gone a tawny beige around the edges with age, but otherwise it was in perfect condition. Ben gave a happy sigh as he gently fingered the dust jacket and opened the book almost reverently to the title page, which had at some time in the book's history been signed by the author.

"You know, I loved those books too. But I've never seen anyone so..."

"Enraptured?" he offered, not looking up at her.

"Obsessed," she supplied instead, "with Paddington Bear."

"It's a first edition!"

"It's a children's book."

He looked across the counter at the woman who had been his friend since they were teenagers and his business partner for the past eleven years. "Frieda, you know I love you," he said with all sincerity, "but you have no understanding of the finer points of collecting or of children's literature, never mind both."

She opened her mouth to protest. Shut it again. Shook her head. "You're right. Hey, there was a message waiting on the voicemail this morning. I forgot to mention it before."

"A message for me or for the store?" His attention was back on his new treasure, but he still heard the impatience that crept into her voice.

"Not that voicemail. PUPI's."

That pulled his attention back to her. "I wish you wouldn't call it that."

She shrugged. "You picked the company name. It's not my fault you didn't stop to think what the initials spelled."

"Yeah, but 'puppy'?" It pained him to say it, and it showed in his face.

"It's better than 'poopy.' I think we should have a mascot, by the way. I'm thinking about getting us a dachshund."

"Used bookstores are supposed to have cats, not dogs."

"Since when are you a slave to tradition? I think having a long-haired dachshund around the place would be cool."

"Why a dachshund?"

"Because it would fit between the shelves, for a start. Can you see a Newfie or a Great Dane trying to maneuver around here?"

Ben burst out laughing. "You're insane."

"That's not news." She smirked back at him.

"So, what was the call about?"

"A possible triple haunting."

"Seriously?" He stood up straighter, his curiosity piqued.

"Yep. And you'll be happy to know the call was from a local business owner. I know how you like it when local businesses support one another."

"Of course I do. What did they want?"

She pulled out a notepad and read the message she'd written down. "The guy's name is Todd Marks, and he said his car is haunted."

That piqued Ben's curiosity further. He'd never heard of anyone haunting a car before. Well, if you didn't count cheesy 1960s television shows. "A haunted car?"

"Apparently."

"So what does he want? If he knows it's haunted, what does he need from us?"

"He also owns a house and a coffee shop. Both on Capitol Hill. He wants to know if the same ghost is haunting them too or if it's a different one—or two."

Now Ben's attention was fully engaged. He carefully slid his new book back into its protective envelope, just in case Frieda suddenly became careless with her big cup of coffee. The merchandise on the counter was one thing, but he wasn't willing to take a chance with his precious Paddington.

She gave him the side eye. "Your book is safe. I'd sooner spill my own blood than my coffee."

"I know. What makes him think his house is haunted?"

"I love how you just accept the car but question the house. I went the other way."

"Of course you did. So? The house?"

"He said in the message that it had to do with spoons."

"Spoons?" echoed Ben blankly.

"Apparently they go missing."

"Missing."

"Usually only from the house. Only now they've gone missing at his coffee shop."

"All of them or just one or two?"

"He didn't say. I would assume all, otherwise it wouldn't be that weird."

"It's odd in either case. I mean, the coffee shop thing could just be a prank. Some high school scavenger hunt."

"I thought that too, although there aren't any high schools in that area. I think the closest is Seattle Prep up near Tenth. The next is Garfield to the south, and that's something like two miles away in a completely different neighborhood. Plus, the coincidence factor is a bit high, you know? House *and* business?" She waited in silence while he considered the few facts she'd given him.

It wasn't much to go on, but they'd had all of one paranormal investigation in the past month and a half. He was willing at this point to grasp at whatever straw was held out to him. "Is that everything?"

"Pretty much. He said he'd like to meet us and talk about maybe having us check it out. Frankly, I'm curious."

"Of course you are. There's coffee involved."

"There is that," she replied with a smile and a sip from her mug. She leaned a hip against the counter and cradled the mug in her hands. "I also want to see if it's the usual seasonal weirdness or if there's something more to it. It's the spoons that intrigue me."

He didn't say it, but that aspect intrigued him too. Why spoons? Was there some spiritual message to be found in the choice of utensil? Had he driven a ghost mad by binge-listening to Soundgarden's "Spoonman"? This wasn't exactly why he and Frieda had founded the company, but it was better than sitting on his hands. Every haunting deserved to be examined. He'd learned that the hard way. "So, when do we get to meet him in person?"

Frieda smiled. "How does tonight sound? I called him back before you got in. He said he'd be there anytime from about ten o'clock until they close."

"What time did you tell him we'd be there?"

"Eleven-fifteen."

"What? Why so late?" Not that he minded so much. He was a night owl just like her. It was just such a random time to pick.

"Why not? They're open late. Until one a.m., in fact."

Ben's eyes narrowed at her as he put two and two together. "You don't want to miss the baseball game, do you?"

"With as long as it's been since our boys last made the playoffs, no, I do not want to miss the game. Life is too short, and this series will be too, if we don't start with the winning," she added with palpable cynicism. "Besides, I think Todd Marks is going to be watching it too."

"Oh?" He gave her a challenging look. "Are you basing this on what you picked up from him when you talked, or are you basing it on your own wishful thinking?"

"The former. I think." She shrugged. "Between the fact that our conversation was over the phone instead of in person and the fact that I really, *really* don't want to miss any of the game, it's difficult to be sure."

A thought struck him. "Wait. Isn't it another early game today?"

"No." She pursed her lips in annoyance. "Late afternoon yesterday, evening today. It's so messed up. I blame the sports networks specifically and the media sponsors generally."

"You know the game probably won't go into extra innings again, right?"

"Are you kidding? I'm counting on it only going eight and a half. But I'm the one who'll be driving, and I don't want to fight postgame traffic across town whatever the case. So..." She left the sentence unfinished, her point clear.

Ben shook his head at her, conceding the argument. "Fine. What's the place called where we're expected at *eleven-fifteen* tonight?"

"Midnight Jones."

Chapter 5

"WE SHOULD CALL AND CANCEL."

"Don't be silly."

Todd and Mona sat at one of the small tables near the front of the coffeehouse, talking quietly over mugs of freshly brewed decaf. The overhead lights were dimmed low enough that they could see the figures of the people who passed by outside the front windows. A little over half of the shop's tables had patrons seated at them. Most were either listening to house musician Willa Murphy playing an old Irish folk standard and singing in her sultry alto on the little stage in the back corner, or they were working away on laptop computers with warmly glowing screens. Votive candles burned in stained glass holders on every table.

"What's silly is letting you talk me into this in the first place," said Todd, more annoyed with himself than with her.

Mona sat back in her chair. "I didn't twist your arm that hard."

"You dialed the number!"

"I had it handy. You're the one who went ahead and made the appointment when they called back."

"Don't remind me."

"Stop worrying so much. They'll come and we'll talk to them. Maybe they can help and maybe they can't. Either way, there's no obligation to hire them. It's worth it just to talk to someone who's familiar with the paranormal. Right?" She gave his arm resting on the tabletop an encouraging squeeze.

"I suppose."

"Pessimist."

"Noodge." He paused long enough to sip his coffee and listen to the end of Willa's song. "I like that one," he said, applauding with the rest of the patrons. "It's cheerier than most. Usually in those folksy Celtic ballad love songs, someone ends up dead."

"If they don't start out that way," Mona added.

The door opened and a trio of people entered, laughing and shaking rain from their coats. Todd recognized two of them as regulars, actors coming in for a drink before heading home after rehearsal at one of the Hill's many small theatres. He waved to them and got a friendly "Dude!" and smiles in return as they huddled up to the counter and placed their orders.

Todd returned his attention to Mona across the little table. "Thanks for coming back tonight and hanging out with me."

"Anything for you, buddy!" she declared. "Of course, getting to meet the people who run Presence Unknown has nothing to do with it." Her indifferent expression broke into a giggle and grin under the scrutiny of his dubious look and raised eyebrows. "Yeah. I didn't believe me either. I can't help it!" She defended herself though he'd ask for no defense. "I love those *Ghost Hunters* guys on TV. The idea that I get to meet the local version is too cool!"

"How did you even hear of them? I never had until you mentioned them. I had no idea we had local ghostbusters."

"You don't watch enough television. You're always too busy tarting up that haunted car of yours. And really, that makes it all the more ironic that you don't know

about Presence Unknown, Paranormal Investigators."
She said the name as if she were a TV voice-over
announcer introducing a particularly intense and scary
program. "They investigated the Harvard Exit last
Halloween. You know how the media like to talk up the
whole haunted movie theatre thing every few years.
Some magazine show wanted to do a spooky segment, so
naturally they called the Harvard Exit, and the Harvard
Exit called Presence Unknown. Honestly, their lack of
imagination is disappointing. You'd think it was the only
haunted building in town." Her tone was both disgusted
and indignant, as if she had her own haunted building
that she felt was being ignored by the media.

"Freak." He said it with all the affection of a lifetime
of friendship.

Her smile was warm. "Loser."

~~*

Frieda turned her '74 Volvo onto Fifteenth East and
began watching for addresses. "It should be on your side
of the street, I think. Are the even numbers on your side?
I always forget the pattern, and I can't see for shit
through this rain."

"You need new wiper blades."

"I know, I know. The numbers?"

"I think…" Ben peered through the dark and the wet
and managed to catch a glimpse of a number on a Thai
restaurant's awning. "Yeah. My side. Two blocks up from
here it looks like. So, park this behemoth of yours
wherever you can find a spot big enough, and we can
walk from there. You might want to try the suburbs."

"Bite your tongue." Frieda pulled her beloved vehicle
into a spot less than a block from their destination. She
shot Ben a too-sweet smile. "The parking fairies are
smiling on us."

Ben gave credit where it was due, nodding graciously in defeat. "Do you give them offerings or something?"

They stepped out of the car. Instantly, a cold wind whipped at his short hair and drove rain into his face. He wished he'd worn a hat like Frieda had. He'd known perfectly well that it would rain tonight, but he'd not wanted to give himself hat-head. He rolled his eyes at his vanity.

Ben wrapped his scarf a little tighter around his neck, zipped his wool jacket up as far as it would go, and shaded his glasses against the rain with one hand. "I could never have found such good parking," he said. "Especially around here."

"It's my biodiesel beams of righteousness. The parking fairies recognize and reward."

He laughed. "You're hilarious." He shoved his free hand into his jacket pocket as they strode quickly along the leaf-scattered sidewalk. Only the earliest of deciduous trees had lost their leaves; the rest still held onto their golden and ruddy adornments. It would be another month before those started to fall in earnest, turning the sidewalks into a slippery mess. Between that and the inevitable winds, November would be littered with leaf attacks. In the meantime, it was cold and wet, but at least it was pretty.

Ben didn't admit it out loud, but he was more than a little excited about the impending meeting. The possibility of investigating not one but *three* related locations was thrilling. Of course, it wasn't a given that this Todd Marks person would want them to do more than check out the coffee shop. He might not even hire them for that, when it came right down to it. Still, a haunted car? That would be a first for them. His mind had been spinning most of the day trying to figure out how they could set up observation equipment in and around the vehicle, how they could control the environment enough that outside factors wouldn't be an issue. They didn't even know what model it was, whether it was kept in a garage or on the street, but he couldn't stop wondering and planning. It would be easier, he thought, if the client had a garage where they could park the car overnight. That way there were fewer chances of the equipment picking up stray noises or reflections or being tampered with.

He chose to ignore the fact that Todd Marks wasn't officially a client yet. This was only the meet-and-greet; nothing was guaranteed.

"There it is. Midnight Jones." Frieda pointed to the dark blue awning with white text over the little doorway. "Try not to look too desperate." She shot him a teasing grin and he knew she'd just read him like a book.

*

The pair who entered the coffee shop looked, at first glance, like any other customers. One was a tall man with short auburn hair that was beginning to silver, a wool jacket, blue scarf, tan slacks, and dark brown shoes. He looked sharp and metrosexual, if a bit soggy and windblown at the moment. The other was a short woman in chunky black boots, an ankle-length gray skirt, a burgundy fuzzy sweater, and a wool wrap made of Black Watch tartan. The golden-brown curls escaping from under her knit hat topped off her Seattle Boho look. They were a sight you could see pretty much anywhere in town at this time of year, and especially in a coffeehouse on the Hill. So why hadn't Todd seen them before? Not that everyone in the neighborhood came into Midnight Jones. There were plenty of other places to get a latte and a scone. He just had the odd sensation that these two had been missing somehow, and their presence here now filled a gap he hadn't previously known was there.

While the woman spoke to the evening barista, Lena, the man dried his glasses with a small cloth. When he put them back on, he turned a casual glance on the coffeehouse and Todd caught a glimpse of his eyes. They were intense and keen behind silver-framed glasses. As if they took in everything he saw and recorded it for later examination. Todd was glad for the lenses between himself and those observant orbs. Absurd as it was—and he fully admitted to himself the absurdity—he couldn't deny the feeling that without that clear plastic protection, those eyes could look right into his soul.

Mona caught him staring and turned to see why. At that moment, the barista pointed to their table. "That must be them!" Mona exclaimed softly. Her green eyes gleamed with barely contained excitement and she bounced slightly in her chair.

"You're squeeing," murmured Todd, trying to maintain enough cool for the both of them.

"Am I?" Her eyes went wide in embarrassment, and then narrowed at him suspiciously. "I am not."

"They're coming this way."

"Squee!"

Todd bit back laughter as she stifled her fan-girlish cry of delight.

"Excuse me. Are you Todd Marks?"

The man looked down at him, and Todd immediately rose and reached out a hand. Jesus, the guy was even taller than he was, and Todd was tall. "That's me."

"I'm Ben Chalfie from Presence Unknown, Paranormal Investigators."

They shook hands, and Todd noticed how strong the man's hand was, and how warm despite the cold weather. He felt a small wave of disappointment when he had to let go. There was a familiarity that exuded from Ben as though they'd known each other years ago and then lost touch. But he would have remembered if he'd ever met the man before. Ben was too striking to forget.

He introduced his companion. "This is my associate,

Frieda Smith."

Todd shook hands with the woman. "It's nice to meet you. This is my friend Mona Ward. She's the baker here. She's the one who recommended I call you." Hands were shaken all around. "Have a seat. Thanks for coming. Can I get you something to drink or a pastry? There's wine, beer, tea, and of course, coffee."

"We're fine, thank you," Ben answered. Frieda shot him a look that spoke volumes and Todd almost laughed. He'd seen the exact same expression on Mona's face countless times over the years, too many not to recognize it. Either the two were married or they'd been friends for a very long time.

"*He's* fine. *I*, on the other hand, would love a soy latte," she said pointedly.

Todd nodded once. "Absolutely. What size?"

"A single short should do the job nicely, thanks. Regular, please. Not decaf." She smiled at him as she pulled off her hat, releasing her long hair. "It's warm in here. Cozy. Nice. I like the musician."

"Thank you." He looked at Mona, who from her expression knew exactly what was coming. "Mona, would you—?"

She rose from her seat. "I'll go order you that latte. Don't start without me." It took her only moments to place the order and return to the table. "Lena'll bring it over when it's ready."

"Thanks," said Frieda. "I would have ordered it myself when we were standing right there, but *someone* couldn't be bothered to wait another two minutes to meet you guys."

Mona chuckled and took a sip of her decaf Americano, lightened to a soft brown with cream.

Ben unzipped his coat and loosened his scarf, then dug into an inner coat pocket and pulled out a small digital voice recorder. "Do you mind?" he asked, looking from

Todd to Mona and back again. "I've found it's easier and a lot more accurate than trying to take notes while we talk."

"No, that's fine," Todd confirmed, all seriousness once again. Mona nodded over her mug.

"So, why don't you start at the beginning?"

It took longer than Todd had expected to explain everything. Ben's intent gaze and his way of actively listening caused Todd to go into greater depth about the spoon-stealing ghost than he had when he'd told the same story to Mona the other night. He tried to ignore her occasional looks of surprise and one very piercing expression of indignation. He would make it up to her later for holding out on her before. Maybe with that new industrial mixer she'd been not so subtly hinting at him to buy. He was planning to get it in the near future anyway; maybe he would make it the even nearer future.

"And you're absolutely certain it all started with the car?" Ben asked.

"Absolutely?" echoed Todd. He shook his head. "No. I know the car is haunted. I discovered that when I finished restoring it. But the rest of it…" He trailed off with a shrug. "I've had the car a few years longer than I've had the house. I don't know if the house was always haunted and I never realized it, or if the spirit in the car has spread out its territory, or if this is something entirely separate and new."

"Spoons, huh?" Frieda put in, a thoughtful expression on her face. "Why spoons? I mean, that's kind of random, you know?"

"Maybe if you can figure out who's taking them, you can ask why."

"Assuming we can even prove the house, or this place, is haunted," said Ben quickly.

Todd stiffened in surprise, immediately defensive. Wasn't that what they'd just spent the better part of an hour discussing? Suddenly Ben Chalfie wasn't as handsome as he'd been when he'd walked through the door.

Sensing Todd's misgivings, Ben explained. "I'm not denying your personal experiences. I've had several myself over the years. That doesn't mean I've been able to prove the existence of paranormal activity in every case. Hard evidence is tough to come by in most cases, even when you can see a ghost so clearly that you could tell someone the color of his eyes."

Something in his voice gave Todd pause. There was clearly history there that he was suddenly very curious to learn. He filed the impression away for later. This wasn't the time or the place. He could hardly expect the man to divulge the whole of his past hauntings to relative strangers. *Get to know him first,* he thought. Then get to know him better and better. Hmm, yes. Those sharp, strong features and sapphire blue eyes were handsome to him again.

Todd forced himself to focus on the subject at hand and allowed no sign of his curiosity or his desire to show on his face. "Of course." He nodded once. Businesslike. Professional. Ben's explanation made perfect sense. Individual belief in something didn't equal fact. "So, what's the next step?"

"We figure out a time when it's convenient for you and for us to set up our equipment overnight so we can make our observations."

"The coffeehouse closes early on Sundays and is closed all day on Mondays," offered Mona eagerly. "I live across the street. I'd be happy to meet up with your team to let you in, lock up afterwards, and whatever else you need."

Todd interrupted before she could start gushing. Even an hour talking with the Presence Unknown people hadn't dulled the fannish sparkle in her eyes. Of course, he was one to talk. He'd been fighting not to openly ogle

Ben Chalfie ever since the man had walked through the door. "We should discuss it with Shell first. Shell Manning," he clarified for Ben and Frieda's benefit. "She's the business manager here."

"We'll check our calendar too," Ben agreed. "If you'd like us to investigate the house and the car too, let us know. We'd be happy to do that as well."

"I don't know what good it would do to investigate the car. I mean, I know it's haunted. I don't need proof. Although it might be cool to see if we can catch the ghost shifting the radio dial or something on camera."

"It's a dial?" asked Frieda, sitting up a little straighter in her chair. "Like a tune-it-in-by-hand, no-digital-readout, honest-to-gods *dial*?"

Todd grinned at her, amused by her enthusiasm. "Yeah. I couldn't get a sixty-three model to match the car, but I did the best I could. After all, I couldn't restore a vintage automobile without a vintage radio, could I?"

Frieda's eyes were wide and her tone heavy with sincerity. "Absolutely not. Most assuredly the fabric of the universe would unravel otherwise."

Todd chuckled awkwardly, uncertain if she was serious or mocking him. He decided it was the former, as her expression held no ridicule. Maybe she was a vintage car buff or something.

"What about the house?" asked Ben, pulling the conversation back on topic.

"Yeah. That's bugging me for sure, but it can wait. I've lived with it this long. But here?" He glanced around the coffeehouse, every protective instinct flaring. "I don't want anything, tangible or intangible, messing with my shop."

"So, do you want to call us once you've spoken to your business manager?"

Todd felt ambivalent. He wished the man was a bit easier going, while at the same time he appreciated Ben's work ethic. In fact, other than being a bit uptight, he couldn't find a flaw in him. Intelligent, well spoken. Tall, handsome. Amazing eyes. Sharp cheekbones, square jaw. Broad shoulders, tight butt, dreamy voice... From the corner of his eye he could see Mona watching him and schooled his expression to something he hoped passed for nonchalant, or at least neutral. "Sure. You check your schedule, and I'll check ours and talk to Shell." He made a snap decision. "You know what? I'd actually love to have you do the house and the car too since you suggested it." He didn't have to check with anyone about those. "Do you want to do it all on the same night?"

"It's better if we do two separate nights, if that's all right. We don't want to spread ourselves too thin. There's only three of us, and it's better to have at least two people on site at all times during an investigation. We want to make sure we do a good job for you."

Todd fingered the business card Ben had given him, picking it up off the table and turning it over. Ben had written a second number on the back. His personal cell phone number. He told himself there was no deep, hidden meaning to that and tucked the card into the hip pocket of his blue jeans. "All right. I'll check with Shell about the coffeehouse. As far as my house and the car go, any night is fine for me. My place isn't far from here, and it's just me, so whenever works for your team is good."

"Great. I'll give you a call tomorrow to set it up."

It was a clear conclusion to the meeting, and they all rose to their feet. Ben and Frieda bundled themselves up against the cold night air as they said their goodbyes.

"Are you sure I can't pay for the latte?" Frieda asked, not for the first time.

"It's on him." Mona nodded toward Todd. "If my boss doesn't like it, he can take it out of my pay." She shot him a grin.

"Did I mention she's not just the in-house baker but

the in-house pain in the butt?" Todd said dryly, and they all chuckled.

"Good night." Ben and Todd shook hands once more and, as before, Todd was disappointed when he had to let go. "Call if anything unusual happens in the meantime," Ben added. "Our daytime number is on the card. There's usually someone around between ten a.m. and seven or eight at night. Feel free to call my cell if it's after hours. Any time."

The way Ben said it gave Todd the impression that he really meant *any* time. But would he still mean it if Todd called in the middle of the night? Sure it was after midnight now, and they were just concluding a business meeting, but that didn't mean Ben made a habit of staying up this late. He wondered if he would ever have the opportunity to find out. "I will, thanks. Good night. Thanks for coming."

The pair of paranormal investigators departed, a chill wind blowing in past them when they opened the door. At least the rain had finally let up.

"Smells like autumn," Todd heard Frieda say before the door shut behind them.

He and Mona both sat down again in the quiet that followed Ben and Frieda's departure. The coffeehouse felt empty despite the half dozen people still scattered about. Willa had long since finished her set and departed, waving goodbye as she'd headed out so as not to disturb their meeting. Todd looked at his watch. It was a quarter to one.

At that same moment, Lena ran her fingers through the wind chime that hung over the espresso maker. "Last call," she announced to the room at large. One woman looked up in surprise and hastily began packing up her laptop. Another glanced languidly at the big clock behind the counter and returned her attention to the man with whom she shared her table. One of the three actors who'd arrived shortly before Ben and Frieda rose and went to the counter for one last round of java poppers. Todd shuddered. How anyone could shoot espresso shots and chomp down jalapeño peppers at any hour escaped him, but after midnight it was just sick and wrong. He'd only added them to the menu to stop Lily bugging him about them.

"You should go home. Don't you usually get here at oh dark hundred?" he said to Mona.

She shrugged. "I had a nap this afternoon so I could come back for the meeting. I'll have another tonight and be back for the baking." She yawned hugely behind one strong, graceful hand. "It may be oh dark thirty tomorrow, though. Assuming the boss has no objections."

"The boss has none."

"So what about them?"

Todd didn't need to ask whom she meant. "What about them?" he echoed. Her subject was clear. It was her meaning that escaped him. Almost.

"Don't be dense. That Ben guy is cute. Looks like he's about your age too."

"And yours," he said.

"I'm not interested in men."

"I know that. I've known that as long as you have. I just... Never mind. I was trying to be funny."

"You were? Usually I notice." She put on a perplexed expression.

"Brat."

Mona stopped short of the usual one-word retort, shaking her head. "I must be more tired than I thought. I have no response." She pushed back her chair, yawning again. She retrieved her coat, hat, and purse from the the kitchen.

Todd helped her into her fuzzy purple coat. "Will you be okay walking home alone?"

"I live a block away," she reminded him. "But if it'll

make you feel better, you can watch until you see my apartment light go on. I know you will anyway." She kissed his cheek. "Good night. I'll see you in the morning."

"Good night, Mona. Thanks again. I'm glad you made me call them, and I'm glad you were here with me to meet them."

"Me too." She smiled and gave him a little wave on her way out the door.

He stood in the doorway, watching through its window until he saw her apartment light go on.

Chapter 6

"HE WAS CUTE."

They were barely inside the car when Frieda made her declaration.

Trying to remain nonchalant, Ben buckled his seat belt as she started the engine. "I suppose so."

She let the engine warm up for a few moments while they talked. "Don't be coy. I saw you looking at him. He didn't notice, of course, because boys are slow. But I saw." She turned on her blinker and edged out into the empty street. "I saw him looking at you too," she added as they drove past the windows of Midnight Jones.

"Did you?" Ben glanced back over his shoulder as if seeking proof, as if he could catch Todd Marks looking at him even now. He could barely make out the figures of Todd and Mona at the little table near the window before the car was too far down the street for him to see more than the coffee shop's awning under the yellowish glow of a streetlamp.

"Oh yes."

He faced forward in his seat and glanced at her. "Are you serious or are you just playing with me?"

"Why do you always ask if I'm serious?" Her question was rhetorical, and they both treated it as such. "Ben, honey, you have no idea how attractive you are, do you? Such a shame that one so handsome should also be so dumb."

"Maybe it's all for the best," he countered, familiar with this particular line of banter. "Maybe if I knew how stunningly handsome I am, I'd be a conceited prick."

"I'd never let that happen."

It was true. Frieda never failed to place a compliment where she felt it was due. Neither did she let him get away with the slightest bullshit. Each time he forgot that fact, she was more than happy to remind him.

"Love you, Frieda."

She shot him a warm smile. "Love you too. Now, what did you think of Todd?"

"You tell me." It was an old challenge, and he couldn't help but bring it up tonight. Her knack for psychically reading people varied by individual. Despite their years of friendship...

"You know I don't read you that well."

"Can't, you mean," he replied with what he felt was a justified level of smugness.

"Can't be bothered, maybe."

He laughed. "You wish."

"All right. Rub it in, clever man. I'll have my revenge someday. Now spill it or I won't tell you what he thought of you."

Ben couldn't help his reaction no matter how she might tease him for behaving like a hormonal teenager. "Did you pick up something?"

She burst out laughing and nearly missed a four-way stop. She hit the brakes just in time or the guy in the red Mazda turning left in front of them would have been toast. "I picked up how you put your cell number on that business card and pretended it was perfectly normal behavior for any paranormal investigation." She checked the intersection, then eased the big sedan through it.

"You noticed that, huh?"

"Oh, honey, it was beyond obvious. I'm pretty sure his friend Mona noticed too. I think Todd Marks didn't think it was anything out of the ordinary—more's the pity. Now come on. Your turn."

"He *was* kind of cute," he said noncommittally. He was glad it was dark and that his friend needed to keep most of her attention on driving. He couldn't rely on her inability to read him and was happy for the distraction. Fact was Todd Marks was stupidly handsome. But did Ben want to admit that yet? Not especially.

"'Kind of cute'?" she echoed in a challenging voice.

So much for his resolution. He caved like a Mexican sugar skull in the rain. "Okay, he was totally hot! That navy-blue sweater he had on? That was cashmere, you know. Soft, warm, body-hugging cashmere. And what a body it had to hug! He must work out."

This time Frieda managed to laugh without endangering anyone's life. "Oh, if he only knew how truly shallow you are," she teased. Ben laughed with her. "All right. You spilled, so I will. Although I didn't get much from him I'm afraid. There were way too many vibes in that joint. Good vibes, but still too many. It made it cloudy. It's hard to pick up anything specific when the atmosphere is that thick. But I can say that he was definitely interested in you."

"Are you serious?"

"You *always* ask that."

"I *always* want to know, and I *always* can't tell."

"I think he was a little intimidated, frankly. That might have been Mona, now that I think about it. She was definitely sending out starstruck energy. But I think some of it was coming from him too, at least at first. Don't ever tell him I said that," she added firmly. "I get the impression he's not starstruck or intimidated by much of anything. You wouldn't want to put him off by suggesting otherwise. And besides, it didn't last long, assuming it was there at all."

"I won't say a word about it. Anyway, I doubt it's true.

Why in the hell would he find me intimidating?" Ben couldn't imagine it. He was a big dork and he knew it. He figured everyone else did too, and it didn't take seeing him in his goofy winter hat for them to realize it.

Frieda spoke to him with the cool edge of someone stating absolute fact. "Ben. Honey. Buy a clue. You're taller than he is, which he's probably not used to, being so tall himself."

"You think everyone is tall."

"Irrelevant. He was definitely over six feet, and you topped him by at least two inches. Besides that, you came across as pretty intense tonight."

"No, I didn't! Did I?" Why could he never judge that sort of thing? Maybe it was why he'd had so few second dates over the past too-many years. "I didn't mean to be intense. I thought I was just being professional. Unlike someone else in this vehicle." He shot her a look she probably couldn't see in the dark, but which he suspected she knew she was getting nonetheless.

"I was perfectly professional. Don't change the subject. And just so you know, he totally checked out your ass as we were leaving."

"Seriously?"

"Seriously."

"I wonder when he'll call back for a date. *With* a date! For the investigation, I mean." Whoops. No way Frieda was going to let that little misspeak slide by.

"Ha!" She put on her best secretary voice. "Paging Doctor Freud. Paging Doctor Freud. We have a full slip, complete with black lace and little red bows, waiting in the front office."

Ben laughed. She'd caught him out, fair and square. "All right, but try to convince me you weren't flirting with Mona."

"I wouldn't want to lie to you, dear." She pulled the car to a stop in front of his skinny three-story townhome and shifted into park. "I'd do her in a heartbeat, and I'd ask her to stay for breakfast. Only I don't know that she'd be up for it. Well, the doing part, I mean. Who would say no to a nice breakfast? I'm an excellent cook."

"All the stuff you can pick up from people and you couldn't tell if she's a lesbian?"

"What can I say? It always works better when it's not for my own benefit. Why do you think I never bother to play the lotto?"

"You could tell me the numbers. I'd share the jackpot with you," he deadpanned.

"You're funny," she replied just as flatly, making him grin. He could never play that sort of game with her for very long before cracking.

She extricated herself from her seat belt shoulder strap and gave him a quick hug. "See you tomorrow at the store. Should I be expecting any more deliveries of vintage children's literature?"

"Not yet. I'll let you know if I win that eBay auction I'm watching."

"Go to bed."

"Drive safe." He climbed out, shutting the door firmly behind him. She waited in the idling car until he flashed the porch light at her so she'd know he was inside safely. He heard her drive off into the night.

He paused in the front hallway, contemplated checking his email before going to bed, and decided against it. Anything that had come in since he'd left for Midnight Jones could wait until morning. He'd taken two steps up the stairs when he stopped and turned back. He should email Adam. It was only right to keep him in the loop, and it would make him less bitchy about missing out on a client interview. Better to let him know right away that PUPI had taken on a new one.

He really did need to do something about that acronym.

Shrugging the thought aside, he turned on the little desk lamp in the office and woke up the sleeping computer. He didn't even have to open a browser window. The moment he logged on, a messenger window from Adam popped up.

Adam: *Dude. You're up late.*

Ben: *look who's talking. met with a new client.*

Adam: *Sweet! whowhenwhere?*

Ben gave a tiny snort of amusement. Adam's typing went to hell when he got excited about something. Not that Ben was much better; he couldn't be bothered to hit the shift key. It drove Frieda nuts whenever they texted; the only capital letters were ones autocorrect put in for him. At least he usually managed to fit in the punctuation.

He answered his friend's questions in order.

Ben: *todd marks. don't know yet. midnight jones.*

Adam: *Midnght Jones? SOunds like a blus band.*

Ben: *come to the shop after work tomorrow. i'll fill you in.*

Adam: *Cool. Dinner first?*

Ben: *we'll order in. pizza?*

Adam: *Sweet! Make sur theres peperoni.*

Ben: *of course.*

Adam: *Seeyu tomorro.*

Ben: *night.*

He closed the window and logged out. He tried to resist the siren call of eBay and failed. He just had to take a quick peek at the auction he was watching. It would close a little over four days from now, in the wee small hours of Sunday morning. That was when he would make his move. He was glad to see that there were no new people watching and no one had placed a bid since someone named bklvr2001's bid about twelve hours ago.

Finally, he shut down the computer for the night, yawning hugely. He was glad he owned his own business.

He wouldn't get in trouble with the boss if he showed up a little late tomorrow morning. Frieda would flip him shit of course, but only if she got in before him. There was little chance of that.

The monitor screen went dark, and Ben clicked off the small desk lamp. The porch light outside the sliding glass doors shed stripes of illumination between the slats of the vertical blinds. He sat in the desk chair for a moment more, enjoying the silence after the computer fan stopped spinning. The rain and wind had stopped over an hour ago. The branches from the dogwood tree in his tiny back yard had ceased their scraping against the vinyl siding. Only occasional drips pinged in the downspouts. It would be dry and clear tomorrow. He could feel it in his skin.

He yawned again and stretched, forcing himself to his feet so he could climb the two flights of stairs to his bedroom on the top floor. The message light on the phone in the kitchen blinked as he passed the second floor. He almost stopped to see if it might be Todd Marks, calling already with a day and time when they could investigate. Good sense told him that was more unlikely than a duck that was afraid of water. Todd Marks didn't have the number to his landline, and it wasn't in the phone book. "You've been single too long, Ben," he muttered, falling into a long-held habit of speaking aloud to himself in the third person. For the first time, it occurred to him that a potential partner might view that as odd and off-putting. He resolved to make an effort to stop.

He turned the bedroom light on to half strength, pleased that he'd had a dimmer switch installed when he'd first bought the house. Even when he wasn't looking for a romantic atmosphere, he found it useful. Big, sleepy eyes looked up at him from the center of the bed. "Go back to sleep, Demon," he whispered. "It's only me."

The fluffy gray cat yawned and took his advice.

"Now it's your... *my* turn for sleep," he said to himself

and began preparing for bed.

The blinking message light followed him into slumber, invading his dreams with its little red flash. First, it was an ambulance light in his rearview mirror as he drove on an otherwise empty freeway. Then it morphed into a cop car that was pulled over on the freeway shoulder where a horse-drawn cart had lost a wheel. Ben rolled over in his sleep, his subconscious trying to dislodge the bizarre images, only to have the urban locations replaced by a swarm of flickering red fireflies in a dark mountain meadow. His mind told him that was very wrong. Wrong color. Wrong setting. There were no fireflies in the Pacific Northwest. He'd never seen one until he'd gone to college in upstate New York, and those were yellow, not red.

The bugs coalesced into a floating ball of fire that resolved itself into a flaming marshmallow on the end of a stick being held by Frieda. She was seated by a campfire and there were chocolate bars and graham crackers beside her on a log. She looked up at him and smiled.

"They're only really good when you've caught them on fire," she said.

The cell phone in his pocket began to play a song by Depeche Mode.

"Your phone is ringing. You should wake up."

Ben woke to his radio alarm. The song was "Waiting for the Night" and he wondered what significance that might have on his day. *Probably none,* he thought. There wasn't another planned meeting with Todd Marks tonight, which would have been nice but implausible. And asking a new client whom he barely knew out on a date was inappropriate. He would have to wait until the job was done before he made that move.

Damned ethics.

Demon meowed in protest as he pushed back the covers.

"You don't have to get up."

The cat looked doubtful, narrowing its yellow eyes at him.

"Go back to sleep. I'll call you when it's breakfast time."

Apparently mollified, the feline yawned and went back to sleep.

As he ran hot water for a shower, Ben wondered if Todd Marks liked cats.

*

It was nearly half an hour later when Ben trudged downstairs. Morning sun poured through the east-facing kitchen and dining area windows and angled obliquely through the sliding patio door to the little balcony that looked out over the yard. Clear and dry today. Just as he had predicted last night. He might not have Frieda's skill at reading people, but he could accurately predict the weather down to the hour, sometimes even the quarter-hour, which was a major asset in the Pacific Northwest.

He scooped food into Demon's kibble bowl, and immediately heard the sound of the overlarge kitty leaping to the floor upstairs. By the time he'd topped up the water bowl, Demon had trotted down the carpeted stairs, found his breakfast, and begun munching happily.

"You're getting fat," Ben said to the cat. "We need to play more."

Demon ignored him and continued to nosh.

Ben poured himself a bowl of sugary, rainbow-colored cereal, topped it with milk, and finally checked the blinking message light that had haunted his dreams.

"Hi. It's just me."

Not the most auspicious of beginnings. Ben recognized the slightly mournful voice and wished he'd checked the caller ID before pressing Play. If he had, he might have been able to convince himself to "accidentally" delete the message without listening to it. Now that he'd started it, though, he felt morally obligated to listen until the end.

"Corey," the voice identified itself unnecessarily. As if Ben would ever mistake that laconic tone for anyone else. He had made the mistake of dating Corey shortly after he had moved back to Seattle. The fact that Corey still called him once in a blue moon had nothing to do with some great friendship they'd maintained over the years and even less to do with any emotional connection they might have shared during the tempestuous three months they'd been together. No. It rather had everything to do with the fact that Corey was completely codependent and lacked even the slightest shred of self-esteem, and that Ben was a total bleeding-heart.

The message played on. Painfully. Inexorably. "So... how are you doing? How's the ghost-hunting business going? I saw that piece you did on the Harvard Exit ghosts from last Halloween and it made me think of you. I thought I'd call and see how you're doing. You looked good. I bet you still do. You always looked so good."

God help him, Ben wanted to leap through the phone line and throttle the man. Unless he was mistaken, the only place Corey could have seen that video segment recently was online somewhere like the network's website or YouTube, in which case he was hardly likely to have come across it by random happenstance. Ben had little doubt that Corey had the link bookmarked and watched it whenever he wanted an excuse to call. Ben should really cancel his landline. Why hadn't he done that yet? Corey didn't have his cell number and never would if Ben had anything to say about it. He'd have to get a new one if that ever happened. And Corey was just smart enough, or had just enough self-preservation instinct, not to call the PUPI line and risk getting Frieda on the other end. No one wanted to witness that conversation. Corey had never visited Hole-in-the-Wall Books, and Ben hoped it stayed that way.

Corey's message prattled on while Ben finished his cereal and silently willed the man to get to his point. He knew it would happen eventually and he didn't care to wait much longer. He needed to get to work.

"I'm okay. I guess."

Ah-ha! Here it came.

"I'm a little down. Jeff and I broke up."

"Again," Ben said to the answering machine.

"Again," the message echoed. "So anyway. Hope you're okay. It makes me feel better to think you're happy. I bet you have some fabulous boyfriend who makes you really happy. I'm sure you do."

Ben rolled his eyes. As if. He hadn't had a proper date in over a year. Hadn't had a second date in longer than that. With a bit of luck, Todd Marks would rectify that situation in the near future. With even more luck, there would be not only a second date, but a third and fourth and Ben would never need another first date with anyone ever again.

He shook himself from pointless happily-ever-after fantasies and tuned back into whatever Corey was saying.

"I hope you and your boyfriend are great. Really. I'd love to meet him sometime. I bet he's fabulous."

Ben gently beat his head against the refrigerator door.

"Okay. Well. Call me or something. You know. If you're bored or whatever. Or, you know, if you just feel like hanging out. We could go for coffee or drinks or something. I'd like to see you, if you want. Okay. Bye."

There followed the blessed click of the connection cutting out, followed by the comforting sound of the digitized voice announcing that there were no more messages.

"That's it. I am cancelling my damned landline." No one but Corey and telemarketers ever called it anyway. Anyone he actually *wanted* to talk to knew to call his cell.

Of course, if he cancelled it, Corey would eventually try to call again and find it disconnected. That brought up the horrifying idea that Corey might work harder to seek him out in person. The last thing he needed was for that particular piece of his past to show up at his present work or, God forbid, home. Aside from the inevitable awkwardness that would ensue, there would be the little problem of cleaning up the mess after Frieda ripped both Corey and him new assholes. The ugly emotional aftermath was more than he cared to contemplate at that hour of the morning on little sleep and before he'd had his coffee.

Why, oh why hadn't he listened to Frieda when he and Corey had first met? He could have saved himself so much trouble in the long run. Looking back, he would have also missed out on some really great sex. But even great sex wears thin when the person you're having it with isn't someone you love. Now Todd, on the other hand, held potential certainly for the former, and possibly for the latter. Frieda already seemed to like him too, which boded well for his and Ben's future together.

God, he needed a date! Here he was pondering an entirely theoretical future—again!—with a man he'd met *one time*, less than twelve hours ago. He was a dork. A sad and desperate dork.

And yet... Where was the harm in a little innocent speculation?

Aside from the obvious things like his handsomeness and personal successes, there were other attributes to attract Ben. For example, Todd struck him as the opposite of a drama queen, and that was definitely a major point in his favor. Ben was adult enough to recognize that he, himself, still had the occasional tendency to be that way, but he usually knew when it was happening and tried to rein it in. He didn't revel in it like he used to. Like Corey still did.

He shook his head. "Enough!" he announced firmly. Reaching out one long finger, he hit the Delete button on his answering machine, erasing Corey's message. He felt the usual wave of guilt that passed by the time he was done putting his dishes in the dishwasher. Then, he put all thoughts of his unstable ex-lover firmly from his mind.

Demon had also finished up his breakfast. After begging for more and being told no, the cat padded silently to the living room where he leapt up into the recliner, curled up in a big ball of gray fur, and fell asleep again.

Ben quirked a jealous smile. "Lucky bastard. All you do is eat and sleep. No wonder you're so fat and happy." He gave the cat a fond scratch behind the ears and was rewarded with a purr that was disconcertingly delicate coming from such a robust animal.

He quickly finished his morning routine and left the house. The air was warmer than it had been in more than a week, and he took a deep, satisfied breath, letting it out in a small puff of steam. Still cold. Just not as cold. At least today, he had brought his hat. He pulled on the ridiculous knit thing Frieda had given him for Solstice last year. It made him look especially goofy, but he didn't care. It took balls for a man his age to wear a hat like that. Hell, it took balls for anyone over the age of six to wear a hat like that. But it kept his ears warm, and it was a gift from his best friend, and he loved it.

He would get coffee at his usual place on his walk into work. The barista would tease him as she always did when he wore his goofy winter hat. There would be a message from Todd on the Presence Unknown voicemail when he got in. And it would be a good day.

Chapter 7

"SHIT!"

Danny swerved up the curb ramp onto the sidewalk to avoid being hit by an enormous SUV whose driver apparently thought that yellow lights meant "turn right really fast in front of the bicyclist."

He tried to stop in a controlled fashion, but it wasn't in the cards. Enough wet leaves clung to the pavement to make it slick, and his tires lost their grip. He skidded, just managing to turn sideways before smacking unceremoniously into a light pole. He caught enough breath to shout "Motherfucker!" at the quickly disappearing vehicle, then he put one foot on the pavement to keep his balance while he caught his breath properly. His heart was racing after the near miss. It always terrified him and pissed him off when someone pulled that sort of bullshit. It was why he wore the helmet cam; in case things went *really* bad and—

"Ow! Son of a bitch!" The adrenaline rush of fear rapidly gave way to the pain of having slammed into a big, metal pole. Worse than that, it was one of those old-fashioned looking ones with a wide, square base full of detail and sharp corners.

"Are you all right?"

"Yeah, thanks," he responded grumpily, too focused on readjusting his clothes and his bike to glance up. "It's not the first time I've been bruised in the line of duty."

"You're a little more than bruised."

"Huh?" He looked blankly at the woman who'd spoken. The back of his mind registered the familiarity of her face, but he couldn't place her in the split second before she pointed down to his right leg. His eyes went wide at the sight of the scraped-up flesh oozing blood from the exposed area of his calf between the edge of his bike shorts and the top of his sock. "Holy—" He sucked in a breath against the stinging pain. "Shit! Fuck! That— Ugh!"

His eyes went wide as he discovered yet another indignity. The lid had popped off his to-go cup, and most of his caramel mocha was now no more than a beige splash on the sidewalk. "Son of a *bitch*!"

"Here. Come with me. You can get cleaned up at my shop. I'm just around the corner."

"Yeah. Okay." He limped behind her down the block, wheeling his bike alongside him and up to an inset doorway with windows full of books on either side. His brain finally put two and two together. But he still didn't know the woman's name.

She unlocked the door to Hole-in-the-Wall Books and ushered him in. "You can leave your bike in front of the shop. No one will bother it."

"Like last time?"

She looked up from disarming the alarm panel next to the door, her expression quizzical. "What happened last time?"

"Nothing really. Some comedian stuck a 'Free Ballard' sticker on the seat. That's all."

She stifled a laugh. "That won't happen again, but you can wheel the bike inside if you like."

Her tone was such that he believed her, but he opted to bring the bike in anyway.

"Follow me. We have a first-aid kit in the back."

"Are you sure? I can wait out here. I don't want to get

you in trouble with the owner or anything." It was half of the truth. The other half was that he didn't want to limp any farther than he already had. He just wanted to sit down somewhere comfortable and not move for a while.

"*I'm* the owner. Well, the co-owner." She gave him a sympathetic smile. "It's not far. There's even a comfy chair you can sit down in when you get there."

There it was again. This woman had an uncanny way of pegging what he was thinking without actually saying exactly what was in his head. It was creepy, but somehow not as upsetting as he felt it ought to have been. Maybe it was her frank and open expression. Maybe it was the smile and the way she talked to him like an old friend when they didn't even know one another's names. Or maybe he was feeling too battered to argue any more. Whatever the reason, he trusted her.

"Thanks."

*

Leaving his bike and helmet just inside the door, Frieda guided him between floor-to-ceiling shelving units full of books. This aisle was primarily science fiction and fantasy. "Circumstances have brought you here twice in as many days. You'll have to check out our stock this time. We have a fair collection of Arthur C. Clarke hardbacks right now. Hardly consolation for being run off the road, of course, but I'm confident you'll find something you've been wanting. Here."

Frieda held aside the heavy velvet curtain and allowed him to step past her into the tiny office. "Sit." She pointed to the well-worn taupe-and-cream striped wing chair in one corner of the crowded room. He happily sat, slinging his satchel onto the floor to one side.

"Thanks. My name's Danny, by the way. Danny Raines. I really appreciate your help."

"Happy to, Danny Raines." She crossed the crowded office to the tiny bathroom where they kept the first-aid kit. "I'm Frieda Smith."

He grinned. "Frieda, huh? Wowie zowie!"

She laughed, immediately recognizing the reference. She responded with a knowing half smile. "Come on, El Kabah, baby. Or do you prefer Captain Jack? Jungle Jack?"

Danny's jaw dropped, and Frieda grinned wider. She hadn't thought people's jaws ever dropped in real life, and she was delighted to be proved wrong. "It's a rare and auspicious day when I meet someone who knows about Jack Flanders without me having to introduce them to him and his compatriots."

"Oh. My. Gods. You know that series?"

"I *love* that series. I have them all on CD—except the ones they only released as digital files, which I also have."

"Me too! Little Frieda is my personal guru."

Frieda set the first-aid kit on the corner of her desk. "Right on. I'm more of a Mojo Sam girl. Ironic, I know. I will admit to a certain delight in discovering a fictional character with the same name as me. That's a rarity. Now, let me see that leg." She knelt on the hardwood floor in front of him.

He tensed and shook his head, saying quickly, "I can do it."

"Suit yourself." Frieda shrugged and handed over the unopened antiseptic pad packet.

He thanked her again and ripped it open.

"Do you want a cup of coffee?" She rose and gestured to the small, automatic coffee pot that stood on top of the tiny refrigerator in the back corner of the room. "It's just about done brewing." She'd set it up on the timer the night before, which wasn't her habit. Now she knew why she'd done it.

"I thought I was imagining the smell of coffee. You don't have to do that." He braced himself and applied the antiseptic cloth to his leg. He hissed at the sting but managed not to pull it away. She watched as he cleaned the scraped area.

The coffee maker burbled to a finish and Frieda poured some into her usual enormous mug. She added in creamer from the little fridge, and then sat in Ben's desk chair so as not to crowd her visitor. It squeaked beneath her. "How is it?"

"I've had worse."

"There's ibuprofen in there if you want some." She nodded toward the kit where she'd left it on the corner of her desk. "If body slamming a lamp post is anything like body slamming a sidewalk, you're going to want it."

"You've hit the pavement that hard?"

"Walking to work one time. Years ago. You know how crappy the sidewalks are in certain places, right?"

He glanced up, nodded, and began digging around in the first-aid kit for a bandage.

"Yeah. Well. I was hurrying and I tripped. Did a full body slam flat into the sidewalk." She demonstrated with one arm, like a tree toppling.

"Ow."

"You're not kidding. It must have looked pretty bad too, because this guy turned the corner and stopped his car in front of me. I was almost to the corner, right? And he asked me if I was okay."

"Someone was that nice?" Danny was surprised, and she couldn't blame him. Then he immediately tried to backtrack. "Not that you didn't just do that for me. I mean, it's not like people here are rude or anything exactly."

"I was surprised as hell. Or I would have been, if I hadn't been in a mild state of shock from the impact."

"I didn't mean—"

She held up a hand and sipped her coffee before going on. "Forget about it. You're not wrong. For the record, it's not that we don't care. It's just that we don't want to invade your personal bubble."

"Huh?"

"If you'd grown up here, you'd know. We're super helpful and friendly, but you have to ask for what you need. You'll learn. How long have you lived here?"

"Less than a year."

"Yeah, you'll figure it out," she said again.

"So, what happened?" He found one of the large adhesive bandages that was pretreated with antibiotic goo and pressed it to his scraped-up leg. That was going to hurt when he tore it off. *Men are such wusses when it comes to hair-removal via sticky things,* thought Frieda with a hint of schadenfreude.

"I went to work," she answered. "I was nearly there anyway. My hands were scraped up, but not too badly. I cleaned up and went on with my day. I don't remember anything else that happened that day, but that could have had something to do with the fact that the job in question was mind-numbingly boring. It was the next day I was sorry."

He stilled, dread radiating from him like heat from a campfire, and looked at her. *Poor kid,* she thought in genuine compassion. *He really is going to be miserable by morning.*

"What happened the next day?" he asked with trepidation.

"I ached from head to toe. My body felt like one giant contusion, even though the only outward sign was my hands and some bruising on my knees and elbows. I spent the entire day on the sofa popping pain killers and watching movies."

Danny gave a chuckle that was half dismissive, half nervous. "That doesn't sound so bad."

"It wasn't—except anytime I had to get up to pee. Moving was a very bad thing. And don't even make me think about going up and down stairs."

He made a face. "Okay. That sounds like the opposite of fun." He sat back, surveying his handiwork. "I guess I should invest in some long, reinforced biking tights."

"I'd recommend it. It's going to be a cold, wet winter." Ben had mentioned it, and he was a better predictor than any Farmer's Almanac or weather blogger.

His leg taken care of, Danny pulled off his half-zip jacket and rolled up his shirtsleeve. A large bruise was already purpling under the warm brown skin of his forearm. He couldn't get the sleeve far enough to see up any higher, but Frieda would bet, based on the way he'd impacted the lamp post, that there was a matching one on his upper arm. He was lucky he hadn't impacted directly on his elbow.

"Sure you don't want some coffee? Or some water so you can take those meds? There might even be an icepack in the kit there for those bruises."

"Are those stick figures on your mug?" His question took her by surprise, which wasn't an easy thing to do, especially one-on-one and in close quarters as they were.

"Yes."

"What are they doing?"

"Shakespeare."

"Oooo-kay." He made up his mind. "I'd love a cup of coffee if you really don't mind. My mocha didn't survive the impact as well as I did."

"I saw. It was in a hell of a state." She rose and poured him a cup of coffee. "Want anything in it?"

"I can get it." He started to rise.

"Sit."

He sat.

"It's too damned crowded in here for gallantry. What do you want in your coffee? I'm sorry we don't have chocolate syrup."

"Just cream and three sugars, please."

"Soy creamer okay?"

"Sure."

She shot him a look as she tore open three little brown packets of raw sugar and poured them into the mug. "Quite a sweet tooth."

He shrugged and turned to dig into the first-aid kit for ibuprofen. "Always have had. No cavities, though."

"Do you put that on your speed dating form?" she joked, stirring his coffee before handing it over.

"Okay. How the *hell* did you know I went speed dating last week?" he demanded, pinning her with an accusing gaze. "I wasn't even *thinking* about speed dating, so you couldn't have read my mind this time."

Whoops. She'd gone too far, and she hadn't even been trying. "I was kidding. I had no idea you'd ever gone speed dating, let alone as recently as last week."

That stopped him short. "Oh." He blushed and hid behind his mug, which was a ZBS Media mug that said "Wowie zowie!" on one side and "Little Frieda" on the other. "I have this mug too." He sipped from it and used the hot coffee to wash down a couple of painkillers.

Frieda eyed him keenly. She liked to pretend she didn't have guilt, but this was one of those moments that put the lie to her. He was wary now when he'd been relaxed before. He was suspicious when he'd been open and friendly. She needed to make amends.

"I'm sorry if I weirded you out."

"What? No! Nothing like that," he lied quickly and changed the subject. "So what is all this stuff? I mean"— his eyes landed on a stack of equipment—"what does a used bookstore need with a thermal imaging camera?"

"Nothing," a male voice answered. "But paranormal investigators use them all the time."

Frieda smiled at the same moment Danny practically leapt out of his skin. It was pure luck he didn't spill his coffee everywhere. He turned in his chair to see Ben looming in the little doorway, latte in one gloved hand and his wonderfully ridiculous knit hat on his head. Danny rose quickly, fighting the wince that came with the movement.

Frieda made the introductions. "Ben, this is Danny Raines."

Danny stuck out his right hand and only then realized that was the one holding the coffee mug. He switched it to his left hand and tried again. "Hi."

Ben pulled off a glove with his teeth and shook hands. Reclaiming the glove, he said, "Ben Chalfie. You're the bike messenger from yesterday. I wondered whose bike that is in the shop."

"Yeah. That's mine. Sorry if it's in the way or anything."

"It's fine. Is there a delivery I don't know about?" Ben looked over Danny's head to Frieda.

"No. He had a near miss with a jerk in an SUV," she answered. "I figured a little first-aid for the body and soul were in order." She gestured with her head to the kit and then the coffee.

"Of course." Ben smiled at Danny.

"I'll get out of your way real soon," Danny said, and then inadvertently contradicted his words by sitting back down. Frieda fought down a chuckle.

"Don't hurry on my account. Finish your coffee." Ben looked to Frieda. "Any messages this morning?" There was more in his tone and expression than simple inquiry, and Frieda knew why. She hated to disappoint him.

"I haven't checked yet."

"Okay." Ben set his coffee on his cramped and cluttered desk, then took off his hat and coat. "Excuse me." He reached behind Danny, who leaned sideways so Ben could access the wooden coatrack tucked into the corner behind the wing chair.

"You don't waste an inch in here, do you?" Danny said.

"I didn't even notice that was there."

"There's not an inch to be wasted." Ben smiled at him and turned to Frieda. "I'm going to open up the store. Let me know if we have anything interesting on the voicemail."

"You bet." Frieda easily recognized the code for *please tell me if Todd Marks called.*

"Thanks." Ben reclaimed his coffee and disappeared out to the front.

Danny piped up the moment Ben had gone. "He said 'paranormal investigators.'"

"Yes, he did."

"Soooooo... On the voicemail, does he mean something ghosty?" he asked in a low, conspiratorial voice.

Frieda smiled and matched his tone. "We have a new client, yeah. We're working on scheduling our investigations with him."

"Investigations, plural?"

"He has a few things that need investigating, yeah."

"Cool. So you guys are *real* paranormal investigators?"

"Ever hear of Presence Unknown?"

His eyes went wide behind his glasses, and he gave up trying to be quiet and mysterious. "That's you guys?"

"That's us guys. And this super-high-tech closet in which you're sitting is our inner sanctum." Her tone was ironic, but Danny was seriously impressed.

"Cool!" he said again. "I know a guy with a haunted car!" He clamped his mouth shut, looking mortified. He fell silent and took a long drink of his coffee to hide his embarrassment.

"Do you?" What were the odds there were two haunted cars in Seattle? In a city of too damned many people with too damned many vehicles, chances weren't that slim. But the added layer of coincidence intrigued her. She was far too familiar with the ways of coincidence to discount it this time.

"Yeah. He's not, like, a close friend or anything. I mean... he owns the coffee shop I go to. My favorite one. Up on Cap Hill."

"Capitol Hill or the Hill." She corrected him automatically. "'Cap Hill' makes you sound like a transplant or a dude-bro douche bag. You're the former. Don't be the latter."

"Oh. Uh. Okay. Sorry?"

"Forgiven. Now tell me about the guy with the haunted car and the coffee shop." She narrowed her eyes and Danny leaned away from her scrutiny.

"Um..."

She was impatient and decided leading the witness was better than waiting for him to spit it out. "It wouldn't happen to be a place called Midnight Jones, would it?"

"How the hell did you know that? Did you read my mind again?"

She ignored his questions and answered his tone. "Relax. It's just a little more coincidence to add to this already highly coincidental day. Tell me, have you ever done any ghost hunting?"

"Me? Well..." He once more engaged in an internal debate that played out on his face. Frieda wondered which side would win—until he spoke. "A little. Sort of. Mostly just heat sensor data and voice recording. But I did determine that my folks' house in Wapakoneta is haunted."

"You got solid evidence?"

Danny took pride in his investigation and it showed in his demeanor. He sat up straighter and puffed out his chest a little. "I got a clearly human female form in the living room, and I got the sound of a little kid laughing in the upstairs hallway. And now one of the ghosts helps my mom decorate with vintage furniture that matches the period the house was built in and the architectural style."

"Interesting." Frieda sat back in the desk chair, which creaked softly under her. She sipped thoughtfully at her coffee and regarded him over the rim of her mug.

Danny drank his coffee in silence and waited for her to make the next move. Which she did.

"You busy tonight?"

"No. Why?"

"Come back here at seven."

"Seven?"

"Can you do that?"

"I guess." He gave her a puzzled look, but she didn't satisfy his curiosity. Let him be surprised that evening. He wouldn't be the only one.

Danny stalled as long as he dared, hoping for more information. When Frieda offered none, he was forced to concede defeat. He downed the dregs of his coffee and rose. "I need to go. There's only so much lost time I can reasonably blame on traffic if someone complains about a delivery or pick-up being late. Thanks for the help and the coffee."

"You're welcome."

He set the empty mug on the nearest desk and pulled his jacket back on over his head, flinching at the motion. He picked up his satchel and donned it more carefully. "Seven tonight?"

"Yep. The store will be closed by then and the front door will be locked, so just ring the bell. I'll come let you in." She rose and once more opened the curtain and motioned for him to precede her.

"Okay. Thanks again," he said.

"No problem. See you tonight."

"Yeah. See you."

They returned to the shop where Ben stood behind the counter, counting the morning till in preparation for customers.

"See you," Danny said to him.

"Sure." Ben smiled. "See you around."

The bike messenger stepped outside, and a waft of fresh morning air filled the space he left behind.

"Did you check the messages?" asked Ben.

"Not yet. Be right back."

*

Frieda emerged from the back once more and leaned on the front counter. She set her mug down and looked at the piece of scratch paper in her hand. "Three UFO sightings. I deleted them. If people can't be bothered to listen to the outgoing message on the voicemail, they deserve no better than deletion. Two potential ghost sightings. One is a UW student who thinks they might have a ghost roommate."

"They wouldn't be the first," said Ben. He'd had one himself when he was in college. It was part of the reason he'd decided to found Presence Unknown. "Do they want us to investigate?"

"I'm not entirely sure. The message wasn't real clear on that point. I'll call back this afternoon and find out what's up."

"I hope they do." He frowned as memories flickered unbidden across his mind's eye. If only he'd paid better attention when he'd been in college. If only he'd paid *any* attention...

He was glad when Frieda went on, interrupting his thoughts. "The other sighting is a woman in Snohomish who thinks she saw the ghost of her old horse in the barn last night."

"She's sure it wasn't just, I don't know, a horse?"

"According to her message, she doesn't have any at the moment. Hasn't had any since the last one died two years ago."

"And she wants us to investigate?"

"So she says in her message. You want to call her back or shall I?"

"I'll do it. It sounds intriguing."

"Sure. If you like horses and stinky old barns."

"How often do we get animal hauntings? Besides, Adam and I can take it if you don't want to come."

Frieda snorted derisively. "Oh yeah. Adam will love you volunteering him for that." But he noticed that she didn't object to the suggestion or offer to accompany him instead.

"Anything else?" He was trying to play it cool. He knew perfectly well that if Todd had called, Frieda would save the message for last just to torment him. Right now, he sincerely hoped that was what she was doing.

No such luck.

"Not yet." Frieda gave him an apologetic look. "We only met him last night, and we were there until nearly one a.m. He may not even be up yet this morning."

"It's after nine."

"Okay, so maybe he's up but he hasn't checked his calendar or talked to his business manager yet. Relax. He'll call today before the store closes." She said it in that tone of voice he'd long ago come to recognize as predicting fact. Otherwise he would have argued with her, letting out all the little doubts and uncertainties in his mind.

Instead, he shrugged. "If you say so."

"I do say so." She pushed away from the counter, leaving the page of messages behind. "I'm going to start inventorying cookbooks. It's been too long since I did anything about that section."

"I'm sure it wouldn't have anything to do with looking for some cool book on pastries or muffins to give to a particular baker we just met." He smiled too innocently.

She pretended she thought he was serious. "Wow. You *are* dumb." Then she grinned back at him. "Shout if you need anything, okay?"

"Sure."

She reclaimed her mug from the counter and began to

head down the aisle that would take her to the corner where cookbooks were shelved. "By the way, we'll be four for the meeting tonight."

Ben didn't have to guess. He'd known her long enough to follow the majority of her non sequiturs. "You hired the bike messenger."

"Not yet, but I'm hoping to. I think we're going to need some seasonal help this year."

"It is that time of year, isn't it?" He sighed. He hated October.

"Yeah." Frieda looked back over one shoulder and shot him a knowing smile. "I love October, don't you?"

Chapter 8

"IT'S DONE." TODD SIGHED AND SHOVED HIS CELL PHONE into his pocket.

"You say that with such a gallows tone." Shell Manning, Midnight Jones's business manager, adjusted her glasses and looked at him across her desk. She tucked her shoulder-length, russet-brown hair behind her ears in a habitual gesture. "You don't have to do this just because Mona wants you to, you know."

"This was my decision," he replied firmly, echoing the words Mona had said to him yesterday morning. He didn't mention that he probably never would have called the Presence Unknown people in the first place if he hadn't allowed Mona to talk him into it. Still, he wasn't sorry. If it did nothing more than stop his spoons disappearing it would be worth it. It was icing on the cupcake that the owner of the company happened to be tall, handsome, and magnetic. Todd was also reasonably sure Ben was single. Mona was positive the man was gay, although Todd wasn't ready to bank on that quite yet. Gay and metrosexual were often confused with each other. Not that any of it meant anything was going to happen, of course. It only meant there was the pleasant possibility. Considering how long it had been since he and Michael had split up, that possibility alone was enough to make him cautiously optimistic.

"I still say you're nuts, but it's your nickel." She fixed

him with a gray-eyed stare. "It *is* your nickel, right? Or do you plan to pay for it out of the coffeehouse's budget?"

"I'm paying from my personal account," he assured her. He knew better than to mess with her budgets without serious advance warning.

"All right then. I appreciate you clearing the coffee shop part with me first." Shell turned her attention back to her computer screen. Hers was the only desk in the little office, and he was forever grateful she'd accepted it. She'd had a good job at his old company even after the dot-com boom had become a crash. And yet, when he'd come head-hunting for someone to manage his fledgling coffeehouse and give it a dynamic web presence, she'd leapt at the chance without a single glance behind her.

He sat in the only other chair in the office, across the desk from her. It had seemed reasonable to make his call from in here rather than out in the dining room. No need to let the patrons in on the potentially haunted nature of the place. On one hand, it might bring in more customers if word got out. On the other, they might not be the sort of customers he wanted. And if it turned out there was nothing paranormal about the place after all, it would only make for disappointment.

"I'm curious. Why are you so skeptical? I know you believe me when I say my car is haunted. So why don't you think my house, or this place, could be too?"

She looked up once more and met his gaze across the desk. "I believe you about the car because I've witnessed it myself. The recurrent theme of 1963's pop hits is undeniable. I have no opinion on your house. I've been there on only three occasions and never once was I in need of a spoon. I have, however, spent many daytime and nighttime hours in Midnight Jones, and I've never once noticed anything supernatural, current missing spoons mystery notwithstanding. I still think it was some sort of prank."

Todd didn't hear most of her speech. He was stuck on what she'd said about the music in his haunted car. "1963?"

"What?" Her gray eyes were blank with incomprehension.

"Are you sure?"

She looked at him like he'd just grown antennae. "Can you narrow it down for me? Sure about what?"

"The music. When the radio comes on to oldies songs, you said it's something from 1963."

Now her expression was one she usually reserved for Flat-Earthers and other idiots. "You didn't know that? It happens every time."

"*Every* time?"

"You seriously hadn't noticed? How long have you had that car?"

He didn't answer. Especially when the answer could just as rightly be "over a decade" or "more than long enough to have figured that out."

"Oh my God. You really hadn't realized." She laughed and then covered her mouth with one hand. "I'm sorry. That's just funny."

"Oh, shut up and code something," he replied, but there was no malice in his tone. She wasn't laughing at him to be mean. He knew that from experience. Shell could have an odd sense of humor sometimes, but it was never malicious. Frankly, he had it coming for having been so slow on the uptake. Now, though, he had to go find out if she was right. He stood. "I'm going to run some errands. Do you need anything for the office?"

She smirked at him, perfectly aware of the motivation behind his sudden errands. "Printer paper. I could use a ream of lavender and a ream of yellow. And a box of blue rollerball pens. The fine point kind."

"Will do. If you need anything else, text me."

"Will do," Shell echoed. "Oh. Before I forget to tell you,

I have four new applications in for another barista. I'll review them all today and set up interviews with the ones worth interviewing. And Lily has a friend she's sending over to apply in addition to those four. Apparently he's worked for both Zoka and Starbucks."

"Which begs the question, why doesn't he work for either of them anymore?"

"Rest assured, I'll be considering that during the interview."

"I wouldn't expect anything less. I'll see you later." He left the office and took the three steps to the kitchen where he stuck his head around the doorframe. Mona was cleaning up, done with the baking for the midday crowd. "Hey, Mona. I'm going out. You need anything?"

"Lunch?" She smiled at him hopefully.

"It's three o'clock."

"Okay, so, lunner?"

He laughed. "Sure. I have errands I want to do. Lunner could be one of them."

"Excellent. Give me one more minute."

"I'll be out front."

"Okay."

There were no customers at the counter, so he leaned against it to wait for Mona.

"Hey, boss man," said Lily with a smile.

"Hey, Lily." He liked Lily, even though her fashion sense made *no* sense to him. She had chosen to accent her usual black wardrobe base with yellow and orange today, right up to the ribbons around her pigtails and the laces in her boots. He supposed the look was nice enough in its own way, and she was never what he would have considered inappropriately dressed to work with the public, so he never commented on it to Shell or anyone else. Of course, his own formative career years had been in a dot-com office, so what did he know about fashion, goth or otherwise? And she was, without question, the best barista he'd ever met.

"You need a drink or a munchy or anything?" she asked with a bright smile.

"No thanks. I hear we're up to the interviewing stage for a new barista."

"Yes!" There was more than a little relief in the single word. "Honestly, I'm so glad Shell's interviewing people soon. It's been insanely busy lately, which is good for business and all that, but the other day it was such a madhouse in here! Even I couldn't predict the extent of it. We almost ran out of drip! And, of course, there always has to be one high-maintenance customer when there's a rush on, and it was so nuts I just wanted to hit someone, and I'm a pacifist! *That* tells you how bad it was. So, yes, please, can you hire another barista?" She looked at him, her kohl-rimmed eyes wide and hopeful.

"Did I hear that you have a friend you're recommending?"

"David, yeah! He's *awesome*! I know he has to go through the interview process and everything," she said quickly. "Got to have everything on the up and up, right? But I just know you're gonna love him!"

Mona emerged from the kitchen at that moment. She pulled her lavender bandana off her head and ran a hand through her short, dark curls to fluff them up. She'd changed from her kitchen Crocs into real shoes and left her apron behind. Stuffing the scarf into the pocket of her fleecy purple coat, she asked, "Ready to go?"

Todd stood up straight. "Yep. We'll be back in a bit, Lily. See you later."

"Bye, boss man. Bye, Mona."

The afternoon air was cool but not cold and neither of them bothered to zip up their coats as they stepped outside.

"Where're we going on these errands of yours?" asked Mona.

"The office supply store. Shell asked if I'd pick up some printer paper for her." It wasn't the whole truth, but it was enough. Or he thought it was.

"Uh-huh." Her tone was skeptical, and he expected her to press the matter, but for whatever reason she let it drop. "So we're headed to your place for the car?"

"Yeah."

"Good. I don't feel like eating in the neighborhood today." The light in front of them turned green and they crossed the arterial, heading into the narrow residential streets that surrounded the neighborhood's retail hub.

"Where do you want to go, then? You have the whole city to choose from." He gestured grandly, then added in a more ordinary tone, "Or at least what there is of it between here and the office supply store."

"In that case, I know just the place. I've been craving poutine for days."

"Of all the proclivities to have picked up when you were living in Canada, that is without a doubt the oddest."

She shook her head. "Not even remotely true. You met Jeanine." They both shuddered at the mention of her ex. "Just count us both lucky that there are more and more places in town that are smart enough to have poutine on their menus, and that one of them isn't far away. Otherwise I'd have to take a vacation day so I could road-trip to Canada every time I wanted some done right."

"That is a long drive just for fries with gravy on them."

"It is *so* much more than 'fries with gravy on them.' You, you silly and ignorant American, will never understand."

"Oh yeah," he pretended revelation. "I forgot there's cheese curds too."

"Smart-ass."

"Canuck."

They laughed as they turned onto the street where

Todd lived. The trees that lined it were in full autumn splendor, their leaves a riot of shades of green, gold, and purple-red.

Mona looked around at them. "Shell is right."

"About what?"

"The leaves do turn the colors of jam. Look." She pointed and named them. "Apricot. Golden raspberry with a dollop of red currant. Plum. Oo! That one's like orange marmalade! Damn. Now I'm *really* hungry. Hurry up." She wrapped her arm around his and picked up her pace, forcing him to walk quicker.

Nearing his house, he pulled his keys from his jacket pocket and hit the remote for the garage. The door rolled up as they entered the narrow driveway.

"Should we place bets on what retro song will be on the radio when we get in the car?" joked Mona, opening the passenger side door.

"I'm going to guess something released in 1963."

She laughed as they climbed in and shut their doors. "That's a given."

That answered that. Was he the only one who hadn't made that connection? Jesus, he would never live it down if Mona found out he'd only just learned about it. Fortunately, there was little to no reason for Shell ever to mention it to her. He flashed her a grin. "Ready?"

She fastened her seat belt and made a show of bracing for take-off. "Ready!"

He started the car. The radio came on immediately although he knew perfectly well he had shut it off last night.

A sweetly lilting group of male voices greeted their ears.

"Oo! I love the Kingston Trio!" Mona turned up the volume and began to sing along.

Todd backed the car out and hit the remote to close the garage door after them. He made a mental note to look up "Seasons in the Sun" the next time he had a minute to himself. He had little doubt he would find that the Kingston Trio had released their recording of it in 1963. But it never hurt to be sure.

At least this discovery, belated though it was on his part, gave him something more to go on in regard to the ghost that haunted his car.

"There's always something good playing when I get in your car," said Mona happily during the soft adieus near the end of the song.

"When you're here, sure. Not so much when it's just me," he replied, remembering the Beach Boys incident the other day.

"No? Well, maybe your ghost just likes me better than he likes you." She grinned at him, and he chuckled.

"You're probably right."

She sang the sprightly final refrain of the rather depressing lyrics along with the radio, deliberately teasing him.

"Very nice." He reached out and turned the radio off.

Chapter 9

THE SHOP'S FRONT DOORBELL RANG EAR-SPLITTINGLY loud in the PUPI office.

"Jesus Christ!" Adam exclaimed, nearly spilling his cola. "What the hell?"

"Did I forget to mention there would be someone else joining us tonight?" Frieda's manner was provokingly mild.

"Yes," he answered, annoyed. "Who and why?"

"Just a potential new hire."

He glared at her from his seat in the comfy chair, irritation and defiance warring for dominance on his round face. "Since when are we looking for new employees? No one told me we were looking for new employees. There's no room for new employees. Literally." He gestured around the tiny office with his slice of triple-meat pizza.

Ben piped up, sighing internally. "It wasn't planned." He loved Frieda and Adam, but their need to push each other's buttons was tiresome at best. He turned to Frieda. "Would you get the door before he rings that bell again, please?"

"Sure." She rose, taking her beer with her and leaving her half-finished slice of customized vegetarian pizza aglio e olio on the chipped plate next to her computer's keyboard. "Be right back."

"Why did you let her hire someone new without

talking to me first?" demanded Adam before the curtain had time to settle behind her. "I thought we were all supposed to be in on that sort of decision. I mean, it affects us all, you know."

"I didn't *let* her do anything, and we haven't hired anyone yet. So just chill out, all right?" Ben could see Adam was only temporarily mollified and hoped Danny wouldn't notice the chill rolling off him. "You might even like the guy if you give him half a chance."

"Hmm. I suppose."

"Just give him a chance," he repeated.

Adam gave an ambiguous grunt in reply.

"Go on in." Frieda reappeared, holding open the curtain so Danny could precede her into the room. "Have a seat. I'll grab the stool from behind the register and be right back."

Danny looked at Ben a little awkwardly, then raised a hand in greeting. "Hi."

"Hi. Have a seat," Ben repeated Frieda's offer and pointed to the chair she'd recently vacated.

"Thanks. I'm kind of sore from this morning, so, uh, yeah. Thanks." He sat on the edge of the chair as if he might bolt for the exit at any second. His rich brown eyes were wary and uncertain behind his glasses, darting from Ben's and Adam's faces to every random item in every corner of the overcrowded room. His manner was reminiscent of a nervous meerkat.

He looked at Adam and repeated the hand gesture that was basically half of a wave. "Hey. I'm Danny."

"Are you." It was less a question and more a challenge.

Ben made the introductions before things could get any more tense. "Adam Shotwell. Danny Raines. Danny, Adam. You can have a pissing contest later if that will make you feel better." The last was directed at Adam. "But you'll have to do it outside."

The big blond man didn't like it, but he got it and

backed off.

"Do what outside?" asked Frieda, returning with the stool. She set it in front of the curtain and sat down.

"Nothing," answered Ben. "Danny, are you hungry? There's plenty of pizza."

"I'm okay. Thanks."

Ben looked the skinny young man up and down. "Are you sure? There's vegetarian if you lean that way."

His face lit up a little. "Yeah? Um, then... yeah. That would be great, thanks."

Frieda picked up her plate, making room so she could open the pizza box and shove it toward him. "It's mozzarella, gorgonzola, and parm with potatoes, spinach, and romas on a garlic and olive oil base."

"That sounds amazing!"

"It is. We get it from Snoose Junction over on Market. There are napkins in the top drawer. How's your leg and your bruises?" She hooked the chunky heels of her boots on the bottom rung of the barstool and took a swig from her bottle of beer.

"Okay, thanks. And, uh, thanks again for helping me out this morning." He picked up a piece of pizza, no longer gooey and hot but still warm and tasty, and took a bite.

Adam eyed Frieda suspiciously. "Helped him out?"

"It was a morning full of many coincidences," she answered without actually telling him anything.

"I had a close encounter with a light pole when an asshole SUV driver ran me off the road," Danny explained between bites.

"Mm-hmm." Adam pursed his lips but said nothing more.

Ben smiled to himself. Danny had adjusted well to the group dynamic already, reading and responding instinctively to keep things on an even keel. He caught Frieda looking across the little room at him, a tiny smile turning up the corner of her mouth. She didn't have to say a word for him to know what she was thinking: *I can pick 'em, can't I?* He couldn't deny it. Saying she had a knack with people was a gross understatement.

"So, we have one big, multi-site job lined up and the possibility of a couple of smaller ones so far this month."

"Plus the wrap-up meeting you and I are doing this week down in Columbia City," Adam reminded him. "Unless you want someone else to go with you." His expression was pointed and accusing, and Ben ignored it.

"Plus that wrap-up. Right." Ben looked at the notes he'd taken during his phone conversation that afternoon. "Todd Marks has asked us to investigate his business, home, and car." Out of the corner of his eye, he noticed Danny sit up straight in surprise. "With four of us—"

Danny looked around at them all, disbelief and delight filling his face.

"—I think it's not unreasonable to try to do everything in one night. We're talking about a two-story Tudor with a half-daylight basement; the car in the garage of said house; and the coffee shop, Midnight Jones."

Danny's disbelief became blank astonishment and Ben fought to hide his amusement. Clearly, whatever the young man had expected from Frieda's invitation, it wasn't to be immediately treated as a member of the company. Not surprising since he hadn't officially been offered a job yet.

Ben went on. "Things are likely to pick up the closer we get to Halloween too, which is why we're inviting Danny to join us for the season. For this first big job, Adam and I can take the house and car. It'll be a challenge, but I think we can manage it. Frieda, can you and Danny handle the coffee shop?"

"Sure," she answered. "No problem. Right, Danny?"

Danny quickly swallowed a bite of pizza. "Uh... sure!"

"You're assuming we have enough equipment to cover

more than one location," argued Adam. "How big is this coffee shop we're talking about?"

"I'm going to go check it out properly tomorrow morning. Based on what I saw there last night, I think we can cover most of the place with two static cameras and a couple of voice recorders. Maybe the night vision camera too. It's not that big, and the suspected activity is limited."

"It's pretty straightforward, architecturally," agreed Danny with a nod. Ben smiled, glad to see him leaping in already. "Just the one big room, the open doorway into the kitchen, the little office, and the back hall where the restrooms are. Midnight Jones is my usual coffee stop on my bike route," he added in explanation.

"Bike route?" echoed Adam with disdain. "Are you a paperboy?"

"Bike courier." Danny was about to say something more, Ben could tell. Instead when he opened his mouth again, he filled it with another bite of pizza.

Temporarily thwarted, Adam turned his bitchiness in a new direction. "So what *is* the activity? Floating coffee cups? A spectral barista?" His tone was slightly mocking, but Ben knew he was genuinely curious.

"Missing spoons."

"Missing spoons," Adam echoed. He looked from Ben to Frieda, ignoring Danny, and looked back at Ben. "Are you serious?"

"The owner is suspicious because he's had a similar problem at his house for some time."

"Missing spoons." Adam's voice dripped skepticism.

"You need to hit reset, Adam," said Frieda. "You keep repeating what Ben says."

Ben ignored them both. "Adam, the owner assured me the car could and would be in the garage overnight, so it should be pretty straightforward for you and me to set up a camera inside it and not have to worry about too many external influences."

"Are there spoons missing from his car too?" His tone had grown sardonic. Ben continued to ignore it.

"It seems the radio is possessed."

"The whole car is haunted," said Danny, breaking in again. "I know him a little. Todd, I mean. The owner of Midnight Jones. And the car." Danny paused, visibly collecting his thoughts. "I've gone to Midnight Jones nearly every day since I discovered it. Well, every workday, anyway. It's my favorite coffee shop and believe me I've tried a lot of them all over the city. Todd's 1963 VW Beetle is totally haunted. Every time he turns on the car, the radio plays oldies music, early rock and roll, that sort of stuff. He doesn't even have the oldies station in his presets."

"You've been in the car yourself?" asked Ben, excited in spite of himself but doing his best not to show it.

"No. Mona told me. She's the baker at Midnight Jones. She's known Todd for ages. Seriously. I think they went to grade school together or something."

"So there are multiple witnesses to the radio thing," said Adam dismissively. "What do spoons have to do with it?"

"That's part of the question we're going to try to answer," Ben replied. "The client is curious to know if he has one spirit expanding its territory or if he has more than one ghost on his hands."

As the meeting went on, they developed a definite schedule and plan for investigating Todd's properties that coming Sunday night. Ben was pleased. It would only work because there were now four of them, two per location, and because the locations were so close together.

"We can set the van up halfway between the house and the coffee shop," Ben said. "They're close enough to each other that it should allow the receivers to pick up the equipment in both locations. We just need to make sure we're switching between frequencies."

"That means we'll only have partial backup records for either location, you realize," said Adam, a note of contempt still in his voice, although it had mellowed considerably over the course of the meeting.

Ben nodded. "I know, but it's just the backup. Assuming nothing goes wrong, the on-site gear will record everything, and we'll be able to download it all to the servers once we get back here. It's either that or spend an extra night in the field."

Adam let the argument drop.

Danny held up a hand, garnering him a sidelong look from Adam. Ben nodded to him encouragingly.

"Can I help with the analysis? I mean, once we've done the field work and all that?"

"You can take my shift," drawled Adam.

"Cool!"

"We'll all take a shift. Or two," Ben said firmly. He shot Adam a sharp look, and Adam once again fell into a disgruntled silence.

Discussion went on about the other jobs. Frieda filled the others in on the haunted dorm room and the possible ghost horse.

"I hope those aren't related," Adam said.

"They're not. Dorm's at the UW. Horse is in Snohomish," Frieda reminded him tersely. "You'd know that if you were listening more and pouting less."

Ben fought not to roll his eyes. The pair of them mostly got along, but Frieda's patience for Adam's drama was always short. Not that she wasn't partly to blame for it tonight. "Can we stay on topic, please?"

Both of them nodded, conceding the subject.

"Thank you."

~~*

It wasn't much more than half an hour later when Ben concluded things. Frieda was thrilled to be done. Adam's attitude had begun to grate on her very last nerve. She took the opportunity of escape offered by escorting Danny to the bookshop's front door to let him out. He moved stiffly. Not surprising after the spill he'd taken earlier and then sitting in one place for so long that evening.

It was full dark out and the sky was clear, the night cut by streetlights and the red-yellow-green of stop lights that dulled and muted the light of the stars overhead.

"I hope you didn't mind Adam too much," she said apologetically. Just because she was fed up with Adam's bullshit didn't mean she had to let Danny know it. *Keep it professional,* she told herself. *Unlike Adam.* "It's nothing personal, I promise you. He was feeling a little left out of the loop. That's all."

"It seemed like more than that to me."

"I should have warned you. I should have warned *him* more than half a minute before you walked through the door. I was messing with him, and I misjudged how touchy he was this evening. He took it out on you. I'm sorry."

Danny shrugged. "I'll survive. I'm not big on grudges. Hopefully he'll get over it, but I won't hold my breath."

"It really isn't personal," said Frieda again. "Adam's just... territorial." She zeroed in on Danny's energy patterns, trying to determine if he truly meant what he said. It was easy; he wore his emotions on his face. As long as Adam got over himself and started behaving like an adult, she was fairly certain Danny would let the whole thing drop. She pursed her lips, irked with herself for letting things get so messy right off the bat.

Shoving those thoughts aside, she deliberately changed the subject. "Did you bike or bus here?"

"Bus."

"Where do you live? I'll give you a ride home."

It was seriously tempting. She could see him weighing his options.

"You don't have to do that. I'm fine," he said eventually.

"You're sure? I'm happy to give you a ride. There's no baseball traffic tonight. It's a travel day. It shouldn't be too bad."

"You don't even know where I live."

"So, where do you live?"

"The north end of Capitol Hill. On Tenth near Boston."

"In that case, you're on your own," she deadpanned. Then she chuckled. "Kidding. Ride?"

Danny hesitated one last moment before... "No. Thanks. I kind of want to process what happened tonight. It's all a little too cool to be real, you know? Bus'll give me time to do that."

"Fair enough. See you later." She let him out and locked the door behind him just as Ben and Adam emerged from the back office. Ben handed Frieda her coat as they traded goodnights with Adam on his way out the door.

Once the door was closed and Adam was out of sight, Ben asked, "Danny gone?"

"Just now. Hopefully in the opposite direction from Adam."

"You smoothed things over with him, I hope."

Frieda pulled on her coat as she replied. "Meh. I think so? Adam was kind of a dick to him. That wasn't just Adam's fault. It was partly mine too. Which I told Danny."

"Good." Ben changed the subject. "He's not biking home, is he? It's so dark out."

"Nah. Bus. I offered to drive him, but he turned me down."

"I wouldn't turn down a ride home."

She smiled at him. "Happy to. At least you're on my way. Danny, not so much."

Ben zipped up his jacket. "Let's go."

~~*

Ben waved goodbye to Frieda, and then flashed the porch light on and off to make sure she knew he was in safely. When all was said and done, it had been a good day, despite Adam's bitchiness and Frieda's irritation with Adam's bitchiness. Book sales had been brisk. There'd been only one misguided message from someone looking for the saucer spotters. PUPI had a plan for the Midnight Jones job and had also scheduled the woman with the haunted barn in Snohomish. Finally, when he checked the eBay auction he intended to win, there were no new people watching it and no new bids. *Yes,* he thought as he climbed the steps up to the middle floor of his townhouse. *All in all, a good day.*

Then he saw the blinking light on his answering machine. There were four new messages. He tried to reassure himself that they would be nothing but telemarketers and wrong numbers, but he didn't believe it.

Sure enough, all four were from Corey and each one was more wheedling and needy than the one before it. He would have welcomed a recorded telemarketing call or even a bogus threat from a computer voice claiming to be the IRS by the time he was done listening to the damned things. The worst part of it was that he felt genuinely sorry for Corey. Okay, so the man was drunk-dialing him from some gay bar on Capitol Hill—God, how early must he have started to be that drunk by ten-thirty on a Wednesday night?—but somehow that didn't stop Ben pitying him. *Face it,* he thought. *The guy is pitiful.* Although he admitted to himself that an equally accurate word would have been piteous. The distinction was slight yet undeniable; there was no contempt connected with the latter.

Against his better judgment, he listened to the last message a second time. It had been left about forty minutes ago and was half-incomprehensible even to Ben, who'd seen Corey drunk enough times to understand most of his blathering. Either he was out of practice (a good thing), or Corey was exceptionally drunk (a bad thing). A second listen brought little enlightenment until the end. Just clear enough amongst the gibberish, and all the more disturbing for that, was the shouted and weeping demand: *"When am I allowed to get over you?"*

And then the click of disconnection. And the machine telling him, "There are no more messages."

Ben's pity was promptly replaced by fury and disgust, turning the pizza he'd eaten earlier into a heavy lump in the pit of his stomach.

"Where does he get off?" he demanded of the empty room. "God*damn* it! Seriously! What the fuck makes him think that's even remotely okay? When is he *'allowed'*? That is so much Goddamned bullshit!" He should delete the messages and go to bed. This was Corey's problem, not Ben's. He was not responsible for an unbalanced ex-lover's inability to separate affection and infatuation.

He reached out a hand, let his finger hover for several seconds over the Delete button, and then in quick succession erased each of the messages. For once, the usual wave of guilt was absent. As an added measure of peace of mind, he unplugged the phone from the jack in the wall. He picked up the receiver and held it to his ear just to hear its reassuring silence. He gave a single sharp nod and set it back in the cradle. No calls from anyone would get through that line again tonight. It was one of the advantages of having a machine instead of voicemail.

Ben took a deep breath and let it out in a long sigh,

willing the tension that had developed while listening to the messages to leave him. When it didn't, he went to the fridge and got a beer. He twisted off the cap and tossed it into the trash before carrying the drink upstairs to his bedroom.

Demon yawned at him from his usual nest of blankets in the center of the bed. The cat blinked sleepily in the sudden wash of warm light from the lamp on the nightstand.

"Hey there. How's my good boy?" Ben sat on the bed, bottle in one hand, and reached out the other to scratch Demon under his bright green collar. The bell on it jingled softly. "Too bad I didn't meet you first. You're a smart kitty. You would have warned me against Corey."

Demon yawned again and meowed once. Loudly.

"Yeah. You're right. Frieda did warn me, and I didn't listen to her, so why do I think I would have listened to you? I never should have gotten myself into that mess. I should have realized how fucked up Corey was from the start. But I *did* get myself out of it. Now if he could just understand that I *am* out of it." Ben heaved another sigh and took a long swig of his beer. "Maybe he will," he said, ever the optimist. "Maybe this latest breakup with Jeff will stick and he'll find someone who actually cares about him and makes him happy."

Demon gave him a disparaging look worthy of Frieda.

"Yeah. I know. Fat chance. No one will make him happy until he's happy on his own. And he's the only one who can make that happen." Irony was rich in his voice. "If only we could run everyone else's lives. We run our own so perfectly, right, Demon?" Ben mused that he was probably the only man alive who willingly and regularly quoted his own mother. But she certainly hit the mark with that one.

He yawned, thinking back on the evening's meeting. Despite Adam's snarkiness, it really had gone well.

Danny would be invaluable this season, and Ben suspected he would be more than willing to stick around come November. With a little luck, Adam would be over himself by then. *Okay,* Ben amended silently, *with a lot of luck.* It was one of the few ways in which Adam was unpredictable; you never knew when he was going to let go of a grudge. It could be three days or three months. Ben hoped it would be the former, although he would be satisfied if Adam split the difference and got over it in three weeks.

His cell phone buzzed in his pocket, and he set down his beer to pull it out. A text from Frieda said simply, "Down and safe." He sent a thumbs-up emoji in reply.

He yawned again, wondering if he could stay awake long enough to finish his beer. Mediating the tension at the meeting had made him more tired than he'd realized, and then the stress of listening to Corey's messages had made it worse.

And I get to deal with Adam's attitude again tomorrow carpooling to the client meeting. Great. At least Adam would be professional enough to keep his complaints to himself *during* the meeting. Ben let out a tiny, mirthless laugh. *Small favors,* he thought.

The car rides to and from the meeting were another matter.

Since Frieda wouldn't be around for him to punish, Adam was sure to find little ways to punish Ben instead. He only hoped it wouldn't be Adam's favorite form of torture: loud show tunes in a closed vehicle.

He took another swallow of beer and reached out again to pet Demon. The cat had snuggled into his nest and barely flicked an ear at the soft touch. "Good plan, buddy boy," said Ben quietly. "Time for bed."

Chapter 10

"I'D SAY THAT WENT REMARKABLY WELL, WOULDN'T YOU?" asked Ben as he and Adam loaded up the gear. The evening was dark and damp, and he was glad when the cases of expensive equipment were all safely stowed in the back of Adam's PT Cruiser.

"For someone who's sure their house is haunted even though we couldn't prove it for her? Yeah." Adam closed the hatchback and they got into the car. "I'm always nervous on cases like this, you know?"

Ben nodded as he buckled his seat belt. "I agree with you. But I thought she took it well. I mean, why shouldn't she believe there's a spirit in her house when she's witnessed it herself? It seemed pretty clear she didn't need our proof for her own peace of mind."

"Which makes me wonder why she called us in the first place." Adam started the car and the radio immediately came on too loudly, blaring the digital Broadway station he had subjected Ben to earlier. Adam shut it off. "Sorry," he said with a suggestion of sincerity. "It didn't seem so loud when we were driving."

Ben didn't agree and didn't say so, nor did he point out to Adam how very predictable he was. That wouldn't do anyone any good. "No problem. I don't ask," he went on with the previous topic of discussion. "As long as she's paying for our investigative services, she is free to keep her motives to herself."

"Good point. You want me to take you home, or do you want to go back to the office to drop stuff off?"

"You know what?" Ben looked out the window at the worn, old houses on the narrow street. "Midnight Jones isn't all that far out of the way from here to Ballard. You want to see the place before the job this weekend? The owner might even be there, and you could meet him too. Maybe grab a coffee. My treat." It was a peace offering, and he was glad when Adam took it.

"Sure. Which way?"

"Head north on Rainier and then take Twenty-third."

*

Ben gave occasional directions until they reached Fifteenth Avenue East. It was a straight-forward trip from where they'd started in Columbia City. "If Todd is there, we can let him know the plan for this weekend."

"You didn't call him yet?"

"Today was too crazy. I never managed to find the time. Just pull over wherever you can find a spot."

Adam didn't have Frieda's parking fairies, but they managed to find a place about three blocks north and across the street from their destination. Not bad at all for a Thursday evening atop Capitol Hill.

They crossed at the nearest corner and strode quickly down the sidewalk. As Ben had known it would, the weather was kicking up, blowing rain at them sideways. *It'll be nice to slip into a cozy coffee shop to warm up and dry out,* Ben thought, ignoring the fact that he'd just gotten out of a toasty, perfectly dry car. He knew he was looking for excuses to potentially run into Todd Marks, and he wasn't ashamed to admit it. But only to himself.

The atmosphere when they walked into Midnight Jones was quiet but energized. The singer from Ben and Frieda's first visit sat on the tiny stage in the back corner, singing an old folk standard and accompanying herself on her guitar. Ben recognized it, but he couldn't put his finger on the title, nor could he recall the singer's name. Maybe Todd hadn't mentioned it the other night. Yes, that must be it. That was Ben's story, and he was sticking to it.

"What do you want?" Ben asked Adam as they approached the counter.

"I'll take a tall chai tea latte."

"All right." Ben recognized the redheaded barista from the night he and Frieda had met Todd. What had he said her name was? Lori? Leslie? Damn. He would need to start taking ginkgo biloba if this name-forgetting nonsense kept up. "Hi. I'd like a double tall latte and a tall chai tea latte," he said.

"What kind of milk would you like in those?" she asked.

"Two percent in mine. Adam, what milk—" He glanced over his shoulder toward Adam, but it was Todd who caught his gaze. Ben barely managed to maintain his casual manner as he nodded a hello across the crowded shop. Inside, his stomach was doing a happy dance that would have made Balanchine weep. Todd's eyes seemed extra blue tonight, even at that distance, and Ben smiled at him. To his delight, Todd smiled back and started coming toward him.

Forcing his focus back to the drinks, Ben finally finished his question to Adam. "What milk did you want?"

Adam glanced from Ben to Todd, and a knowing look crossed his face. He stifled it behind his usual wry demeanor. "Cow's?" he said dryly, and then added to the barista, "Just kidding. Whatever is fine. Two percent, I guess, since you're steaming it already."

"Coming up," the woman replied with a smile. "For here or to go?"

On his own, Ben would have said "For here." With Adam as his ride home, he figured he'd best not push it.

"To go, please."

"Lena," said Todd, reaching the counter, "go ahead and put those on my tab for this week."

"You don't have to do that," Ben quickly protested.

"I know, but I'd like to. Call it a retainer fee. Or something."

Todd laughed a little shyly, and Ben smiled wider. He couldn't help it. It was silly of him, but his heart was a little aflutter at the idea of his very handsome new client buying him a drink, even if it was just a latte, and even if he was buying one for Adam too. "Well, thanks."

Adam cleared his throat in a less than subtle fashion. Ben shot him a tiny look of annoyance but said nothing other than, "Todd, you met Frieda the other night. This is my other Presence Unknown associate, Adam Shotwell. Adam, Todd Marks." There. That should please Adam. The subtle implication that Danny wasn't officially a part of the team. God, he disliked petty office politics.

"Pleasure to meet you." Todd put out a hand, and Adam shook it.

"So, this is the place without the spoons, huh?" said Adam.

Todd nodded. "It is. Fortunately, we don't serve soup."

Ben laughed more exuberantly than the quip warranted. He reined himself in and took the drinks the barista, Lena, set on the counter. "Thanks." He handed the chai to Adam, and added to Todd, "And thank you."

"You're welcome. I'd offer you a table, but—" He gestured around. There wasn't a single empty chair in view.

"It's fine," Ben said. "I see business is good."

"Willa usually brings in a nice-sized crowd. So, is this visit business or pleasure?"

Both, thought Ben. Aloud, he said, "Business. If it's all right with you, we'd like to go ahead and run both locations at the same time."

"Sure! That's great, actually. One less night of waiting for data to come in is good."

"Our thoughts exactly."

"Excuse me," said Adam. "I see someone I know. I'm going to go say hi. Just let me know when you're ready to head home."

"Right. Thanks."

Adam drifted off into the crowd to a table where he was greeted warmly by one of the women there. That was good, thought Ben. He didn't want to think Adam was making things up to deliberately give him and Todd a little alone time. He didn't want to believe he was that obvious about his attraction to PUPI's new client. Although, come to think of it, that sort of subterfuge wasn't Adam's style. He mentally shrugged it off and smiled again at Todd.

"Adam and I were in the neighborhood tonight. Finishing up a job for someone a little south of here." It was stretching the truth, but not to the breaking point. But was that subtle enough for Todd to get that he and Adam were nothing more than coworkers? He hoped so.

"You had an investigation tonight?"

"No. We only do those overnight. This was the post-investigation meeting where we delivered our findings."

"Ah. Gotcha." Todd smiled at him and Ben felt a happy wibble in his stomach. He covered his momentary distraction by taking a sip of his latte.

"Great coffee. Excellent foam."

Todd's smile widened. "Good! We like to hear that around here."

Ben was dimly aware of the singer, who he now knew was named Willa, finishing up her song. People applauded. She said something Ben didn't catch and began another tune. It sounded Celtic to Ben's ear, not that he was really listening. The better part of his attention was on Todd.

Silence fell between them. It felt like they were caught in a cozy, slow-moving pocket of time. A little drop of stillness in the ocean of energy around them. It was nice.

And then it went on a little too long and became awkward.

Crap.

"We're all looking forward to the investigation this weekend," Ben blurted, just to have something to say.

"Me too. I'll be glad to know what's really going on." There was something in Todd's tone Ben couldn't quantify. Maybe, given a quieter ambience and Frieda's people-reading skills, he could have figured it out. As it was, it was too brief and too elusive for him to catch.

Soon, he told himself. He would have more information to go on after the investigation. And they would be that much closer to finishing the job. That much closer to when he could ask Todd on a date. He smiled again and took another swallow of coffee.

The bell over the door jingled as several customers left and a few more came in.

"I should get going," Ben said. Not that he wanted to, but it was time. "I shouldn't hold my ride hostage any longer." Although... He glanced over at Adam who didn't seem to be bored. Still, it was getting late, the rain was easing up, and he did want to drop off the gear at the shop before heading home.

"It was good to see you. Stop in again sometime when it's pleasure rather than business."

Judging from the light in Todd's eyes, he wasn't just saying it to be polite.

Or maybe Ben was projecting his own desires onto the other man. It wouldn't be the first time. He fought back the demons of self-doubt and pulled up one more smile. "Thanks. It was good to see you too. We'll see you again in a few days, and remember, if you need anything from us before that, just give me a call. Any time." He stuck out his free hand and Todd shook it, his grip strong and warm, just like Ben remembered from the other night.

"See you this weekend."

With great reluctance, Ben let go, nodded one more goodbye, and went to collect Adam.

*

Todd watched the two investigators depart and smiled to himself. *So they're not a couple,* he thought in satisfaction. He was smart enough to have picked up on the hints Ben had dropped. But the little green-eyed monster in him still wished *he* was the one taking Ben home tonight, and that he wasn't just dropping him off there.

"Don't be stupid," he muttered under his breath. *Client, consultant. Client, consultant,* he thought over and over again.

Mona bustled through the door at that moment. "I'm back! Did you miss me?" She grinned, unwinding her long blue scarf as she came to meet him next to the pastry case.

"I did. Desperately. But you missed me more," he teased.

"Did I? Why?" She unzipped her fuzzy purple coat.

"Because while you were gone, I got to see Ben Chalfie, and you didn't. And that means you wish you'd been here, hanging out with me."

"Bitch!" she exclaimed.

"Loser," he gibed back.

"Damn!" She laughed. "My timing sucks. Well that, and the checker at QFC was so slow I think she might actually have been running in a different time stream than the rest of the world."

"How *Star Trek* of her."

More people entered the coffeehouse, and Todd and Mona retired to the privacy of the kitchen. Mona flipped on the light so they weren't standing there in the dark. Todd was glad; he found dark industrial kitchens creepy.

"Did you get whatever it was you were getting?" He didn't see any bags in her hands, but then he didn't know what she'd been after at the grocery store.

"Yeah. I dropped it off at my apartment. I should have come back here first. Ah well." She took off her coat and stuffed her scarf into the sleeve. "Or should I just put this back on and we can go?" The expression on her face suggested what answer she wanted to hear, and he obliged her.

"Might as well head out. I'm getting hungry, and if you're still up for dinner tonight—?"

"I didn't get a better offer from the checker at QFC, if that's what you mean," she joked.

"You have a knack for making a guy feel so special," he said dryly.

She grinned at him. "I know. Let's go." She bundled back up while Todd got his coat and hat from the coatrack in the corner of the kitchen. Not for the first time, he wished they had a proper break room. The coatrack and the little cupboard next to it were the best he could manage with the current architecture. Maybe when he opened a second coffeehouse he could make sure there was room for stuff like that. And a new office, with windows, for Shell. Then he could convert her little closet of an office here into a closet of a break room.

But none of that was going to happen anytime soon. Eventually, someday, yes. But not this year.

"Good night, Lena," he called to the barista. She waved at them as they passed through and out onto the sidewalk.

"So," Mona said before the door had even closed behind them, "how was Ben?"

They turned left to walk over to the neighborhood pub. "Cute," he replied, echoing her playful tone.

"Uh-huh. And?" she prompted, and he laughed.

"And I'm really looking forward to this job being done so I can ask him out."

"Good, good."

They crossed the street in silence. Then Mona shot him a quick, almost furtive glance. "Was, uh, Frieda with him again this time?"

So, that's what was going on. She wasn't just curious for him, she was curious for her too. He should have guessed.

"Not this time. He had another associate with him. Adam something."

"Shotwell," Mona promptly supplied. "He's the third member of the Presence Unknown team."

"How, and more importantly why, do you know that?"

"Duh! Local celebrities!"

Todd chuckled again. "Right. If you say so. Come on." The wind gusted, and Todd shivered inside his leather jacket. "Let's get inside and get some dinner."

Chapter 11

TODD PULLED INTO HIS GARAGE AND SHUT OFF HIS engine. He sat in the driver's seat, listening to the soft jazz on one of the local noncommercial radio stations until long after the garage's motion sensor light turned itself off.

It had been a long day. A week of long days when he thought back on it. And it wasn't over yet. Tomorrow was Saturday, commonly a busy day at Midnight Jones. In addition to that, it was the fifth and last game of the five-game playoff series the Mariners were in. He would be a stress puppy all day until that game was over, won or lost. Fortunately—or unfortunately, depending on one's priorities—the game was out of town and therefore relatively early in the day. The city would know by dinner time if the season was over or not.

He continued plotting out his weekend in his head while the music played on. Sunday should be relatively low-key during business hours. It would only be after dark, when the Presence Unknown people came to do their investigations, that it would get exciting.

Since he couldn't be in his home or the coffeehouse while they were working, he would be hanging out with Mona at her apartment until Ben called with the all-clear. He chuckled softly. Mona was as excited as a kid before a trip to Disneyland. She was anxious to see as much of the investigation as possible. Although she couldn't be on site while it was going on, Todd saw no reason to keep her away while they were setting up. He certainly intended to observe the process, and he would welcome her company.

The piece of music came to an end. He turned off the radio and got out of the car, the motion sensor light coming on again when he opened the car door. The garage smelled of cold cement and the last of the car's exhaust. Entering the basement through the interior garage door, he reset the house alarm and climbed the narrow stairs to the main floor.

It was quiet in the old house. *As always,* he thought with a hint of self-pity. He tossed his car keys and a small collection of spoons from the local thrift store onto the counter and opened the fridge. He would throw the spoons into the dishwasher in the morning. He was in luck. There was one beer left from that six-pack of IPA Mona had brought over the other week. He popped the top off the bottle and took a long drink of the crisp amber brew. A nasty little voice in the back of his head told him he shouldn't be drinking alone. He told it to shut up, it was one damn beer. It wasn't like he was tossing back a half rack while listening to Morrissey whine about how it sucked to be alone.

Or downing a fifth of cheap gin while beating up on his wife.

He clamped down on the bleak childhood memory and shoved it back into the tiny corner of his mind where it belonged. But it continued to niggle at him, throwing a cloud over his mood, chilling his thoughts, and tightening his belly. He should call his mom. See how she and her husband were doing in the great desert of the southwest, Phoenix, Arizona. He hadn't talked to her in a couple of weeks. He resolved to call her tomorrow morning. Before the game.

The resolution was enough to lighten the dark cloud,

although it didn't disperse completely.

He moved from the dark kitchen to the slightly less dark living room. The streetlight across the road cast creepy shadows through the big oak tree that loomed over the parking strip in front of the house. At least there was enough of the spooky ambient light to see him across the room. He continued around to the stairs that led up to the top floor and the converted master suite. It had once been a landing leading to two bedrooms and a tiny half bath. Now it was his sanctuary. He flipped on the overhead light with his free hand and sat heavily on the side of the big bed. The down comforter billowed up on either side of him as he sat. Downing another quick swig of beer before setting the bottle on the nightstand, he leaned over and untied his shoes. Comfortable as they were, he was more than happy to be free of them at last as he kicked them off, wiggling his toes inside his socks.

He contemplated taking a bath in his Jacuzzi tub, but glancing at the bedside clock, he decided otherwise. Chances were excellent that at this hour and as tired as he was, a single beer would put him right to sleep. That was fine if he was in bed, less so if he was sitting in a full tub of hot water. Leaning back against the big pile of pillows and stretching out his long legs, he reached for the remote and switched on the flat-screen television. Surely there would be something on Food Network he could half watch while he finished his drink.

Luck was with him again. Reruns of *Iron Chef* were on—the Japanese one that Canadian TV had dubbed into English. The various US incarnations of the show were all right, but he preferred the original. There was something wonderfully surreal about it that the American programs lacked. Tonight's rerun was Battle... something fishy, he figured, sipping at his IPA. He couldn't always tell right away when he missed the initial reveal, and on the Japanese version of the show it could be damned near anything. He'd once seen them cooking with swallow's nests. To this day he wasn't sure if they were real bird's nests or just something they called that. A part of him was afraid to know the answer, so he'd never bothered to look it up.

Abalone. Huh. That's what they were cooking? Okay. He liked episodes like this one that used nothing he would ever cook with himself. It made it easier not to pay too much attention—perfect late-night viewing. Now if they ever used boxed mac and cheese, he'd be riveted to the screen for the duration.

His eyes felt heavy and gritty. He should get up and take out his contacts before he fell asleep in them. He hated when that happened and he woke the next morning to a white film over his vision. Aside from the inconvenience and having to wear his glasses the next day, it was the knowledge that he'd been that dumb that bothered him most.

He swallowed the last of his beer and set the empty bottle on the nightstand.

Was that crab brains on the TV? Please say they weren't using crab brains again. That grossed him out every time they did it. No matter what the judges said or how many kinds the iron chefs used, crab brains were nasty, not "luxurious."

He yawned hugely. Even the train-wreck fascination of abalone and crab brains couldn't keep him awake. He dozed against the pillows, eyes drifting shut, remote held loosely in one hand...

He woke with a start, jerking upright and dropping the television remote onto the duvet. On the television the Chairman was just doing the lead-up to announcing the winner. Todd turned off the set. It didn't matter who'd won. He needed to get ready for bed.

Naturally, by the time he'd taken out his contacts and done all his other usual pre-sleep activities, he was wide awake. He laid in the dark under the bedclothes, hair mussed against the dark blue pillowcase, and stared nearsightedly up at the ceiling.

He was finally beginning to drift off again, at almost half past two, when a noise downstairs startled him back to wakefulness. He sat up and listened.

The house had settled a lot over the more than eighty years since it had been built. Most of that had happened long before he'd bought the place. Still, he heard the occasional creak and groan and was familiar with its usual sounds. This was probably just more of the same. He decided to ignore it and rolled over onto his side.

The noise came again.

He froze.

That didn't sound like settling.

What was that? A footstep? No. It had sounded more like something falling. Or being dropped. What could fall amidst all his stuff downstairs? There were plenty of possibilities. Lots of stuff could be knocked off shelves; pictures could fall off walls—if he owned a cat or if there were an earthquake. But he had no pets, and he felt no telltale shiver of a quake or its aftershocks.

Had he reset the alarm when he'd come in through the garage? He thought so, but it was such a habitual motion he could easily convince himself he had when he hadn't or vice versa. The nearest alarm panel was by the front door. He'd have to go downstairs to check it.

Pushing back the covers, he swung his flannel-clad legs over the side of the bed and shivered as the chilly air hit the bare skin of his chest. He reached for the t-shirt he'd discarded onto the hardwood floor earlier and pulled it on, shivering anew at the touch of the cold cotton. Before he could go any farther, he had to be able to see where he was going. He fished in the nightstand, found the case that contained his glasses, and put them on. Better.

He moved cautiously, uncertain if he was alone in his house and imagining things or if there was some genuine threat awaiting him downstairs. Some junkie looking for something easy to steal and sell so he could get drug money maybe. Or a professional looking for the sort of pricey loot successful ex-dot-commers like Todd often had in abundance. In that case, whoever was down there would be disappointed. He had a few collectable pieces. Large furniture mostly. Like his dining room set. Vintage stuff that wasn't likely to go over well with the sort who shopped out of the backs of vans in dirty back alleys. Although there was his computer setup in the den. The equipment itself wasn't anything special, but the information on the hard drive was valuable to any identity thief smart enough to break into the files.

He shook his head at his wild imaginings. And Mona thought he didn't watch enough television? Oh, please.

Moving stealthily on bare feet, he trod silently to the top of the stairs and listened again.

Nothing.

He counted to twenty.

Still nothing.

He sighed with relief and relaxed, feeling more than a little silly. It was probably just the house settling after all. Or someone passing by outside being raucous and obnoxious. That sort of thing was unusual but not unheard of in this neighborhood.

He reached out a hand toward the light switch, prepared to turn it on and bathe the upstairs landing in light and common sense. A hair's breadth from the switch, his hand froze. The air was like ice. No. Colder than ice. Biting into his fingers. Stinging cold pain. He pulled his hand back and tucked it into the opposite armpit to warm it.

Okay. That was odd. He put out his other hand, slower this time, and this time the air around the light switch was no different than the rest of the room. He hesitated, uncertain, and decided not to turn it on after all. He couldn't say why, but something in that momentary chill had struck him as a warning.

Wiggling his frozen fingers under his arm, he felt the sting of blood returning to revive them. Pain was better than numbness.

Resting his free hand on the railing, he descended the hardwood staircase one slow step at a time, being careful to avoid the spots he knew would creak under his weight. He'd heard nothing since that second sound, and yet he couldn't help feeling that he wasn't alone in the house.

But then of course, technically, he wasn't.

Could it have been his spoon-stealing ghost who'd made the noises? He'd left a handful of thrifted spoons on the kitchen counter. Perhaps the ghost was over-eager, couldn't wait for him to wash them and put them away in the drawer where one could easily be separated from the stack. She—he couldn't help thinking of the spirit as female—might have knocked them onto the kitchen floor, causing the falling sound he'd heard. Only that didn't add up; nothing had sounded like the clatter of metal.

At the bottom of the stairs, he once again stopped, waited, listened. A new sound came to him through the darkness. The soft scraping of something across a hardwood floor. As if someone were shifting one of the chairs in the dining room. But why? To sit on or to climb on were the obvious reasons that leapt to mind. Only there was no reason to go climbing on chairs in that room. Everything of value was within easy reach. There was a fair amount of Norwegian silver in the china cabinet drawers, but nothing was stored on top of the cabinet.

Not that a burglar would know that.

Shit. Why hadn't he grabbed his phone before coming downstairs? Hell if he was going back for it now. It would take too long and give an intruder time to get away with whatever loot he could grab. He could handle some punk kid if he had to.

Todd moved forward, one cautious step at a time, across the living room and toward the small formal dining room. Three feet from the archway, he stepped into a wall of freezing air. It sank instantly into his bones, chilling him inside and out. He gasped at the shock of cold, his breath misting before him, and took a reflexive step back, shivering all over. Something didn't want him to go any farther. He was certain of it. Why? Was it an attack? Or was something trying to stop him for his own safety?

Never had the old house felt so eerie, so imposing. The light from the streetlamp that shone through the waving oak branches cast terrifying shadows against the window shades. Todd shivered again, and it had nothing to do with the temperature. That seemed to have returned to normal. Sixty-four degrees had never felt so toasty. He put out a cautious hand and touched only cool room-temperature air.

Moving forward once more, he found nothing spectral nor tangible barring his path. Stepping into the dining room, he looked around. The light from outside was stronger here with no tree to dapple it and no shade over the bay window seat to filter it. At first glance, everything seemed ordinary. The china cabinet was closed, its contents apparently untouched. The light fixture above the table hung dark and still. The painting on the opposite wall was unmoved.

Then he saw it. The chair at the head of the table across the room was pulled away as if someone were sitting in it, and yet there was no one there. Goosebumps rose up and down his arms and his stomach felt sick. Footsteps sounded behind him and he spun in place, stomach lurching. Queasy and dizzy, he grabbed the open doorframe for support. A shadow darker than anything caused by the furniture loomed up out of nowhere. Vaguely human in shape. Ominous. Threatening. There was nothing he could do. He couldn't move. Couldn't breathe. Couldn't defend himself. Hell, he wasn't sure there was anything physical to defend against.

The shadow form wafted toward him. He gasped in a shallow breath and held it. The thing swept over him. Around him. Through him. He choked at its passing, turned to follow its path into the dining room where it reached the opposite wall and vanished.

Todd sank to his knees, gasping for breath, fighting not to vomit up the meager contents of his stomach. When he could trust himself to move without throwing up, he shifted onto his butt and sat with his back against the archway. Knees bent with his arms atop them, he let his head fall back against the cool, solid, reassuringly real wood.

Chapter 12

TODD SHIFTED POSITION UNDER HIS WARM AND COZY comforter and squinted at the bedside clock, surprised to see it was only a quarter past seven. He didn't remember much about the night after his ghostly encounter. He'd managed, once his queasy stomach and racing heart had calmed, to check the burglar alarm and found it active and undisturbed. Then he'd shivered his way up to bed and barely managed to take off his glasses before crashing out, physically and emotionally exhausted by the terrifying spectral visitation.

He rolled onto his back and closed his eyes. He would almost have preferred to have found an intruder in his dining room. A burglar or a junkie would have been straightforward, if dangerous. Something he could report to the police and be done with it.

Why was life never simple? And why in the hell was he awake so early?

By all good sense, he should be fast asleep. He was wiped out after last night's goings-on. His body was exhausted and wanted more rest, but his brain was alert and racing, ready to face the day that was dawning outside his windows.

He needed to tell someone about last night if only for the sake of peace of mind. *I mean, Jesus Christ!* he thought. An angry ghost had attacked him and left him shaken and nauseated on his dining room floor!

And wasn't *that* on the wrong side of humiliating?

In the light of day, dark memories flooded in. Memories from decades ago that were triggered by last night's frightening encounter. He'd never been the one lying battered on the floor back then. That had been his mom. And it wasn't some disembodied spirit that had put her there. It was his father.

He didn't want to think about that. Why was he thinking about that? His guts twisted while, against his will, his mind dredged up images of his mother crying over the kitchen sink, washing away blood from a cut lip or gingerly icing a bruised eye, all the while muttering prayers of forgiveness. The guilt of years of childhood helplessness built within him.

"No!" He sat up sharply. Pressing the heels of his hands to his closed eyes, he forced the memories away. His father was long gone. It had been more than twenty years since they'd gotten free of him. For all Todd knew, he was dead and good riddance. His mom was happy in Phoenix with a man who loved her and treated her like a queen. He would not let his childhood hold him prisoner like this.

He dropped his hands and opened his eyes again, willing sunlight and reality to force the painful memories back into the dark corners of his mind. Several deep breaths later, he felt he'd regained some control. He laid back and folded his arms under his head against the pillow, thinking hard about last night and *only* last night. Not letting his mind wander any further back in time than that.

Was it necessary that he tell whomever he talked to *everything* that had happened? It depended whom he told, he supposed. If he simply wanted to confide in someone, it would be Mona, and she would know if he was holding something back. If he wanted help determining exactly what had happened and possibly dealing with it, it would be Ben from Presence Unknown, and Ben would need all the data he could get in order to make a thorough investigation. Either way, Todd would have to recount every humiliating detail.

A third possibility occurred to him. He could talk to Shell about it and leave out the more embarrassing bits. She was analytical and skeptical. The ideal outside observer. Yes. Perfect! He would talk to Shell and... and risk Mona's disappointment and hurt feelings when she found out. No. Not a viable option.

Watery morning sunshine began to trickle around the edge of the pleated shades, while the light that filtered through them cast a blue glow over everything. He rolled over, determined to fall back to sleep. It was too early even for a normal Saturday morning. On a morning following the night he'd had, this was stupid early.

Forty minutes later, he gave it up as a lost cause. His mind was awake, replaying in the light of day the strange occurrences of the night before, and there was no shutting it down. Maybe, he thought, a good long run would be enough to clear his head. It was a fifty-fifty chance. Either the vigorous exercise would clear the cobwebs of disturbing memory from his mind or it would focus his thoughts to the point of solution, or at least rational explanation, for what had occurred. Whatever the result, it was more welcome than this pointless tossing and turning of mind and body.

Another quarter of an hour later, he was outside the house, breathing in the fresh autumn air. The day had dawned clear and unseasonably warm. It promised to be a beautiful day out for baseball. Too bad the Mariners were in Kansas City for game five instead of at home.

Even now as he stood on his front walk and stretched a little, he deemed it too damned early. He descended to the sidewalk and turned north, beginning a slow, loping pace to warm up his muscles and get his blood flowing.

Mornings were one of the many things he didn't miss since leaving the corporate world. They were why, when he'd decided to open up a coffeehouse in a city already littered with them, he'd chosen to go the late-night route. Midnight Jones was never meant for the early birds, the morning people, the corporate drones, or anyone else who rose before dawn. He'd deliberately set it up to catch the midmorning coffee-breakers, the after-work customers, and the late-night theatre crowds coming over from the myriad fringe, community, and semi-pro theatres that were tucked into spaces ranging from small to positively wee in buildings all over Capitol Hill. He'd seen the gap in the market and seized it, and now Midnight Jones was one of the most popular night spots on the Hill.

Which was why he was so anxious to make sure the place wasn't being disturbed by paranormal phenomena. Nothing had happened since the spoon incident, and he dearly hoped that would be the end of it. The more time passed, the more he suspected the theory that it had been some sort of prank or student scavenger hunt was the right one. His house, on the other hand... That wasn't so easily explained. Particularly not after last night.

He paused at the corner of Fifteenth and Aloha, waiting to fit himself into the pattern at the four-way stop and surprised to see how many cars were on the road at this hour on a Saturday morning. A glance at his watch reminded him that this wasn't all that early by most people's standards, even if it was the weekend. Checking all directions, he jogged across the street one way and then the other and on toward Volunteer Park.

His thoughts inevitably shifted back to last night's weirdness. He was hesitant to call it a haunting. That sounded melodramatic and silly. Not to mention naming it also gave it an air of truth that he wasn't quite ready to accept. He could handle the fact his car was haunted.

That was small, simple, and so far as he could tell, safe. Besides which he was used to it; it had been going on for years.

The matter of the missing spoons was mildly annoying but essentially harmless. It would be nice, though, to confirm that ghost's existence—assuming the Presence Unknown people could do that. It would be nicer still to communicate with it and get it to return the more valuable pieces it had pilfered. Maybe he could cut a deal with it. He could offer to bring home spoons especially for it, if it would just leave his good silver alone.

Jesus! Now he was pondering bargains with disembodied spirits. This didn't bode well for his sanity. Mona would undoubtedly find it perfectly reasonable. Shell would find it both absurd and amusing. What would Ben Chalfie think?

It wasn't just his position as cofounder of PUPI that brought Ben to mind, although if questioned, Todd would have insisted his motivations were entirely professional. He would have argued his perfect rationality. In truth, Todd *wanted* to confide in Ben, and it was only partly due to his knowledge of the supernatural. Ben exuded a stillness and a passion that, rather than contradicting one another, blended seamlessly together. That alone was enough to draw Todd's thoughts to him, to desire his presence not just because of the ghosts at home, but because, plainly put, being around him felt good. Ben's presence made Todd feel centered in a way he hadn't even realized he lacked.

When they'd met that first time, Ben had said Todd should call him any time if anything unusual happened before PUPI came to investigate. He had reiterated it when he'd stopped by Midnight Jones the other night.

Last night certainly qualified as unusual.

Todd paused on the dirt-and-gravel path. He could do it right now, right here. His cell phone was in his pocket, and PUPI's number was programmed into it. For that matter, so was Ben's cell number. He unzipped the pocket, pulled out his phone... and hesitated. Why? Was he afraid that sharing the incident, like naming it, would make it more real somehow? *Face it,* he told himself. It was real whether he called it a haunting, a weirdness, or nothing at all; whether he told anyone about it or whether he took it as a dark secret to his grave. It. Had. Happened.

Was he concerned Mona would feel hurt if he didn't tell her first? Possibly. She was still disappointed not to have heard about the spoons at his house earlier than she had. She hadn't said it in so many words, but he could tell.

Was he nervous to speak to the handsome, magnetic Ben Chalfie without someone there to chaperone them for fear he would overstep the bounds of client/consultant propriety and kiss him?

Todd did a mental double take. Had he seriously just thought what he thought he'd thought? There were so many layers of wrong to it, he could hardly credit it. He and Ben had only just met, and Todd had never been one to fall into bed with someone he barely knew. Besides that, Ben was doing a job for him. He'd said to Mona just the other night that he wanted to ask Ben out *once the job was complete.* Any romantic involvement was out of the question while they had a business relationship. Finally, it was a *phone call,* for Pete's sake! He had managed one before, to schedule the investigation, and nothing untoward had happened. How could it? He couldn't kiss the man through the phone!

When Ben turned up at Midnight Jones out of the blue, Todd had been pleasantly surprised at his unexpected appearance, but he hadn't gone overboard or gushed over him or anything. Had he? No. Of course not. Had he wanted to? Well, *yes.* But the point was, he hadn't acted on it. So why was he so hesitant to contact Ben now?

He shook his head. He was being ridiculous.

Get a grip, he told himself firmly. *Make the damned call.*

This whole freaking out over a phone call thing was so... high school!

He shuddered at the thought.

Of course, come Monday, the job would be done, right? He could ask Ben out then. They could go for lunch. Or drinks. Dinner would be too much too soon. Better to start slow. See if Ben even agreed to a first date.

They could start picking china patterns later.

He gave a self-deprecating chuckle. There were ways in which he freely admitted he was an incurable romantic. Candle-lit dinners? Check. An unexpected bunch of flowers? Check. Rose petals scattered in a path that led to the bed? Big check. But china patterns? That was going too far, too romantic-schoolgirl-scribbling-hearts-on-a-Pee-Chee, for him. Did they even still make Pee-Chees? God, he felt old. And, he silently insisted, none of that had anything to do with the fact that he already owned his grandmother's gorgeous antique china, which he wouldn't part with under any circumstances.

Nope.

Nothing to do with it at all.

Yeah. Right.

He *loved* looking at china patterns. Jesus, he was such a girl! A house-remodeling, vintage car-restoring, Food Network-watching, baseball-loving girl. Shit. He was a lesbian. Wait until he told Mona! He laughed out loud, startling a bicyclist who swerved away from him and nearly sideswiped a tree. The woman shot him a dirty look and he waved a hand in apology. He took a moment to collect himself, then dialed the phone.

Chapter 13

"DUDE! WHAT THE HELL?" ·

"Am I late? The game's already started, hasn't it?" Ben entered Frieda's house with an apologetic look and a chilled six-pack.

"Curve Ball seasonal? Excellent choice." She took the beer from him, heading back down the hall to the living room so quickly that her oversized Mariners jersey billowed around her. "Yes, it's started. We're in the top of the third inning already and we came out swinging. It's three to one in our favor. Where the fuck have you been?"

He closed and locked the front door behind him since she was clearly too preoccupied to think of it. He sniffed the air as he followed her. It carried the heady scent of her special game-day nachos. He loved those things. "I got held up on the phone, so I was late getting to the store for the beers."

"You could bring the phone with you. It's not like you were driving."

"It was Todd Marks."

"He called during the game?" She plopped down on the sofa and twisted the cap off a bottle. "That seems unlikely." She stretched out her denim-clad legs and crossed her stockinged feet on the teak coffee table.

"Will you please put your feet somewhere that isn't right next to the nachos?" asked Ben.

"Yes, Mom." She lowered her feet to the floor, shoved a

bite of cheesy chips with pickled jalapeños and guacamole into her mouth, and asked around the mouthful, "So? Todd?"

"Oh my God. Swallow first, please!"

She looked at him with a mischievous and slightly evil expression on her face. She was contemplating opening her mouth to show him the half-masticated mess inside. He just knew she was. "Don't you dare, or I'm not telling you *anything*."

She wrinkled her nose at him, but she chewed the bite and swallowed it. She even took a moment to wash it down with beer. "Happy now?"

"Todd called before the game started," he said by way of an answer. He sat next to her and reached for a beer of his own. She beat him to it, opened it for him, and handed it over.

"So? What'd he call about? Business? Or plea-suuuuure?" She drew out the second syllable, shooting him a smile and wiggling her eyebrows before turning her gaze back to the game.

"Considering he only called my cell because he didn't think it was a good idea to try explaining things to the Presence Unknown voicemail? Business. I know what you said before, but I don't think he's interested. I mean, for a while I thought maybe, but now I don't think so again." He took a drink and sat back, eyes on the screen where men in tight pants were playing a game he only vaguely understood. But, hell, as long as they showed plenty of shots of the catcher's ass, he was fine with the rest of it.

"Yes, he is. He's just being professional. Like you. You know, while I totally respect your ethics and all that shit, you need to get over it where Todd is concerned. And so does he."

"Thank you, Yenta." His tone was both sarcastic and resigned. How many years had she been trying to match him up with someone? Never mind her own single state; his seemed to weigh heavily on her mind. He'd long since given up pointing that out to her. It only ever led them around in conversational circles. He was glad he hadn't mentioned the brief visit he and Adam had made to Midnight Jones the other night. Of course, there was no guarantee Adam wouldn't mention it or that Frieda wouldn't pick it up out of his aura or whatever it was she read, but he would deal with that if, or when, he had to.

"When will you learn to listen to me? If you'd listened to me after college you wouldn't—Oo!" She interrupted herself and sat up abruptly, shouting at the screen, "Go! Go, go, go, go! Yes!" at the same time the announcer on the television was calling, "Goodbye, baseball!"

She pumped her fist in the air. "Two-run bomb! Sweet! Five-one. Take that, Kansas City! Not so royal now." She did a little happy dance in her seat and swigged down half of her beer in celebration. Leaning back again, she picked up where she'd left off. "You wouldn't still be getting phone calls from Corey."

"I didn't tell you. He called and left another one of his mournful messages the other night."

"Jeff dump his skinny, codependent ass again?"

"What do you think?"

"I think I don't have to meet that guy to know he's a prick. A manipulative, opportunistic prick. I don't like Corey, but that doesn't mean I think he deserves to get jerked around by some fucker on a power trip. Of course, that's not to say he should be calling you to cry over his bullshit either. Dude needs professional help. Why don't you cancel that landline?"

The question was rhetorical, and they both treated it as such, returning their attention to the screen. Ben decided there was no point mentioning the drunk-dialed messages. It would only support her argument, with which he fervently agreed.

"I'll do a protective spell for you tonight. I know it's not your thing," she forestalled any argument, "but it can't hurt."

When the inning was over, Frieda muted the commercials and turned to him. "So?"

"So what?" Ben asked blankly.

"Hel-*lo*! What business did Todd Marks call you about? What was so complex that he had to talk to you rather than leaving a voicemail?"

"Oh! He had a haunting last night."

She sat up straight again, and this time it had nothing to do with sports. "Seriously? Like, how? What? What the hell happened that he found it worth calling before the gig tomorrow night?"

There was a short pause while Ben waited for her to continue her babble. "Are you done?"

"Yes, and so are the ads so you'll have to talk over the announcers." She unmuted but was gracious enough to turn the volume down a little and actually face him while he spoke.

"Sounds. Icy patches in the air. A chair that wasn't where he'd left it. And what he called 'a malevolent shadow manifestation.'"

"Oooo! Dude." She nodded appreciatively. "That sounds way cool. Did it do anything?"

"Other than move the chair?"

"Yes, other than move the chair. You're such a literalist shit sometimes." It was said with equal amounts of affection, irritation, and honesty.

Ben merely smiled smugly and answered her question. "It went through him." He was gratified to see her eyes widen in shock. "Took his breath away and knocked him to his knees. He said it made him sick to his stomach to be near it, and he nearly threw up after it hit him. That was how he knew it was malevolent. He felt it when the thing touched him."

Frieda gave a low whistle of awe. "That's some serious shit."

"If it's real."

"I can tell you that much without instruments. I just need to get into that house."

"You're doing the coffee shop with Danny, remember?"

"Shit. I forgot. I don't regret it though," she added quickly. She looked at him pointedly for a brief moment before something on the TV screen caught her eye. "Oo! Get under it! Get it! Yeah! *That's* what I'm talking about. I love it when one of our guys climbs the wall and steals a home run from whoever's at bat." Her grin was wicked, and it sparkled in her eyes. "I love watching the opposing batter round first base thinking he's got it made, and then have to trot on back to the dugout in defeat."

"Oh my God, you're vindictive."

"Yes. Yes, I am," she confirmed with a nod of her head.

"What about that Wiccan thing? Like Karma coming back to bite you in the ass?"

"What you put out into the universe comes back to you three-fold. Yeah. I'm not always so good at that. Lucky for both of us my vindictiveness is usually reserved for baseball." She looked suddenly thoughtful. "Maybe that's why the M's tend to lose. Then again, I've never done anything against an opposing team or player. I never wish *anyone* actual harm. Not even the Yankees. So it can't be me. Danny will be a great addition to the team."

"Whose? The Mariners or Presence Unknown?" He followed her non sequitur with alacrity. He just liked messing with her.

Her tone was flat. "You're so funny. Right on! Three up, three out! I love an easy inning for my boys." Another commercial break began, and she muted the game once more. "So, what's the deal?"

"We do the investigation tomorrow just like we planned."

"Seriously? You're not going over there tonight to see if it happens again? Or even just, you know, to keep him company so he won't be alone?"

"Frieda. He's. A. Client." He pronounced each word with the sort of clarity used by ignorant Americans when talking to foreign tourists who speak flawless English.

"So?" He gave her a look she knew all too well. He'd been giving it to her periodically since the day they'd met back in high school. She backed off. "Okay, okay. But *after* we're done with the investigation, you no longer have any excuse."

"Why do you care so much if he and I go out?" Sometimes it amused him. Sometimes it charmed him. Sometimes it puzzled him. This time it was starting to annoy him.

"Because I want you to be happy!"

He gave her the look once more.

She caved. Again.

"And because I like him. I'm as selfish as a human being can be and I want whoever you end up with in your life to be someone *I like too*. Satisfied?"

"Okay."

"I mean, can you blame me?" she went on, on the defensive although he'd just agreed. "He's cute. He owns a coffee shop that is open after midnight. He has a vintage radio in his vintage car. He likes baseball—"

"You don't *know* that he likes baseball."

"I can tell. I bet you five bucks if you called him right now, he'd be watching the game."

"Then I'd better not. I know how you fanatics don't like being interrupted during a big game."

"Damn right." She turned on the sound and opened another beer. "Now shut up. We're up again."

~~*

Todd was all smiles as he burst into Midnight Jones. "Hey, gang! Fantastic game, right?"

The weekend afternoon barista looked at him like he was speaking in Latin. The young man wasn't a sports fan and as such was unprepared for Todd's random burst of sports-fannish excitement. Todd ignored him as Mona and Shell both emerged from the kitchen, grinning like mad.

"Hell yeah!" exclaimed Shell. They took turns embracing him while the patrons who had been startled from their caffeinated little worlds by his exuberant entrance returned to those worlds, their ruffled feathers settling.

"We had it on the radio in the kitchen," said Mona, adding with a laugh, "You'll forgive me if we didn't get quite as many key lime tarts baked as I had intended."

"Are you kidding? We're going to the ALCS for the first time in *decades*. I'd forgive you if you'd burned the kitchen down!"

"Seriously?"

"No!"

They all burst out laughing, Todd and Mona falling on one another in their glee and excitement.

"Good," said Shell through her mirth. "Because I do *not* want to file the insurance paperwork on that!"

"I can see the headlines now." Todd mimed a giant banner in the air before them. "Woman Toasts Win and Bakery in Capitol Hill Celebration Conflagration!"

Shell snorted and Mona barked out another laugh. Todd turned to the barista. "Arjun, a round of drinks for anyone who wants one. On me!"

That got the attention of everyone in the coffee shop. The line at the counter was suddenly lengthy, and Arjun shot Todd a disparaging look. "Thanks so much," he muttered, grinding beans and filling metal pitchers with various dairy and nondairy beverages in preparation.

"You couldn't have waited until Becky got back from her break?"

Todd merely laughed again and flashed a grin at the room.

"One of you could get back here and help me," Arjun hollered to be heard over the noise of the steamer.

"Fair's fair," added Mona.

"You're right!" With that, Todd leapt over the counter and called out, "Who needs a beer or a glass of wine? Step right up! Ri-ight here, ri-ight now-ow! This is where I wanna be-hee-hee!" He sang the misquoted bit of the Jesus Jones song rather badly, but no one complained. He was the one footing the bill. The line split into two, and he began pouring the adult beverages.

"I'll just stay out of the way, shall I?" suggested Mona, smirking at the controlled chaos.

"The hell you will! Get back here and serve pastries to people who want them. You have to pay for those," Todd called out so there would be no confusion. "I'm covering the drinks. One each. You'll have to wait until we win the American League pennant before I splurge any more than that."

Mona muttered good-naturedly, while Shell joined in and took over the cash register.

In minutes, the line was clear and so was the pastry case.

"I think that's my cue to get back into the kitchen and do some proper baking," announced Mona.

"You want to close out your tab now, big spender?" Shell asked him.

"No. Give me the bad news later. Right now, I'm in too good a mood." He grinned at her. "I'm gonna go see if I can give Mona a hand with the baking. Seems only fair, since it's partly my fault the pastries are all gone."

"Partly?"

He ignored the good-natured gibe as he turned and

gave Arjun a pat on the back. "Well done. Nice to know you're reliable in an emergency," he joked.

Arjun looked frazzled, but he chuckled. "Just give me a little more warning next time, please?"

"I promise."

Todd slipped out from behind the counter and followed Mona to where she'd disappeared into the relative calm of the kitchen.

"Hey." She looked up at him and smiled, already measuring out flour to the accompaniment of the postgame show. "Turn down the radio, would you? I'm almost afraid of what will happen if we *do* win the ALCS. I'll be stuck baking nonstop for a week."

"*When* we win," he corrected her firmly, doing as she asked. "Gotta think positive." He leaned back against the Hobart dishwasher and crossed his arms over his chest.

She glanced over at him, not pausing in her measuring. "Uh oh. What happened?"

"You doing anything tonight?"

"After work?"

"After work."

Her tone was teasing. "I don't know. I have this asshole boss who just gave away lots of drinks."

"Sounds like a great guy to me."

"Yeah. You should meet him. It's his liquid generosity that wiped out my pastries too. Now I have to make more before I can go home."

"I'll help." He pushed away from the dishwasher.

"You will not. I trust you with boxed macaroni and cheese, grilling steak, opening beers, pouring wine, and pulling espresso shots. You are not going anywhere near my ovens, thank you." She turned on the enormous mixer and began creaming together butter and sugar. "But you can get more butter out of the fridge and put it on the counter next to the oven to soften faster."

"I'm getting you a new one of those on Monday." He

tipped his head at the mixer as he crossed to the fridge and pulled out a chef's cut of butter. "One or two?"

"One will do. That's almost as good as today's win. Now tell me what's going on."

Instead of answering, he set the butter where she'd said to and asked her another question. "What are you making?"

"Oatmeal chocolate chip cookies. What's. Going. On?"

"I got haunted last night."

She reduced the mixer to slow and added the mixed dry ingredients to the wet a bit at a time. "You're always haunted. I've been in your car. And then there's that spoon issue you failed to mention."

"This was different."

She stopped what she was doing and looked at him properly. She even shut off the mixer. "Bad different?"

He considered the question carefully before answering. He didn't want to upset or scare her. How much should he reveal? Probably not how sick he'd felt. No. No need to mention that. He settled for, "Creepy different."

"Let me finish mixing, then you can tell me about it while I scoop out dough. Okay?"

He nodded. "Yeah. Okay."

*

Mona didn't hesitate once he'd finished telling his tale. "You're staying at my place tonight." Her tone brooked no argument, yet he felt compelled to give one.

"I think that's overreacting, don't you?"

"No. I think it's being practical and cautious. It freaked you out enough to call Ben over at Presence Unknown, and you're still freaked out now, aren't you?"

Todd couldn't deny it, but he didn't want to say anything more that might give weight to her belief that it was too dangerous for him to go home tonight.

"So, if it's disturbing enough for you to discuss it with

the paranormal investigator who is about to investigate your home and your business *anyway*, I think that makes it disturbing enough for you to stay at my place for one night."

"Two. You said I could stay with you the night they investigate. That's tomorrow."

"Oh my gods, it is." She couldn't contain her fangirlish giggle of glee. "They're coming to investigate *tomorrow night*. That is so freaking cool!"

"Can we get back to the fact that I was attacked by a disembodied spirit last night?"

"Attacked?" She was suddenly serious and frowning, a bizarrely incongruous expression as she stood there in her lavender bandana and purple apron, a number twenty-four disher in her hand, poised mid-scoop above the big bowl of cookie dough. "You never said you were *attacked*. You were *attacked*?"

Shit. He hadn't meant to use that word. He'd just wanted her to focus. Now she would be even less inclined to give up her argument. "It wasn't really an attack. I mean, I have no proof, or even concrete evidence, that it intended any actual harm. It was just... freaky. Okay?"

"No! Not okay. You just said 'attacked'!" Her protective instincts were on overdrive, and they'd always been strong where Todd was concerned. She pointed the disher at him like a weapon. "You are staying at my place tonight, so stop arguing about it."

"Can we compromise?"

Her eyes narrowed in suspicion, but she went back to scooping out cookies. "Go on."

"Why don't you come stay at my place tonight? If nothing else, should something happen you'll be there to confirm it." He didn't voice it out loud, but a part of him wanted her there and hoped the black shadow thing would appear again. Not that he wanted to put her in danger. Never that. He only wanted a witness to it, so he wouldn't be the only one.

So he would know he wasn't completely out of his mind.

"What do you say?"

She considered for several moments before answering. "You buying dinner?"

"Anything you want."

"I want something really good. I want Indian."

"It's yours."

"I'll be there."

Chapter 14

TODD AND MONA SAT IN TODD'S BIG BED TOGETHER, watching movies and drinking shiraz while tucked under the down comforter. The tree out front cast spooky shadows through the blinds on the upper floor just like it did downstairs. Todd was inured to them after several years living there alone. Mona, on the other hand, jumped whenever a particularly strong gust of wind hit the branches or an occasional creak of the house settling caught her ear.

"How do you stand it?" she asked when she couldn't take it anymore.

They were two thirds of the way through *Earth Girls Are Easy*. Todd glanced over at her, paused the movie, and shrugged as he looked back at her. "I admit it isn't high art, but I think it's cute. And you have to admit it's pretty much the only movie where Jeff Goldblum could legitimately be described as hot."

"Not that! You know I love Julie Brown. I meant this house. How do you sleep alone in this place?"

He kept the same calm tone, hoping to diffuse her fear by pretending it didn't exist. "Pretty well usually. I paid a lot for this fancy mattress, and it's totally been worth it. Don't you think it's comfy?"

"You know what I mean." She shot him a withering look, and he gave in.

He shrugged ruefully and took a sip of wine. "Usually

it's only missing spoons and 1963's Billboard hits that I have to worry about. This whole spooky haunting thing is new to me. Up until last night, it was just an old house with the occasional creak and a ghost with a spoon fetish."

Mona sighed, mollified. "Okay. I get it. Play the movie."

~~*

It was after one a.m. when Todd finally shut off the TV. Mona had crashed out about twenty minutes into *Bill and Ted's Bogus Journey*—a testament to the film's high quality. He'd always thought the first one was better, but none of the streaming services he subscribed to had it. He knew he shouldn't have settled for the sequel. With a few notable exceptions, sequels were never as good as the originals.

He rose from the bed and went quietly into the adjacent bathroom, not turning on the light until he'd closed the door behind him. He didn't want to wake Mona if he didn't have to. She would only fret over every little nighttime noise.

He brushed his teeth and got as far as removing one contact lens when he felt a chill brush over his skin. He shivered in his pajama pants and t-shirt and continued with what he was doing. The chill swept over him again, sending a shiver down his spine and raising goose bumps all over his skin.

Shit. It was only now that he had both contacts out that he remembered he'd left his glasses in the nightstand.

Was that misty haze he saw in the mirror just the result of his tired, dry eyes, or was it something more substantial? He looked directly at his reflection. No haze there. He shifted his gaze to the white, amorphous cloud

141

that hovered behind and above his right shoulder. Denser than steam, not as dense as mayonnaise, his blurred vision told him. Beyond that, he could make no determination.

Feeling half stupid, he spoke in a hushed voice. "What do you want?"

No answer was forthcoming. What did he expect? It was a fucking cloud! It looked like something from an episode of the original *Star Trek*, for Christ's sake.

And then, living up to his memories of more than one gaseous lifeform on the classic *Star Trek* series, it moved. As the dark shadow had last night, it swept over, around, and through him. It left him shivering with its icy passing, but unlike before, he didn't feel sick. This was not the same entity that had attacked him last night. Never mind the denials he'd made to Mona earlier; he definitely felt that encounter had been an attack. That was why he'd told Ben he thought it was malevolent. This thing now wasn't angry; it was just damned cold.

He hurried from the bathroom and, in the wedge of light cast through the doorway, scrabbled in the nightstand until he found his glasses case. He grabbed his glasses and put them on. The cloud was still there, hovering next to the light switch. He approached cautiously, one hand outstretched, braced for the biting cold.

"Mona!" he hissed. "Mona!"

She stirred on the bed but didn't wake.

He couldn't tear his eyes from the cloud for fear it would vanish. He called out louder. "Mona!"

No response.

"Perfect." He pursed his lips and took a step forward. Even expected, the icy chill was a shock to his skin. It sank deep into his muscles and all the way to his bones.

Danger.

Keep back.

Don't go downstairs.

Why not? he wondered. *What's down there?*

There was no response.

He'd never been someone who backed down from a challenge or tried to avoid a necessary confrontation. If this spectral cold front couldn't give him an answer, he would have to go find one for himself.

He tried once again to rouse his sleeping friend, but she only mumbled and rolled over, burying her face in the pillow such that Todd wondered how she didn't smother herself. Was she *really* that sound a sleeper, or was something spectral keeping her asleep? Maybe it was the wine that had knocked her out. In the end, it hardly mattered. She wasn't waking up, and he was on his own. Warning though he believed it to be, he passed through that cold, white cloud and went to discover what awaited him downstairs.

~~*

Mona woke to a choking fear that chilled her limbs and stopped her throat. She sat up like a shot, heart racing, and her eyes lit on the bedside clock: 1:32. The problem was, it wasn't her clock. Now she thought about it, this wasn't her bed. And on top of that, it wasn't her fear.

Todd.

Memory rushed to her waking mind. She looked to the side where Todd should have been and wasn't. Where was he? How long hadn't he been there? She reached out a hand and felt between the sheets. His side of the bed was chilly.

Slowly, she processed the emotions enveloping her, separating them from her own confusion and concern. Her heartbeat slowed little by little and the clamp around her throat eased. She looked around the room, taking in all the information she could from what she could see.

The TV was off. The lights in the bedroom were out. Her empty wine glass stood next to the bedside clock as did a small plate with the traces of the syrup that had glazed the *gulab jamun* they'd had for dessert. The bathroom light was on and the door was ajar. She could just see where Todd's bathrobe hung on the hook inside the door.

Where the hell was Todd, and why was he so scared?

A scream cut the silence. Definitely masculine. Definitely terrified. She was out of the bed and down the stairs before she knew she was moving. Her feet in their fuzzy socks slipped on the polished hardwood, but she didn't check her headlong pace.

She found Todd curled into the fetal position in the doorway between the living and dining rooms. His arms were clutched around his head, and he shook so badly for a moment she was afraid he was having some kind of seizure.

"Sweet Mother Goddess!" She fell to her knees beside him and gathered him into her arms, wishing she'd grabbed his big fleecy bathrobe off the bathroom door. She could really use it now. Although... he didn't feel cold to her. Far from it, in fact. He was shivering as if he'd been out in a blizzard without a coat, but his body felt warm against hers. Rubbing her hands up and down his back to calm him, she murmured soothing nonsense sounds and rocked him back and forth as if he were her child rather than her childhood friend.

She didn't know how much time passed as they huddled there together. It was so quiet. Even the grandfather clock in the front entryway seemed to have ceased its incessant ticking. Finally she felt Todd relax against her and unclench muscles he had clenched... In fear? In defense? His position suggested a physical attack and an attempt to protect himself against swinging fists and feet, but there was no evidence that anyone else had been there. No alarm shrieking. No broken windows. No door busted off its hinges. Not even a picture askew on a wall.

"Hey," she said softly, brushing his blond hair back from his sweat-dampened forehead. "You okay? Yeah? No? Talk to me, buddy."

Todd took a deep, if shaky, breath. That alone was enough to ease some of her anxiety. But he still hadn't spoken.

"Todd? Say something. Can you tell me what happened?"

He uncurled slowly, sitting back a little, moving his limbs as if the motion pained him. Maybe it did. He had been curled up pretty tight. His glasses were askew on his face, and the frames had left an imprint where he'd pressed them against his temples. She adjusted them for him and felt better to see that small indication of a return to order.

"That... shadow. It's not... It's bad. It... I don't know what it wants, but... it doesn't like me."

She pulled him back into her arms and resumed rubbing his back to get his blood flowing through him. He didn't protest. Big strong man. Classic tough guy. Her boss. Her best friend. It was his lack of resistance that worried her more than anything else. He was the most determinedly self-sufficient person she'd ever known. His willing acquiescence to her care did more than freak her out. It downright scared her.

"Wuss." She whispered the epithet. Desperate for a hint of normalcy. Relieved when she heard his softly muttered reply.

"Bitch."

~~*

"Hi. Is this Ben Chalfie?"

"Yeah, speaking," Ben replied, only half listening.

"It's Mona... Ward. From Midnight Jones?"

"Oh, right. Hi." He glanced at the time in the corner of his computer screen. "It's awfully late..."

"Yeah. I know... Sorry. There was another attack."

"What?" In his tiny study on the ground floor of his townhome, Ben sat up straight in his desk chair. The room was lit only by the small desk lamp and the computer screen where the minutes ticked down to the end of the particularly exciting eBay auction he'd been watching all week. Now, though, all his attention was on the voice on the phone.

"Yeah. Todd said he told you about the first one? He said he called you? Um. I don't know what to do. Your number was on the back of the card, and I..."

"Is he all right? Are you both all right?" His heart raced and not just from the unexpected call at a quarter past two in the morning.

Mona's voice came hollowly through the cell connection. "He's back upstairs. I drew a hot bath for him and made him some tea. He was shaking like a leaf in a November windstorm."

The thought of Todd lounging in a tub of steaming water with a mug of tea in his hand did not enhance Ben's attempts to remain detached. That was a mental image he'd be more than happy to make real as long as he was allowed to join in.

He ordered himself to focus. "When did the attack happen?"

"Just a little bit ago. Less than an hour, I think. I don't have a clock in front of me."

Something didn't quite make sense. "Did he call you?" They lived close to one another. She could realistically get there right away if he needed help.

"No. I'm here. At his place. I was here when it happened, but I didn't know it was happening until afterwards. He wouldn't stay at my place, and after what happened last night, I wasn't gonna let him stay here alone." Her words came out in a babbling rush. She was obviously still riding the adrenaline wave of panic from the attack.

Ben kept his voice steady and businesslike, hoping his own calm would find its way to her through the phone connection. "I can be there in forty-five minutes. I'll call Frieda, and we'll be over with some equipment. If that's all right," he added, not sure if PUPI's presence would be welcome at this hour despite her call.

"Good! Yes!" She spoke with a mix of relief and hysteria that quickened her speech to the point that the words practically tumbled over one another. "You have no idea how much I was hoping you'd say that. Todd didn't want me to call you so late, but I figured if you guys could get here at all then the sooner the better. Right? Like there might be traces of something you could pick up with your equipment or something. Maybe. I don't know, but I thought it had to be worth a shot, you know?"

So much for infusing some calm into the situation, Ben thought as he listened to her babbling. He shot a final look at the computer screen. Either his bid would hold or it wouldn't. There was nothing to be done about it now. The investigation at Todd's was too important to postpone. If he lost the auction, there would be others. It wasn't the last autographed copy of *Paddington At Large* there would ever be in the world. He shut off the monitor and hurried upstairs to his bedroom to change into proper clothes.

Mona jabbered on over the phone. He had to move it from his ear while he yanked a long-sleeved sweater on over the t-shirt he had planned to sleep in. "Mona?" he said when he put the phone back to his ear. She was still talking a blue streak. He held the phone against his shoulder while he changed from sweats into a pair of jeans. "Mona?" he tried again more sharply.

She stopped mid-sentence. "Yeah?"

"I need to hang up and call Frieda. Will you and Todd be all right until we get there, or do you need one of us to call you back and talk to you until we arrive?"

She hesitated for a second. "We'll be fine. I've turned on every light in the house," she added with a self-deprecating laugh. "I'll be up all night anyway. I couldn't sleep now if you drugged me. I'll keep an eye out for you."

"Great. We'll be as quick as we can."

Chapter 15

BEN COULDN'T STAND FRIEDA'S SELF-SATISFIED SILENCE any longer. "Spit it out. What do you want to say?"

"Nothing." Her tone was too innocent. She was lying. He might not have her advantages when it came to reading people, but he wasn't an idiot.

"You're feeling, what? Pleased? Vindicated? Full of yourself?"

"If you knew that already, why did you bother to ask?" She turned the big Volvo up the hill and stopped at the light across Broadway.

"Why? Because you get to check out Todd's house after all?"

"See? You keep asking questions to which you already know the answers."

"I wanted to clear the air. The smug satisfaction rolling off you was starting to fog the windshield."

The light turned green and she snorted a laugh, continuing up the street toward their destination. "I admit to the satisfaction, but I would say 'smug' is pushing it. I'm excited to get a chance to check the place out. Two malevolent hauntings in as many nights? You have to admit it's compelling."

"That's one word for it."

"What word would you use, then?"

He had to think about it. She expected an answer. "Curious. Disturbing. Scary. Fucked up. Pick the one you like best."

"Well, yeah. Can't argue with any of those." Several blocks later, she turned right onto a narrow residential street lined with wide parking strips, mature trees, and many parked cars. "What's the house number again? Never mind. I think I see it."

One house about halfway down the block on their right was awash with light. The windows were glowing, beacon-like, in the darkness of the small hours of the night.

Parking on the street was an impossibility. Fortunately, Todd's driveway was empty, if a bit narrow for the old sedan.

"I've parked in tighter spots," Frieda said, pulling in expertly. "And aren't you glad Adam isn't here to comment on that dubious statement?"

Ben chuckled. "Yes."

They squeezed out of the car and Frieda went to open the back. The instruments that would be most useful waited in a pair of equipment cases in the trunk. One contained a stationary camera and its accompanying monitor for catching a single angle of a room. The other held an infrared thermometer, an EMF detector, and thermal imaging and night vision cameras. He'd grabbed a digital voice recorder too and slipped it into his coat pocket as they'd hurried out of the PUPI office. "You could fit a body in this trunk," he said, picking up both cases and hefting them out.

"Oh, two and a half at least. More, if you cut them up and stack them efficiently," she confirmed with a casualness that would have disturbed an unsuspecting passerby. Fortunately at that hour there were none.

Mona met them at the front door before they could knock. She was dressed in pajamas and a flannel bathrobe that reached to the ears of her fuzzy blue bunny slippers. Steam rose from the chartreuse Fiestaware mug she cradled in her hands. "Thanks for coming. Todd's asleep. I didn't want you to ring the doorbell and wake him up. Come on in." She stepped aside and kept talking. Ben wondered if constant chatter was her standard reaction to panic. Evidence suggested it was. "He wanted to be up to talk to you when you arrived, but he was totally wiped out after what happened. He crashed out pretty quick once he hit the bed. I'd rather not wake him unless you really need me to."

"We'll see what we can learn first," said Ben.

Once they were inside, she shut and locked the door behind them. The alarm chirped once, warning that it was ready but not active.

"Was the alarm on before we arrived?" he asked, glancing over his shoulder at the control panel.

"Yes." Mona's reply was definitive. "I watched Todd set it. I wanted to be sure if anything corporeal tried to get in, we'd know, you know? At least we know for sure it wasn't that sort of intruder, eh? Do you want some tea? It's chamomile mint. Or there are others if you want. I can brew you a cup."

"No, thank you. Where was it that you found him?"

"Over here. In the doorway to the dining room." She led the way and stood to one side so they could see. "Everything is just as it was. He was curled up right there." She pointed to the left side of the archway. "He was..." Her voice caught and she cleared her throat with a swallow of tea. "He was curled up right there. He had his arms over his head like he was protecting himself from a beating, you know? His glasses were all wonky when he finally straightened up. It scared the shit out of me."

Ben pictured the scene in his mind: Todd huddled in a protective ball on the floor, being battered by an invisible enemy. Unable to defend himself. Unable to stop it. Ben's stomach did an unpleasant flip-flop. Damn his imagination. It had served him poorly in the past, and here it was making life difficult once again.

Frieda shot him a furrowed-brow look both inquisitive and concerned. He shook his head. It was nothing. He was fine. She gave a tiny nod of understanding in reply.

"Can we move the furniture around at all?" she asked Mona. "That little end table maybe? I want to set up a static camera to try to catch the whole room."

Mona nodded. "Like an establishing shot. Sure. When I lived in Vancouver, BC, my girlfriend at the time worked at a TV studio," she explained. "I can get you some books if you need to raise the camera up higher."

"That would be great."

Mona collected a stack of sturdy hardcovers from somewhere down the hall and put it on the little table. Once they had it set up to best advantage, they could move forward with the rest of the investigation. Ben unpacked the night vision camera and the EMF detector as well as a couple of small but sturdy Maglites. He left the thermal cam in the open case on the floor by the sofa, handy if they needed it, but out of the way.

"You set?" he asked Frieda.

"Good to go."

Ben turned to Mona. "We need to go dark. Can you turn out the lights, please?"

"Which ones?" she asked.

"Everything on this floor. Will you be okay with that? Or do you want to go upstairs while we do this?"

She shivered but shook her head resolutely. "I'll be fine." It took her a minute to shut off all the first-floor lights, starting with the rooms down the hallway at the other end of the house. Coming back, she hit the switches to the table lamp and torchière in the living room and then the wall switch that controlled the dining room chandelier. She returned to where they waited. "Is that better?" she whispered, compelled to quiet by the darkness.

Ben replied softly. "Much, thanks. Can you get the kitchen lights too, please?"

"Oh! Right." She hurried off to the kitchen and the rest of the floor went dark, lit only by the ambient light from the streetlamp.

Frieda switched on the EMF detector and turned her flashlight on the screen. She began scanning the area between living and dining rooms for electromagnetic field fluctuations. Ben turned on the night vision camera, looking for anything that might indicate a presence.

"I'm getting some spiking here," Frieda said in a soft voice. "It's increasing the higher I go. Two point six. Two point nine." She rose up as high as she could on her toes in her chunky heeled boots, holding the meter over her head with one hand. "Three point two. Are there any major electrical wires that go through this wall?"

It took Mona, standing in the kitchen doorway several feet away, a moment to realize the question was directed at her. She approached the dining room and spoke in a whisper. "Shit. I have no idea. Sorry."

"It's okay. I didn't expect you to have memorized the house's blueprints." Frieda shot her a smile of reassurance and comfort and Mona smiled nervously back. "What's upstairs here?"

"Umm." Mona frowned, thinking. "The master bath, I think."

"Is there anything in there that might cause a spike? Is it wired to a house stereo system maybe? Or is there radiant heating in the floor?"

"There's a Jacuzzi bathtub."

"That's probably it." Frieda continued her scans down the other side of the wall. "Readings falling. Two point two. One point six. Point seven."

Ben stood just inside the dining room, filming anything and everything and trying to ignore the image in his mind of Todd in the bubbles of a hot tub, a bottle of champagne close at hand, lights dimmed to a romantic level. Maybe there would be candles lit around the room. A red rose in a vase. Todd smiling, beckoning to him from the water...

Goddamn it! What was up with his imagination these days? He needed to concentrate.

Ben forced his thoughts back to the investigation, finding focus in his annoyance at the mundane: the light bulbs in the chandelier were still cooling down and therefore distorting his readings; there were no shades over the big bay window, allowing in light from outside that also distorted his readings as it reflected off the glass in the china cabinet doors and all the crystal within it. Todd Marks had an impressive array of wine glasses and cut crystal. Ben wondered if he collected it.

Keep your mind on your job, he ordered himself silently. Aloud, he asked *sotto voce,* "Is that light in the far-right corner coming from somewhere inside?" He couldn't see from this angle if there was another light source or perhaps another entry on the other side of the big china cabinet.

Mona jumped at his soft inquiry. "Oh! Yeah. That's the other way into the kitchen. Sorry. It's the light over the sink. I must have missed it before. I guess I'm kind of scattered. Do you want that off?"

"Please."

"I'll go get it. Can I do anything else? Tea?" Mona's voice was just above a whisper in the darkness.

Ben was too busy trying to focus on his instruments to answer her, so Frieda did instead. "You know, I'd love a cup of tea. Maybe you could fix me one? Since you're headed into the kitchen anyway."

Mona perked up. "Sure. You want chamomile mint? Or I think I saw vanilla chai, or English Breakfast, or Good Earth, decaf Market Spice, rooibos—"

Frieda cut her off. "I'd love a mug of Market Spice if it's not too much trouble."

"Not at all! It'll just take a minute to get the water back up to boiling. I'll be right back." She disappeared into the kitchen. In a moment they saw the light bleeding in at the far end of the dining room go out.

Ben noticed at a level just below conscious thought that Mona went the long way around back to the kitchen instead of cutting through the dining room to the closer door. He could put it down to her not wanting to get in his way, although he suspected she simply didn't want to walk through the room where the shadow had attacked her friend. On a more active level, he realized Frieda had just given Mona the distraction the woman needed to keep her relatively calm and also out of the way while they ran their investigation.

"Nice job," he said in an undertone.

"What?" Frieda glanced up from her instruments.

"Her." He gestured toward the kitchen with his head and said again, "Nice job."

"It seemed like the best option at the moment."

He nodded. "You getting anything?"

"I've got dick on the EMF detector," she announced in quiet frustration. "Other than what I picked up from the hot tub upstairs, the variation is minor and consistent with standard electrical wiring. No spikes. No drops. Nada. There's nothing going on. Okay. I take it back." She looked at him with watering eyes. Emotionless tears ran down her cheeks and she dabbed at one with the back of her hand. "Something's active. Just nothing electromagnetic in nature, apparently. How about you?"

"Nothing. Wait—" He shivered. "I'm feeling a cold spot." He put out a hand in front of him. "Do you feel it?"

She reached where he was reaching. "No—"

"Get the thermal cam."

She did, dropping the EMF meter into the padded case

and taking up the small camera. She turned it on and aimed it at Ben, following the warm line of his arm toward the cold spot.

"It's moving. This way." He walked between the table and the china cabinet, one arm out, the other still aiming the night vision camera. Nothing untoward appeared on its screen. "Are you getting anything?"

"Yeah. Seriously chilly area moving toward the far end of the table," Frieda confirmed. "It's swirling. Doing some seriously weird shit with the colors, though. Not staying visibly cold, you know? It's coalescing at the far end of the table, hovering above the chair."

"I see it. Like a cloud at the head of the table."

"Do you have the infrared thermometer?"

"Yeah. Hang on." Wishing for more hands, he set the night vision camera on the table, still filming and aimed at the cloud. He pulled the thermometer from his pocket and turned it on, then took his flashlight out of his back pocket, shining its light on the little screen.

He held up the thermometer and first checked the ambient air temperature. Narrating for Frieda's benefit and that of the camera they'd set up on the little end table they'd moved into the corner of the room. "Sixty-five. Sixty-four. The temperature change is nominal so far. Still sixty-four. I'm aiming it at the far end of the table and moving toward the cloud. There it is. Temperature just dropped significantly. I'm reading forty-one, thirty-eight." He shivered. "I can feel the cold spot. It doesn't seem to be moving at all. I'm still approaching. It just dropped to twenty-one degrees Fahrenheit."

"That's consistent with what I'm seeing on my screen." She raised her free hand and wiped her eyes on her sleeve. They were still tearing up and would continue to do so while anything paranormal remained active. "These colors are psychedelic. You should see this. It's bizarre."

"I'll see it in playback when we get back to the office." Ben raised his voice and spoke to the air. "Is there someone here who wants to communicate with us?... Can you tell us your name?... Or give us a sign? Something to indicate who you are or what you want?"

No answer was forthcoming.

The chill spread through the room and he shivered.

"Can you see me on the screen?" he asked Frieda in a low voice.

"Yep. You're reading warm and living."

"That's a good sign."

"Fuck, it's cold," she said through chattering teeth. "I can see my breath."

"Thermal reading just fell again. It's down to twelve degrees."

"Put your arm out into it. Tell me what you feel."

"I'm putting my flashlight and thermometer away. Hang on." He shut off the instruments and tucked them into his pockets. "Okay. I'm reaching out my right hand toward the cloud."

"I see it. It's clear on the thermal. There's your arm, your hand, your fingers." Frieda sucked in a breath of icy air. "It is butt-cold in here. I think my cheeks are freezing, and I'm out here at the edge of the field. How's your hand? It still looks relatively warm."

"Relative, yeah," Ben said wryly. He could no longer feel his fingers. "Do you have what you need?" he asked through clenched teeth.

"Yeah. Come take a look."

He retrieved his arm from the deep cold and the two of them edged back to the archway, shivering. He exhaled warm air on his right hand, trying to breathe life into his numbed fingers. "I hope you got something useful."

"Check this out." She handed over the camera on which she'd spun the recording back. He played it at normal speed. There was a sudden dark area where the cold spot manifested. There was the warm shape of him as he came around the table. There was his arm, outstretched into the deep blueness of the cold patch. He shuddered at the tingling in his fingers. It was painful, but at least it was feeling.

Then something caught his eye. "Look at that!"

"What?" Frieda jumped at his sudden, soft exclamation.

"Look at the outline of my arm. Do you see it?"

"See what?" She frowned at the image. He rewound it and played it again, pausing it so she could see what he had seen.

"There!"

Finally, she grasped it. "There's no transition zone. There's a definite demarcation line between your arm and the cold spot. There's no gradation whatsoever between the warm colors and the cold. No green."

"Exactly. But I felt the cold. It affected my whole arm."

"There should be green."

"There should."

"There isn't."

"No." He massaged his arm. The tingling was subsiding to warmth at last.

"Okay, that's just weird. What do you think it means?" asked Frieda. "In the grand scheme of things, I mean? Does it matter?" She wiped her cheeks again with her sleeve; her eyes had stopped tearing, at least for the moment.

"I don't know. You go stick your hand in there." He started recording again, aiming the camera toward the empty chair.

"What? Fuck you." But the protest was nominal. She did as he asked.

"What does it feel like?" he asked, suspecting the

answer before she spoke.

"Nothing. Same as the rest of the room."

Ben sighed in disappointment. "That confirms what the camera says. The cold patch is gone."

"I'm not crying anymore either, by the way. I'd say whatever it was vanished while we were reviewing the recording." She returned to him again. "Did Mona say anything about cold areas? Mona?" Frieda turned to where the other woman had just appeared in the shadows of the living room. "Did Todd say anything about cold patches in the air?"

"No. But he didn't really say much about anything." She handed over a blue mug the same shape as her own chartreuse one, full of steaming hot tea. Frieda took it in both hands with a smile and a quiet thanks.

"How about you? Have you felt any particularly cold areas in the house tonight?"

"Nothing that stands out beyond normal nighttime chill. Should I have?"

"Not necessarily, but we picked up a cold spot over there." Ben pointed to the far end of the dining room. "A big one. Frieda, do you have the voice recorder on you?"

"Yeah." She shifted the big mug to one hand and dug the small device out of the pocket of her jeans. "You want it?"

"Just turn it on and hold it out." As she did, Ben held up the thermal imaging camera, slowly panning around the dining room. "Is there someone here?" he asked the air.

Frieda and Mona were silent, watching him and waiting, straining to hear any possible response. They heard none.

He tried again. "Is there someone here who wants to communicate with us?" Another pause. "We're here to listen. Tell us what you want." Silence. "Can you tell us your name? Just your name. I'm Ben. This is Frieda and

MAIA STRONG

Mona." More silence. "We want to help you. Can you tell us why you're here? This house belongs to Todd Marks... Is there a message you want to give us? A message for Todd?... Can you show yourself?"

Nothing.

Frieda spoke softly. "Do you want me to try to agitate it? See if I can provoke a response?"

Ben shook his head and turned off the thermal imaging camera. "I don't think so. Not at this point. You can stop recording."

She turned off the digital voice recorder and pocketed it.

"Hopefully it caught something. I'll get Adam to scan it for EVPs tomorrow."

"EVPs?" said Mona, eyes wide and voice hushed. "That's electronic voice phenomena, right?"

He gave her a nod of confirmation. "Right. There's always a chance the recorder caught something our ears missed." He turned to Frieda. "Are *you* picking up anything?"

She shook her head. "No. Not since the cold spot disappeared. Whoa." Tears suddenly streamed down her cheeks, apropos of nothing. "I take it back."

Ben spoke in an undertone. "The night vision camera?"

"Where you left it on the table." She set her mug of tea down next to the static camera on the end table and took the thermal cam he held out in her direction. She aimed it into the dining room and began filming.

Ben picked up the night vision camera and slowly panned around the dining room once more.

"Are you getting anything?" she asked.

He watched the screen closely, black shadows and shapes reflecting various shades of green. The bay window with its cushioned seat; the dining room table and chairs; the picture on the far wall; the light from the

160

doorway to the kitchen; the antique china cabinet full of glassware and dishes...

"Hang on." He was nearly past the china cabinet before his brain registered what his eyes had shown him. He backed up. There in the corner where the kitchen entrance was mostly hidden by the china cabinet, there was a darker patch amid a lighter one. "Mona?" he said softly. "Is there a light on in the kitchen?"

"Shit! Gods, I did it again. Sorry! It's the little one over the stove. On low. I turned it on when I was making Frieda's tea. I'll go turn it off." It all came out in a rush as she was moving back toward the kitchen.

"Wait, don't."

Mona froze where she was, halfway across the living room.

"Frieda, what do you see in that corner?" He pointed with his free hand. "Not the thermal cam. You. What do *you* see?"

"Okay. Hang on." She set the camera aside and peered into the dark room. "The china cabinet is on the right," she said. "Full of stuff—dishes, wine glasses, cut crystal. There's nothing on top unless it's hidden by the finials. There's the empty corner beyond that where the archway opens into the kitchen. On the back wall there's a framed picture, about two by three feet, I'd guess. It hangs above the chair that's at the head of the table."

"Stop. Go back to the doorway."

"Okay. I'm looking."

"Are your eyes still watering?"

"Like a leaky sink."

"I think I know why. Look closer."

"What am I supposed to be seeing? It's dark—Hang on." Her quiet tone grew intent.

"Do you see it?"

"What the hell is that?"

"What?" asked Mona in a frightened whisper. She

edged back to stand beside Frieda and peered into the dark corner of the dining room.

"There's light around the top of the doorway," Frieda answered.

"I told you. It's the stove light from when I was making your tea. I can go shut—"

For once Ben was glad someone had dropped the ball and left a light on. "No, don't. Frieda, you see it, don't you?"

"I see... something... Oh! Whoa!"

"Mona, is there anything—a half door, a curtain, *anything* that might block light through that doorway?"

"No," said Mona. "It's open just like this one. So?"

It was Frieda who answered. "So there's light at the top of the doorway, but the rest of the opening is dark. Holy shit!"

With a speed too quick for the eye to follow, the shadow in the doorway swept toward them, around them, past them.

Ben tried to follow the movement with the camera. It was so fast! He wouldn't know until they analyzed it if he'd been even remotely successful.

Mona shrieked, splashing tea everywhere as she nearly jumped out of her skin. Frieda gasped and choked.

"Shit! I lost it. Frieda, can you see it anywhere?" He scanned the area with the night vision camera. Nothing. "Frieda? Did you see it?" he asked again more urgently.

It was Mona who spoke. "She's... she's not..."

Ben lowered the camera and turned to see the two women: one standing stock still and clutching her tea mug like a security blanket; one grasping the doorframe as if it were the only steady point in a whirling world.

"Frieda?" He shut off the camera, setting it quickly aside in the open case near her feet. Her knuckles were white against the dark wood. He laid a hand on her arm, not sure if he should try to pry her fingers from the frame or let her release her grip in her own time. "Frieda?" He called her name quietly but insistently. "Frieda, talk to me. Frieda!"

Finally she took a deep, shuddering breath and turned her head to look at him. Her cheeks were wet, and her pupils were so wide her blue irises were nearly all black in the darkness.

"Are you okay?" He took some of her weight as she released her death grip and slowly found her balance.

She coughed and cleared her throat. "My mouth tastes awful. Like cigarettes and—" She made a disgusted face. "Ugh! What is that? It's nasty."

"But you're okay?"

"I'll be fine. But that thing…" She looked where it had passed into the living room and vanished. "It's not happy."

"I know."

She shook her head, and then winced in pain. "No. You really don't. My head is killing me."

"Then tell me. I need data I can't get from the cameras."

"I know, I know."

"Could you feel something in its energy pattern?"

She gave a small laugh that held an edge of hysteria that scared him far more than the shadow had. "Oh yeah. It's recent. So recent, I'm not sure it even knows it's dead. And it's seriously pissed off."

Ben shivered as though someone hadn't merely walked over his grave but Riverdanced on it. "I fucking hate October."

Chapter 16

BEN PACKED UP GEAR WHILE FRIEDA SAT ON TODD'S SOFA, sipping her hot tea and making only token protests at not being allowed to help him.

"We need to speak to Todd," Ben said to Mona. She looked up from where she knelt mopping up the tea she'd spilled.

"Are you sure? I don't know. I think we should let him sleep."

"It would be best to get his impressions on the entity tonight while it's still fresh in his mind. Maybe he and Frieda could compare experiences."

She rose, fiddling absently with the damp kitchen towel. "I don't know," she said again.

"Please?" said Frieda. "It could be invaluable to the investigation. The sooner we can identify the spirit, the sooner we'll know how to proceed."

Ben recognized her tone. He called it her sales-pitch voice. She'd never said she could influence people beyond normal means, but he wouldn't be surprised if there wasn't something of her psychic abilities in that tone.

There was silence while Mona debated internally. Finally, she said, "Okay. I'll try to wake him, but if he doesn't want to talk to you right now, I'm not going to make him. Okay?"

"Of course. Thank you." Frieda smiled.

Frowning, Mona turned and hurried upstairs.

"Working a little magic?" asked Ben softly.

Frieda turned a blankly innocent gaze on him. "I don't know what you're talking about. I asked. She agreed. She's very protective of him, but she knows this is for the best."

"Hmm. Sometimes I wonder about you." She could be as calculating as she could be compassionate. This was one of the times when he wasn't sure where the line lay.

He was saved from further pondering by the return of Mona. Todd followed behind her, wrapped in a thick bathrobe. His hair was tousled, and his eyes were sleepy behind thick-lensed glasses.

"I'm sorry to have Mona wake you, but I need to ask a few questions while your memory's still fresh," Ben said.

Todd nodded and hid a yawn behind one hand. "No, of course. I'd've been annoyed if I hadn't gotten to speak to you before you left."

"First off, what brought you downstairs originally? A noise, a feeling?"

"A warning," Todd said without hesitation.

"A warning?"

"Yeah. I was taking out my contacts when I felt an intense cold and saw a sort of misty cloud. Mona was asleep, and I couldn't wake her up."

Mona startled at that little revelation, but Todd went on without noticing.

"It was at the top of the stairs, telling me not to go."

"So naturally you went," said Mona, her opinion on the matter clear in her tone.

Todd looked at her, unapologetic. "Of course."

"And what did you find when you came downstairs?" Ben encouraged him to continue before the conversation could get sidetracked.

"It was dark. Just like last night. But different from last night, nothing was out of place."

"It was the chair that had moved then, correct?"

165

"Yeah. I came across the room here to the dining room entryway."

"Why there?"

"That's where it was before."

"There wasn't anything guiding you or suggesting it this time?"

"No. It just seemed like where I should go." Todd yawned again. "Excuse me."

"Can we wrap this up soon?" Mona asked. She twisted the dish towel in her hands distractedly. Ben didn't think she was aware she still held it.

"Of course. I'm almost done." Ben turned back to Todd, who was looking at his friend in annoyance. "So, you were standing in the doorway to the dining room, and then what happened?"

Todd hesitated and Ben heard Frieda shift on the sofa behind him.

"I don't exactly remember. I think... I think it came at me like it did before, but it... stayed this time." He shivered and tugged his robe tighter about him. "I was scared. Terrified. I... That's all I remember until Mona found me."

Ben suspected it wasn't the whole truth, but he let it go for the time being. He would ask Frieda what she had picked up that Todd hadn't said in words.

"Okay. Thank you."

Todd only nodded and shoved his hands into the pockets of his bathrobe. "Sorry I can't help more."

Frieda rose from her seat. "It's fine. You've been very helpful. We should get out of your hair now." She handed the big mug to Mona and smiled. "Thank you for the tea and all your help."

"You're welcome."

Ben and Frieda collected up the equipment cases and Todd ushered them to the front door. "Are you still planning to do the regular investigation tomorrow night?"

"Absolutely," answered Ben. "Unless you'd rather postpone it."

"No. Tomorrow's good."

"Our full team will be available. We'll explain the setup then. Will you both be here?"

Todd glanced at Mona, sharing some silent secret. "Yeah. Count on it."

"All right. Good night. Make sure you rearm that after we go." He pointed to the alarm control panel.

"Oh I'll make sure of it," Mona said. "For all the good it'll do."

"Good night. And thanks again," said Todd from the open doorway.

Ben nodded and stepped outside. Frieda was close behind him, but before Todd could shut the door, she paused and turned back. "Do you smoke?"

Todd looked surprised but answered readily enough. "No."

"Did you ever?"

"No. Never."

"Okay. Good night."

With the door finally shut behind them, Ben and Frieda descended the stone steps to street level and the car.

"You want to open the trunk?" he asked when they reached the driveway and she only stood there, lost in thought.

"Oh. Yeah. Right." She pulled her keychain from the pocket of her long wool coat and opened the trunk so he could put the equipment cases away.

He eyed her dubiously. "Do you want me to drive?"

"Do you have a license?"

"Not a current one, but I can get us back to base. At this hour, who's going to be on the road for me to run into anyway? It's an automatic, right?"

She shot him a wry half smile that did more to calm his concerns than any verbal reassurance she might have given him. "You inspire such confidence. And yet, I think not."

They got into the car, and Frieda started the engine. He let her back out of the narrow driveway and onto the similarly narrow street before he chose to distract her with discussions of the investigation.

"So, what do you think?"

"I think..." She paused as they turned onto the cross street that led to the arterial. "I think I'm starving. You want to go to Beth's?"

"You're driving. I'll go wherever you want. I wouldn't say no to a burger and a cup of coffee."

"Good. I'm suddenly dying for a mushroom and cheese omelet and a strawberry milkshake."

Ben laughed outright at that. "Are you hung over or pregnant?" he asked through his mirth.

She chuckled, finally coming back to her usual self. "The former is a hell of a lot more likely than the latter. Preferable too. But the last drink I had was that beer during the eighth inning this afternoon."

"God. Was that only this afternoon?" It felt like days had passed since they'd sat on Frieda's sofa, cheering the Mariners and consuming too much beer and too many game-day nachos. Exhaustion landed on him like a box of rocks. The prospect of a cheeseburger, fries, and coffee at the twenty-four-hour dive, Beth's Café, was as alluring as manna and ambrosia. His stomach growled loudly enough for Frieda to hear it.

"Word to that. I am *ravenous*." She sped up as they headed down Tenth toward Eastlake and from there over the University Bridge. At any other time, her speed across the grated bridge deck would have made him nervous. Right now, he was all for getting to food as quickly as possible.

"What did you pick up from Todd there at the end?" he asked as she cruised on up Eleventh. "I could tell he didn't like admitting he was scared, but there was more, right?"

"Yeah. It was hard to pin down, though. There was something he didn't want to talk about in front of... me? You? Both of us? I'm not sure. But—" She took a breath, thinking, and exhaled slowly. "I think he knows who the ghost is. Or maybe the ghost reminds him of someone he knows. Or, I mean, someone he knew."

"That's not very specific."

"No. It isn't."

They fell silent for several blocks, each caught up in private musings. Ben was certain they had encountered two separate entities tonight. He was frustrated at his inability to communicate with either of them. It seemed like that was always the way of it. No matter how hard he tried and how open he was determined to be, he could never make a direct connection with a ghost. It was like he was doing penance for not listening the first time someone from the next plane of existence had come seeking his help. But he'd been doing that penance for years. When was he ever going to atone for his sins?

He frowned and forced his thoughts away from his failures, seeking pleasanter ponderings: Todd sipping champagne in his Jacuzzi tub. Red rose petals scattered around. Candles glowing warmly.

Yeah. That was particularly pleasant.

The Todd in his mind's eye rose and stepped from the tub. His skin pebbled in the cooler air and Ben mentally wrapped him in a fluffy bath sheet to keep him warm. He took dream-Todd by the hand and led him to the bedroom.

His thoughts took an unexpected and unpleasant turn. Mona was spending the night with Todd. She would spend tomorrow with him too, at her place, while

Presence Unknown ran their investigation.

Frieda broke the silence, startling him.

"They're not sleeping together."

Only then did it occur to him that she'd been following his train of thought. Of course she had. Close proximity like this and few distractions, she wouldn't have to work hard to pick up on what he was feeling, where his thoughts were leading.

Whoops.

He attempted a prevarication that was doomed to failure. "I never thought they were." It was such a blatant lie he was surprised she didn't laugh at him.

"Sure you didn't. Although I suppose, technically, they might be tonight. I mean, I wouldn't sleep alone in the guest room of that house after what we saw. I'd knock back some scotch, crawl into bed next to my best friend, and do my best to sleep without nightmares. Wouldn't you?"

Would he crawl into bed with Todd Marks? Stupid question. *In a heartbeat.* Instead, he said, "I'm not much of a scotch drinker."

"Funny."

"So, what's your point?" He could guess it, but he wasn't the one who had voiced the subject. He was more than happy to let her do the work of putting everything into words for him. She was better at it anyway.

"My point is, while they're likely sleeping in the same bed for the night, they are not, and I believe never will be and never were, anything other than very good friends. Besides, you've clearly forgotten that girlfriend in Vancouver she mentioned."

"So?" If she was determined to stick to this topic, which he would much rather forget had even come up, his best option was to make her keep going until she ran out of talking points. Anything he said in support or denial would be evidence she would jump on to fuel her arguments that he and Todd were meant for one another. Better to let her wear herself out nattering on to her eventual conclusion.

"So? So?" She echoed him in obvious frustration. "So your path to him is totally clear once we finish this job!"

That was quick. "You can stop pestering me on that point any time now. I'm already planning to ask him out on a date once we're done with the investigation."

She shot him a stunned glance and then forced herself to focus again on the road. "You are?"

"Yes. Now can we drop it and talk about the job?"

To his relief, she nodded. "Sure. I've made my point."

"Right." He rolled his eyes and had no doubt she could sense the sarcasm pouring off him. "We should call Adam. Once it's a decent hour for calling anyone, I mean."

"He'll be bummed he missed out tonight."

"I think he'll get over it when he isn't the one mainlining coffee just to stay awake past noon."

Frieda laughed. "Too true. How about you call him and I'll call Danny? See if he's available to do some desk work tomorrow." She glanced at the clock. "I mean later today."

"Good idea. Maybe if we stick the two of them in the office together it will give them time to get to know each other a little. Break the ice."

"Or blow up the room."

"You're so cynical."

"I'm *so hungry*." She stopped at a red light, muttering curses and tapping the steering wheel impatiently as she waited for the green. "Honestly? They'd get along fine if Adam would stop being an ass." The light turned and she gunned it through the intersection.

"He'll get over it," said Ben. "Eventually."

"Maybe once he figures out Danny's kind of into him."

Ben looked at her. She kept her eyes on the road. "Are

you serious?"

"You always ask that." It was the old routine.

"I always wonder."

"Yes. I'm serious. Not that he's said so. I'm just making one of my keen observations. They might even be good for each other. A fun fling, you know?"

"I don't know. Do you really think an office romance is a good idea? Especially considering the size of our office?"

"I'm not talking about a romance. Did you hear me say anything about romance? No. I'm talking a friendly fuck-fest between the two of them. It'd clear the tension from the air, at any rate."

Ben burst out laughing. "Oh my God, Frieda, you crack me up!"

"I'm serious!"

"I know! That's why it's so funny!" A lit sign outside his window caught his eye. "Thank God we're here. I'm *starving*."

Chapter 17

DANNY SAT AT BEN'S DESK, BIG HEADPHONES OVER HIS ears, listening intently and staring at the frequency readout on the screen. They'd given him the digital voice recordings and thermal imaging results to examine, while Adam sat at the other desk reviewing night vision and standard video footage. Danny knew Adam still wasn't thrilled to have him on the team—or at least he wasn't happy with the way Danny had been brought on board. They'd barely exchanged a dozen words all day and the atmosphere in the little office was chilly. Maybe if he could find something on the recording, it would help. Prove to Adam that he was good enough to be there.

He saved a section of thermal imaging footage that struck him as significant. It started with psychedelic swirls of color that made no thermal sense and ended with what looked, based on the rainbow colors on the screen, as though Ben had his arm stretched into an iceberg. He'd not had much experience with thermal imaging in his own amateur work and hoped he hadn't just highlighted something mundane that was simply outside of his sphere of knowledge. He wished there were sound with it, but that would be on the standard camera footage Adam had.

Next, he called up the digital voice file. It wasn't long. Just a few minutes of Ben trying to make verbal contact with whatever it was he'd caught on the thermal cam.

Danny heard nothing but static in between Ben's questions. He dragged the cursor back to the beginning, upped the volume, and tried again. And again. Maybe if he mixed up the treble and bass a bit, tweaked the middle down this time rather than up, he'd catch something on his fourth listen. But he was beginning to think it was a lost cause.

"Dude! Dude!" Adam yanked off his headphones and spun in his chair to face Danny. "Dude!" he exclaimed a third time, prompting Danny to think there might actually be a good reason for his outburst. He paused the voice file and lifted one side of his headphones.

"What? Did you find something?"

"You've got to see this!" Adam's eyes were alight with excitement. He waved Danny over to join him at the other computer.

Leaving his headphones on Ben's desk, he crowded in next to Adam. "What is it?"

"Okay. You know how Ben said they got some good thermal data, right? But he didn't think they'd caught much on the infrared."

"Yeah," said Danny, adding, "I isolated the sections of thermal image data I think he must be talking about. Why? Did you find something?"

"Okay, so I took the infrared, right, and I synched it up with the footage the standard camera picked up." Adam shook his head as if he couldn't believe it. "You tell me what you think." He rose from the chair, and sat Danny down. "I don't want to say anything in case I'm imagining it, you know?"

"Sure. Don't taint the sample. Or something like that."

"Right. Here. Put those on." He pointed to the headphones, and Danny picked them up. "I've synchronized and linked the sections so they play simultaneously. Tell me what you think," he repeated. He leaned across Danny to the mouse and clicked Play.

It wasn't until he'd played the clip from start to finish three times that Danny finally removed the headphones and looked wide-eyed at Adam. "Holy shit!"

"You heard it, didn't you? Did you hear it?"

"Yeah. I heard it." Danny was as elated as he was stunned. He hadn't been this excited since he'd caught an image and an EVP at his parents' house. "That's... Wow!"

"That's what I'm saying!" Adam dug into the pocket of the coat he'd thrown on the wingback chair and pulled out his phone. "Did you get anything off the digital voice recording?"

Danny shook his head. To his astonishment, Adam gave him a look of sympathy and said without a hint of sarcasm, "Don't sweat it. It happens a lot. We all find nothing a hell of a lot more often than we find something, you know? I'm texting Ben."

~~*

Ben and Frieda walked along Market Street, each carrying an enormous to-go latte.

"Do you think they've had any luck?"

Danny and Adam had been alone at the PUPI office since maybe nine o'clock that morning, going over the footage collected at Todd's the previous night. So far neither had texted to say they'd found anything. Ben hoped that meant they were too busy reviewing data to get into a pissing match.

Frieda yawned over her coffee, following his concerns despite her exhaustion—or perhaps because of his. "Relax. Either they'll kill each other or they'll fuck each other."

"Either way, I don't want it happening in our office, and I really don't want to walk in on it."

"You don't want your own private gay porn show?"

"Gah! No! Not when it's people I *know*!"

Frieda snorted a laugh. "No argument there." There was a brief pause before: "We should get tickets to Hump Fest next year."

"No." Before she could argue her case, his phone chirped. He dug one gloved hand into his coat pocket and pulled it out. "It's Adam."

"What's he say?"

"They've got something."

"That's it? How informative," she said dryly.

"Let's go see what it is."

It wasn't much farther to the door of Hole-in-the-Wall Books. They picked up their pace and covered it in less than three minutes.

Ben didn't even have to let them in; Adam was watching out for them.

"There you are! Finally! Come check it out."

Frieda quickly locked the front door behind them and followed the men into the cramped office.

Danny was seated at Frieda's desk. With nowhere else to go, he rolled back as far as he could until he ran into the wall so the others could squeeze in before the screen.

"I've synchronized and linked the sections so that they play simultaneously in addition to what Adam put together," Danny said. "Night vision is on the right and still camera on the left."

"We still don't know what it is you guys have found," Ben pointed out.

"Oh! An EVP and an image on the stationary camera. We synched it with the infrared footage."

The static camera image was aimed diagonally across Todd's dining room toward the kitchen entrance. Ben's infrared footage was pointed in roughly the same direction. Ben remembered it perfectly. "Put it through the speakers and play it."

Adam unplugged the headphones they used while reviewing raw footage and turned on the speakers. He nodded to Danny. "Play the clip."

Danny clicked Play, but the volume was too low to hear anything. "Shit. Sorry." He cranked the volume and restarted the clip.

Frieda's voice came through the speakers first. *"There's light around the top of the doorway."*

Then Mona's reply. *"I told you. It's the stove light from when I was making your tea. I can go shut—"*

Then Ben cutting in. *"No, don't. Frieda, do you see it?"*

"I see...something... Oh! Whoa!"

"Mona, is there anything—a half door, a curtain, anything *that might block light through that doorway?"*

"No. It's open just like this one. So?"

Frieda answered her. *"So there's light at the top of the doorway, but the rest of the opening is dark. Holy shit!"*

Frieda's exclamation startled everyone, even though they all knew it was coming. Ben jumped, trying to follow the blurred green images on the right side of the screen.

"Shit! I lost it. Frieda, can you see it anywhere? Frieda? Did you see it?"

The linked clips stopped where Danny had marked them.

"What am I supposed to see? Or hear?" asked Frieda, her patience short from lack of sleep. Ben agreed with the questions and the sentiment but kept silent.

"Watch the still cam footage at the end." Danny backed it up and played it again.

There it was. "Whoa!" Ben exclaimed. He'd lost the shadow on infrared as it swept across the room, but the static camera hadn't. It passed in a blink across the table and out of the camera's range. "Back it up a few seconds. I want to check something."

Danny did, and Ben watched again to make sure he wasn't imagining things. Nope. "That thing went *through* the table."

"Did you hear it, though?" asked Danny.

"I heard *something*," said Frieda.

"What?" Ben had been too focused on the visual, and had missed the EVP. "What did you hear?"

"Hang on." She knelt down in front of her desk, jamming Danny farther into the corner and forcing Ben to back up a half step to make room for her. She took control of the mouse and backed the clip up a fraction. Then she reached out and cranked the speaker volume up high. "It's just as you're panning the infrared across the room. Wait for it."

She clicked Play.

This time he heard it. An almost animalistic noise. Spectral and spooky as all hell. A single word.

"Oooout!"

Ben shuddered as though someone had hopscotched across his grave. He tried to play it cool despite the chill running along his spine. He clapped Danny on the shoulder. "Good work. Nice catch."

"It was Adam—" Danny began.

"It was a team effort," Adam interrupted.

"I have a question." Frieda's expression was contemplative, her eyebrows drawn together in a thoughtful frown.

"What?" asked Ben.

"It said '*out*,' right?"

"Yes. We all heard it that time."

"Okay. So I'm just wondering if it meant us...or itself."

"What do you mean?" Ben eyed her keenly.

"Out," she repeated thoughtfully. "It's pretty ambiguous, don't you think?" She rose to her feet and leaned one hip against the desk.

"What's ambiguous about it?" asked Adam. "It wanted you guys out."

She looked at him. "Did it? One word isn't much to go on. If it had said, 'get out,' then yeah. The meaning would be relatively clear. But it just said 'out.'" She shrugged.

"It's vague."

"*As far as we know*, it only said the one word," Adam persisted. "You don't know that it didn't say a whole lot more the equipment just didn't pick up."

Before Frieda could respond, Ben's cell phone rang. "Excuse me, you guys." He opened the phone as he went out into the shop letting the curtain fall shut behind him.

He heard the discussion in the office start up again and put as much distance as he could between himself and the curtained doorway without actually leaving the building.

"Hello?" he said and was doubly glad for the interruption when he heard the voice on the other end.

"Hi, Ben. It's Todd Marks."

"Todd, hi. What's up?" Ben's heart raced. Personal or paranormal, this was definitely a call he was happy to take. It had shown up as "Blocked" on his caller ID. He hadn't programmed the unlisted number in yet to identify it as Todd's. He would have to remedy that when the call was over.

"Listen, this may sound pointless and please tell me if I'm wasting your time."

"Not at all. What can I do for you?"

"I wondered if you wouldn't mind coming over early today. Before the investigation. On your own. I'd like to talk to you about what happened last night and the night before. Just the two of us." Even through the hollowness of the cell-to-cell connection, his uncertainty came through loud and clear. So, Frieda was right again. Last night, Todd had been hiding something he didn't want to share with both of them.

"What time?" asked Ben.

"Anytime. Now would be great. If you're not too busy that is. Or just sometime before the investigation. I don't want you to have to make two trips over."

"No, it's fine. I'm not that far." He glanced at his

watch. It was a quarter past noon. He'd managed to grab about three hours of sleep after Frieda had dropped him off at the shop to download the footage to the PUPI server. Not for the first time, he was grateful he lived so close to where he worked and could easily walk between them.

He fought down a yawn. "I can come over now. We can talk over lunch, if that's okay." There were several good independent restaurants in Todd's neighborhood, any one of which would likely be open for lunch on a Sunday.

"I'd like that. Meet me at my place, and we'll walk over to Fifteenth, okay? There's a new Thai place that I've been wanting to try. It's a couple of blocks from the coffeehouse."

"I think I know the one you mean. I'll be over as soon as I can."

"Thanks. Bye."

"Bye." Ben disconnected the call. He took a moment to program in Todd's name and number before closing it, all the while knowing exactly what Frieda would say when she found out about this lunch date. And she would find out sooner rather than later; he needed to borrow her car.

~~*

Frieda leaned nonchalantly against the bookstore's front counter as she dangled her car keys at the end of one outstretched finger. She didn't bother to conceal her smirk of satisfaction as she swung them lightly back and forth like a carrot before a donkey. "Normally, I wouldn't let you do this. I'm a law-abiding citizen, you know. But since it's for a good and noble cause…"

"I don't know if I'd call it that."

"You're meeting a client, who is undoubtedly in some distress, in order to help him through a difficult time."

Ben claimed the keys and gazed down at her with a raised eyebrow and doubtful purse of his lips. "That's reading a lot into it, even for you."

"Yeah, well…" She trailed off, her manner suddenly evasive.

He grew wary and a little concerned. She'd never been one to keep her feelings and opinions to herself. Quite the opposite, in fact. Whether you wanted to hear them or not. "Well, what? What's going on?"

"I have a bit more insight on this one than usual."

"What do you mean?" Had she spoken to Todd and not told him? No. That was ridiculous. More likely she'd spoken with Mona and gleaned something from her.

"I didn't mention it before because, well, I didn't want to upset you and because I wanted time to deal with it on my own first."

"Deal with what? Frieda, what's going on?"

"I caught the brunt of that shadow last night. When it flew past and you lost it on the infrared. You know?"

"Yeah. I'm not likely to forget." It had been a supremely disturbing sight: Frieda gasping and clutching at the doorframe like it was a life preserver hanging on the bulkhead of *RMS Lusitania*. He shuddered at the memory and wondered briefly if that was how Mona had felt when she'd found Todd in the same place after the same sort of event.

"That entity…" Frieda shook her head, her golden-brown curls bobbing with the movement. "It's seriously angry. That sort of residual emotion… it sticks with you. I don't mean *I* felt angry like *it* felt angry, but… Gods, what do I mean?" She paused, collecting her thoughts into something she could coherently express. "You feel the emotion but at the same time it isn't your emotion. Does that make sense?"

"Yeah." Ben nodded. "I get that." He'd never felt anything like it himself, but he understood it theoretically. He'd had his fair share of emotional turmoil in his ghost-hunting life and was glad to have been spared that particular sort.

"Good, because I'm not sure I could explain it any better. The thing is, Todd might not recognize it as something separate or outside of himself, and it could manifest itself in a variety of ways. He could act out in anger for no apparent reason. He could fall into depression because of it. Being pissed off all the time can really wear you down. I should know. I was really good at it when I was in high school and college."

"And yet I've loved you since the day we met," Ben said with a smile.

Frieda returned it with wry amusement. "More fool you. It says something for your tenacity, though. *I* certainly didn't love me back then."

"Is there anything else I should be ready for?"

"It's an extreme reaction, but it's possible that, left unsorted, the imposed emotions could drive Todd crazy."

Ben started in surprise. "Seriously?"

"Seriously. The closest analogy I can think of is split personalities, only in this kind of situation, it's split emotions. The entity's anger has been superimposed over Todd's real emotions. If he doesn't recognize that, he can't deal with it. If he can't deal with it, it'll keep gnawing at him. And if he already has a temper of his own, it's likely to compound things further."

"Okay. I see where you're going. I'll talk to him. Tell him what you said. Hopefully I can explain it as clearly. I'm not completely unfamiliar with personal encounters, even if I haven't experienced exactly what you're talking about."

"I know. I just wanted to make sure you knew, you know?"

"Yeah, I know."

Her demeanor changed suddenly to flippant normalcy.

"And of course I could just be talking out of my ass. It's entirely possible nothing spectral stayed with him once he got past the immediate physical aftereffects of the attacks."

Ben wasn't fooled. He'd known her too long and too well to be put off by her abrupt changes in manner. His expression grew once again serious. "What about you, though? Are you okay?"

"I'm fine. Thank you." She smiled at him reassuringly. "I did a basic cleansing last night—or this morning. Whatever. Before I went to sleep. I'm planning to do another once this case is done. A proper one. You're welcome to join me if you want to."

He never had before, and still she asked every time. "Maybe."

"Okay. Tell Todd too. If you think he'd be okay with it, I'd be happy to include him as well."

"I will."

"I really think it would do him good. If you ask me, he could have used one before all this happened."

"Why do you say that?"

She shrugged. "There's something bothering him. His energy is...muddled. It's like an eel in the bottom of a muddy pond. It doesn't visibly disturb the surface, but it's down there mucking up the waters."

"Yuck."

"Yeah. We all have some of that, but with Todd there's definitely more going on than there is for your average Joe Lunchbucket." She turned flip and dismissive once more and, as before, he followed her twists and turns with the ease of years of practice. "Now go before I change my mind about loaning my beloved car to a man with an expired driver's license."

"I thought you said it was a good and noble cause," he joked, jingling the keys in his hand.

"Only if it eventually gets you laid. Now go! I want to

close up the office and get some more sleep before tonight's gig."

"You could leave Adam and Danny to close up."

"They were here alone all morning. They seem to have reached a détente, but I think much longer would be pushing it, don't you?"

"Yeah." He glanced toward the back of the shop and the velvet curtain—which wasn't actually visible from where he stood—that hung between them and the subjects of their conversation and lowered his voice. "I trust them with the equipment, but…"

Frieda matched his quiet tone. "Agreed. Things have definitely thawed between them since they found that image and EVP. But there's no telling how long it will last." She made a dubious, pinched-up face.

Ben chuckled and opened the bookstore's front door, letting in the crisp autumn afternoon. "I leave matters in your capable hands," he said as he made his escape. "Have fun."

"Don't crash my car!" she shouted after him out the open door.

"Don't you have a baseball game to watch?" he called back, walking backwards away from the storefront.

"Travel day followed by an off day between series. Tuesday, though, you won't see me for love nor money while the game is on."

"It'll rain Tuesday."

"We have a roof! You should come to my place and watch the game with me after work."

"I might. You know I love those tight pants they wear!" Ben laughed again and waved before turning around to see where he was going. He found her car parked around the corner and got in, adjusting the seat and mirrors for his greater height. He couldn't help feeling a little zing of excitement at the prospect of meeting with Todd one-on-one over lunch. Maybe he would order a midday glass of wine. He liked sweet white wine with spicy Thai food. Would the restaurant have a liquor license? Surely it must.

"It is not a date." He spoke the words out loud in a firm tone in order to make them stick. It didn't work. "He's a client," he went on, turning on the car's engine and signaling to pull out. "We have a professional relationship. He wants to discuss a professional matter that relates directly to the case. This is *not* a *date*."

Of course, if things progressed naturally from a not-date to a date, well, who was he to argue with that? Maintaining one's ethics was one thing. Failing to seize a moment when the universe presented one was something else entirely. He smiled at the possibilities. He was a professional, but he wasn't a fool.

Chapter 18

"I'M GLAD YOU COULD MAKE IT ON SUCH SHORT NOTICE. I really wasn't sure if I should bother calling or just wait until you guys came over tonight."

Todd and Ben walked side by side, long legs striding efficiently along the sidewalk.

"This is fine. I'm glad you called."

Ben shot him a quick look that Todd couldn't quite interpret. Thoughtful? Curious? Friendly? Concerned? Damn the chilly breeze that had caused him to pull his scarf up so high. Why couldn't today have been one of those warm, Indian summer sorts of autumn days? At least at lunch they would be sitting across from one another. A much better setup for observing someone you wanted to get to know better.

Not that that was Todd's primary motive in calling. It might be his *secondary* motive, but it was not the most urgent reason he wanted to talk to Ben. In truth, the attacks he'd experienced had left him more shaken than he liked to admit and he wanted reassurance from someone with more experience with this stuff than him. Assuming he could bring himself to voice his fears. Life had taught him not to let down his defenses that way. It was a hard habit to break.

"So, what did you want to talk to me about?" Ben asked as they crossed the arterial and Todd pointed to their right.

"The restaurant's just up in the next block. You're okay with Thai, right? I don't want to pressure you into anything." And if that didn't sound like some sort of passive-aggressive come-on, Todd didn't want to know what did. He cringed internally. Fortunately Ben took the comment at face value.

"I love Thai food," he answered with a quick smile.

"Great."

They fell silent for the rest of the short walk and didn't pick up the thread of the conversation again until they were seated with menus in front of them.

A waitress in a classic black and white ensemble accented with a purple apron typical of Thai restaurants set glasses of ice water before them. "Would you like something to drink?"

"I'd like a glass of Riesling, please," said Ben immediately.

Todd was surprised, although he didn't know why. It was nearly one in the afternoon, they'd walked to the restaurant, and no one was driving anywhere any time soon, therefore, there was no real reason not to have a drink with lunch. He just hadn't taken Ben for the Riesling type.

"Do you have Singha?" Todd asked the waitress.

"We do."

"I'd like one of those, then, please."

"A Riesling and a Singha. I'll be right back with your drinks."

Once she was gone, Ben surprised Todd by saying, "I'm really glad you called."

"Oh?"

"Yeah. I'll tell you why later. First, tell me why you called."

Todd hesitated, internal debate raging in the span of a few heartbeats. Avoidance won out over honesty in the end, and he asked, "Do you cover many hauntings?"

"As many as we can."

"So, you get a lot of calls?"

Ben shrugged. "Depends. In a normal month, we might get one or two. Some months we have none. This time of year, though, things pick up."

"Really?"

"It starts around the autumnal equinox, builds until Halloween, and then slacks off again in November."

"Weird."

"Actually, it isn't. According to Frieda, it's an expected seasonal variation."

The waitress returned with their drinks, setting them in front of each man. "Are you ready to order?"

"We haven't even looked at the menu," Todd said.

"That's okay. Take your time. I'll check back in a few." She smiled and went off to see to other customers.

"We should probably decide now, huh? Before she comes back again."

"It's easy. I have a policy," said Ben.

Todd's stomach fluttered for no good reason. Policy on what? Thai food? Business lunches? First dates? "What's that?"

"The first time I go to a new Thai place, I always order chicken pad thai. It's a good baseline for comparing all the different Thai restaurants since everyone has it on the menu, but no two are exactly the same."

Ah. So his first guess was the right one. Todd wasn't sure whether he was relieved or disappointed. "That makes sense." He closed his menu and caught the waitress's eye.

She finished filling water glasses at another table and approached. "Decided already?"

Todd nodded to Ben. "Go ahead."

"Chicken pad thai, please."

"How spicy? Zero to five stars," she informed him.

"Three stars."

She scribbled a quick note on her order pad and looked over at Todd. "And for you?"

"Swimming Rama, Rama Garden, Rama Angel—whatever you call it here. With chicken," he added.

"With chicken. How spicy?"

"Four stars."

"Brown rice or white?"

"Brown."

"All right. Rama Garden with chicken, four stars, brown rice. Chicken pad thai, three stars. I'll be back when it's ready." She took their menus and left them to themselves once again.

Ben took a sip of wine and regarded Todd with his intense blue eyes. They were that much more daunting without Mona or Frieda there to divide Ben's attention.

Todd took a swallow of his beer, mentally bracing himself. *I can do this,* he thought. *It'll be fine.* "So... like I said on the phone... I want to talk to you about the past two nights. They were a bit...outside of my normal sphere of experience." He gave a wry half smile hoping to hide deep uneasiness he felt saying even that much out loud.

"I'd be worried if they weren't." Ben returned the smile easily, giving Todd courage.

"I've never experienced anything remotely like that before. I mean, the ghost in my car is one thing. All it does is mess with my radio. And the ghost that steals my spoons..." He shrugged. "It's annoying, but I can deal with it, you know? Although I'd really like to get back the good Norwegian silver ones. Do you guys ever communicate with these"—he sought the right word—"beings? Is it possible I could make a deal with it?"

"Frieda's the one to talk to about that. The few times when we've had direct, extended communication with an entity, she's been the one to handle it. She has a knack for it that I lack. Sometimes we call in a friend of hers who's an actual medium. It depends on what sort of energy she's getting from the paranormal entity and what the client wants, of course. According to her, he's attuned like she is but from a different angle."

Todd wasn't sure what that meant but nodded as if he did. Now that it came to it, he wasn't sure what he wanted to say or if this was even the right venue in which to say anything. Ben seemed okay with discussing the subject here, but he dealt with this sort of thing on a regular basis and was undoubtedly inured to it.

Or was he?

Todd took another swallow of his beer and set the glass down before asking, "Does it ever get to you? Freak you out, I mean?"

"What? The hauntings?"

"Yeah."

"Hell yes." Ben gave an exhale that was half chuckle, half sigh. "Sometimes it's no big deal, but other times it can be seriously scary. Mostly, though, it's somewhere in between. We rarely get anything as extreme as what we experienced at your house last night. I blame it on October. The craziest ones always seem to hit in October."

"And yet you keep doing it." He didn't quite feel it was his business to ask why, but the question was there, couched in his reply.

"Well, someone has to, right?" Ben sipped his wine and Todd couldn't help feeling that he was missing something.

"I don't know about that, but I'm certainly glad someone is. Otherwise, I'd be at a total loss for what to do right now."

They fell silent once more. Todd wondered what Ben was thinking and wished he could see the patterns that connected people as well as he saw those that influenced his business decisions. Running a company was so much easier than dealing with personal matters.

He took a long swallow of his beer and contemplated the man across the table. What was behind those eyes? Why, all of a sudden, had they become so veiled? Moments ago, he'd been open, taking in everything around him, actively watching and listening. Now it was like he'd shut off that function and with it any chance that Todd might see beyond the surface.

The waitress returned with two loaded plates, interrupting his increasingly puzzled thoughts. "Pad thai," she said, placing one in front of Ben. "And Rama Garden." The other went down before Todd. "Let me know if you need anything else." And she was gone again.

While Ben squeezed lime juice over his pad thai, Todd mixed some spicy peanut sauce into a huge mound of brown rice. He added a bit of chicken and took a bite. The flavor of the sauce hit first, then the chicken, followed by the slow burn of the four stars of heat. It was all he could do not to roll his eyes in delight. "Mmm! So good!"

"Is it?" Ben spun rice noodles onto his fork and popped the bite into his mouth. He smiled around the mouthful, his face suddenly just as friendly and open as it had been earlier. "Mmm-hmm!" He swallowed the bite and followed it with another. "Oh my God. That's excellent!"

"Everything good over here?" It was the waitress again, topping up their water glasses that were still essentially full.

"Delicious. Thanks," answered Todd.

The woman slipped off again, leaving them in peace with their food.

Several pleasant moments and tasty bites passed with no sound between the two men beyond the clink of forks on plates and happy noises made over a truly delectable meal.

Ben chased his pad thai with ice water. "This has really good spice. I can't believe you went with four stars."

"I like things spicy." Todd grinned—and then realized how suggestive that sounded. He took a swig of beer, silently cursing his subconscious. "I mean... That is... Peanut sauce is never as spicy as the number of stars suggest. I think it's because there's coconut milk in it," he ended in a rush.

When it came down to it, he still wasn't one hundred percent positive Ben was gay, never mind interested in him, no matter what Mona said. He used to be better at reading the signals. When had he lost that skill?

"I'm not so sure about that," said Ben lightly. "I mean, I like spicy food too, but four stars is a bit much for me. Clearly I'm not as macho as you. Of course, I'm not as macho as Frieda either, so that's not saying a lot," he finished with a joking smile.

Todd laughed. "Macho is overrated."

"You think so?"

"Are you kidding?" He set down his fork so he could tick off points on his fingers. "I spend six months or more out of every year following Major League Baseball. I restored my vintage car myself, and I change my own oil regularly. I never stop to ask for directions. Oh, and I do my own home improvement projects. That's more than enough macho for me, thanks, and in the end it's what drove my last partner away." Cripes! Why had he said all that? He might as well have announced it: *I'm single and I like graceful, bookish guys who wear glasses.* Okay, so the last part probably wasn't so obviously inferred, but still. And the part about his failed relationship? What the fuck was he thinking bringing that up?

Ben laughed, startling him from his spiral of self-recrimination. "Frieda was right."

Of all the things he'd just revealed, Todd couldn't imagine which one Ben was talking about. Or maybe Frieda had been right that Todd was lonely and looking for love. Jesus, he hoped it wasn't *that* obvious. He kept his expression and tone as neutral as he could. "Oh?"

"Yeah. She said you were a baseball fan."

"Oh!" He laughed with more than a little relief. "Did she? How did she figure that?"

"Honestly, I think she figures everyone is until they prove her wrong. Or I should say, until they disappoint her."

"And you? Are you a fan or a disappointment?"

"I'm a fan of the tight pants." Ben grinned.

Todd laughed again, thinking, *that answers that, at least.* He was inordinately pleased with this small revelation. "We should go to a game sometime. I usually get a sixteen-game package for the season. I'd go for more, but I just don't have the time."

"Thanks. I might take you up on that. I just need the right motivation, I suppose."

Todd looked back at his plate, took a bite, chased it with beer. He was going to need another drink if he didn't slow down. Or maybe he shouldn't. He was such a lightweight—ironic considering his family history. Did he really trust himself buzzed around Ben? Probably not the best idea right now. Maybe a Thai iced tea would be better. He tossed back half of his glass of ice water in one long draught and returned his attention to his meal.

It was Ben who broke the silence that followed. "We got some good data at your place last night."

"Yeah? That's good."

"It didn't take very long either. When a space is that active, you don't have to wait long before you get something definitive. If you're going to get anything at all."

"And did you?" Todd asked, not entirely sure he wanted to hear the answer. "Get something definitive, I mean?"

"We got some interesting footage on all the cameras.

Standard, night vision, and thermal imaging. We got an EVP too."

"EVP?"

"Electronic voice phenomenon."

"You got a voice?" Todd's eyes widened and he leaned forward over his plate.

Ben shot him a grin, just as excited with the discovery. "Yeah."

"What did it say?"

"Out."

"Out?"

"Out." Ben nodded once and took a bite of his lunch. "It's clear and, to be honest, damned creepy. We'll play it for you when we do the final examination and analysis at your place. It'll be a few days. It'll take time to go through the footage we get tonight, and it's more practical to show you everything at once."

"Sure, sure. That makes sense."

"But how are you?" Ben changed his tone so abruptly, Todd wondered how he didn't give himself the mental equivalent of whiplash. "You experienced that shadow twice, and from what I understand, it was head-on both times. Are you doing all right? Frieda said the entity was angry."

Todd let out a laugh that lacked most of its humor. "I'd say angry is an understatement."

"And what about you?"

There was more in the question than lay on the surface. Todd was certain of it. He decided the direct approach was the best one. "I'm fine. Why? Shouldn't I be?"

If Ben was at all surprised by his question, he didn't show it. "Frieda was concerned you might be feeling some aftereffects from the contact. It can happen sometimes. She recommended a cleansing. She did one herself this morning after she got home from the investigation."

"A cleansing? Why do I think you're not talking about a shower?"

"Yeah, no. It's a witch thing. I don't know what all it entails, but she finds it helpful to cleanse her energy after an intense paranormal encounter."

Ben's response wasn't what he'd expected. "Witch things" didn't automatically leap to Todd's lapsed-Catholic mind. "Oh. Thanks, but I think I'm okay."

"Sure. If, you know, you start feeling...not quite yourself, though, she said you'd be welcome to join her when we're done with the job. For a cleansing."

Todd frowned. "How do you mean not quite myself?"

"She's concerned there might be some residual spectral energy clinging to your aura. Or something like that. Specifically, she said there might be left over anger."

"That can happen?" The idea had never occurred to him, but then he wasn't a witch or a paranormal investigator.

"Definitely."

"Huh. Okay. Thanks," he said again. "Tell Frieda thanks too." There didn't seem much more to be said on the subject, so they fell silent. Todd decided digesting this weird new information required another beer. He flagged the waitress and ordered one. With luck the food would cushion the alcohol sufficiently to keep him from getting tipsy. Once she'd brought it and departed, he cleared his throat.

Ben looked at him expectantly.

Todd had no idea what he wanted to say.

"Have you ever been haunted?" The question came out in a rush, surprising both of them. "I'm sorry," Todd added quickly. "That's sort of a personal question, isn't it?" He didn't know why he felt that way. He'd never been shy about his haunted Beetle. Why did he think Ben would be offended by his curiosity?

Ben was silent, his expression inscrutable.

Shit. Todd was pretty sure that he'd just blown any chance he might have had. "It's none of my business. Forget I asked."

"No, no. It's fine." Ben's eyes regained the intensity they'd had earlier, and Todd was held by them, unable or unwilling to look away. "It can be a personal question, but I don't mind discussing it." Ben fell silent again and took a sip of wine. "Do you want the short version or the long version?"

Fair question. What did he want? Ben owed him nothing and was under no obligation to answer at all. And yet here he was, asking Todd how much of his past Todd wanted him to reveal. That was a serious offering of trust, and Todd didn't want to abuse that offer.

"I want to know as much as you want to tell me." It sounded like a cop-out once it was out there, but so be it. He could only hope Ben would see it for what it was—a bridge built from one side of a gap in an attempt to meet another coming from the other side. Now if the two sides would only align properly...

"I had a ghost roommate in college."

If Todd had had any expectation, this wasn't it. He waited, wondering if that was as far as Ben's bridge was going to go. There was still a fairly big gap between sides, in his opinion.

Then Ben went on. "I went to college in upstate New York. A private university in a smallish town. A lot of the buildings are pushing 150 years old. The dorm room I had my senior year was meant for two students, but the roommate I'd been assigned dropped out fall quarter and I never got a new one. So I was on my own. Mostly. There was a ghost who would come in sometimes. Randomly. Usually at night. I would hear the door open and close when it clearly stayed shut, and sometimes I would see someone sitting on the extra bed. I can tell you what he looked like, down to the color of his eyes and what he was wearing."

Todd let out a low whistle. "Wow."

"Yeah." Ben gave a smile both wistful and melancholy. "That's what I would have thought too, had I acknowledged it at the time."

"You mean you didn't...I don't know...do something? Tell someone?"

"What was there to tell? That I was being haunted? That I was hallucinating? I didn't want to think about it enough to figure out which answer was right. So I ignored it. I'm not proud of it, but that's what I did."

"What about Frieda? You knew her back then, right?" Todd had no reason beyond instinct to suspect it, but he had gotten the impression that she and Ben had been friends for a long time.

"Sure. We met her freshman year of high school. My sophomore year."

"So, why didn't you tell her?"

"Eventually, I did. But she was here. I was across the country. On the wrong coast as she calls it. I told her all about it while I was home for the winter holidays that year. She told me to talk to it. To him. She wanted me to ask who he was and what he wanted. I couldn't do it." He paused, looking pensive and, Todd thought, regretful. "She called me at least once a week. Bugging me to talk to him. I still didn't listen to her, and then it was too late. He must have needed something, or he wouldn't have been haunting the room, you know? But I never found out what it was. I owe him my life, and I don't even know his name or how he died. And I only have a guess as to when he lived, so researching who he was would be very difficult."

"But can't you go back?" Todd was thoroughly into the story by now. It was like something out of a movie. "I mean, it's been years, right, but what's linear time to a ghost? Maybe you could take some equipment, take Frieda with you—"

"The dorm is gone. They tore it down eight years ago. Damage from a heavy snowfall caved in the roof. It was too expensive to restore the whole building or something. I don't know. It doesn't matter why, anyway. I've seen pictures of the construction they've done since. There's an environmental sciences building on that site now."

"Oh man. That...sucks." The statement was wholly inadequate, and Todd knew it. But what more was there to say? Ben's revelation had given him some answers and at the same time raised a number of new questions. Like, Ben owed the ghost his life? How did that work? Owed in what way? He wanted to know, but after what he'd already learned, after the way Ben had trusted him, Todd didn't feel he could ask any more. Not yet. Maybe later. After the job was over. When they could go out on a real date. Or maybe over drinks back at Todd's place. They could talk, get to know one another, and if it ended in a long night of steamy, sweaty sex, who was he to argue?

Jesus Christ. Where had *that* come from? There went his damnable subconscious again, rearing its horny head. What sort of asshole was he to take the confidence Ben had shared and rather than respect it, exploit it by considering how he might use what he'd learned to get Ben into bed? He hated himself in that moment. Ben had opened up to him and all he could think about was how soon he could get him alone and get into his pants. Jesus! He was a total jackass who was thinking with his prick! That was no way to treat someone who'd just spilled their guts to him. He was such a fucking jerk! He was—

He looked at his hand where it gripped his beer glass, knuckles gone white as the blood was forced out of them. Had it been a can, he'd have crushed it and spewed beer all over himself. Looking up, he saw Ben regarding him with his too-blue eyes. Wary. Expectant. Concerned.

He took a deep breath, exhaling heavily and expelling with it the sudden and extreme wave of anger. He had a temper when he was riled, sure, but this was beyond anything Todd counted as normal. "I think," he said, prying his fingers from his glass one by one, "I might take Frieda up on her offer of a cleansing after all."

"It might not be a bad idea."

Todd sat up straighter in his chair. "In fact... would you mind a change of plans tonight?"

Ben looked surprised but shook his head. "What kind of change?"

"Can we do just the house? Save the coffee shop for another time? I know it's why I called in the first place, but I'm starting to agree with Shell that it was some sort of prank."

"Can I ask why?"

"Nothing's happened there since the spoons went missing. I mean, zilch. Not even a sudden chill. Besides, if it *wasn't* a prank and it *is* the same ghost that's stealing spoons at my house, we can kill two birds with one stone. So to speak." He felt silly for using that particular analogy talking about beings that were already dead, but he shrugged it off. Better to feel silly than unaccountably ragey.

"Sure. Actually, that simplifies things so, yeah. Great." Ben smiled over the last of his wine.

Todd's shoulders relaxed and he smiled back, echoing, "Great."

Chapter 19

TODD STOOD IN FRONT OF HIS HOUSE, WATCHING BEN drive off in Frieda's battered old car. When he'd gone, rather than heading inside, Todd decided to pop into Midnight Jones to find out how the day was going there. He tried not to bother his staff too much on his days off, but Sunday afternoons were a quiet time, so he shouldn't be in their way. He'd just get a coffee, see if Mona was still around, and let her know that the new mixer he'd promised would be delivered a week from Tuesday.

The bell over the door jingled as he entered the coffee shop.

"Hey, boss man!"

"Hi, Lily. What're you doing here on the weekend?"

The weekday barista greeted him with a big smile. "Filling in and picking up some extra hours. Becky called in sick. What can I get for you?"

"Just a grande double Americano, thanks."

She pulled a pouty face. "That's all? I don't get to show off my fabulous foam picture skills for you? I learned how to make an elephant at Coffee Fest. You should see what my time off from here bought you in return. Plus I need the practice, and it's totally cool!"

He chuckled but shook his head. "Maybe next time."

"All right," she said with an exaggerated sigh of disappointment.

"I'll take a scone, though."

"Pumpkin ginger or almond poppy seed?"

"Pumpkin ginger."

"Hey, did the Beaverton Police Department find you yet?" She got him the scone on a little plate and pulled a double shot for him as they talked.

"No. Why would they want to?"

"I don't know. They called for you earlier. I handed them over to Shell, and I think she might have given them your cell number."

"I've had it on Do Not Disturb. I was at lunch." He pulled his phone from his pocket. Sure enough, there was a notice that he had a missed call and a voicemail waiting. Why had the Beaverton police called him? He didn't know anyone in Beaverton. Did he? "Do you know what they wanted?" He pocketed the phone again.

"No. They might have told Shell."

"Is she still here?"

"No, but she might have told Mona."

It was like pulling teeth. "So *Mona's* still here?"

"Yeah. In the kitchen."

"Thanks."

He took the coffee and scone and went to find Mona. He relaxed considerably the moment he stepped through the doorway. Mona had a way of making her space comforting, even when that space was an industrial kitchen. "Hey there."

Mona looked up from a pan of cookies she was transferring to a cooling rack and smiled at him. "Hey, yourself. What Oregon laws have you broken lately?"

"None that I know of," he replied. "I haven't even been to Oregon since that road trip we did to see Depeche Mode. Although we did break a few then if I remember correctly."

She made a dismissive noise. "Minor traffic violations."

"We chased the Depeche limo through the streets of

201

downtown Portland," he reminded her dryly.

"Right. Like I said." She shrugged.

He chuckled. He set his coffee on an out-of-the-way countertop and took a bite of scone. "Delicious as always."

"Thank you. So, if you haven't taken any lawless day trips south of the border, what do the Beaverton cops want with you?"

"I'd hoped you knew."

"Nope. According to Shell, they were all sorts of professional and need to know, and she didn't need to know."

"I guess I'm reduced to listening to voicemail. You don't mind." He pulled his cell phone from his pocket.

"Are you kidding? I'm dying to know what's up."

Setting down the scone next to his coffee, he accessed his voicemail and sipped his coffee as he listened to the two new messages: the first was a brief word from Shell telling him the Beaverton police would be calling; the second was from the police themselves.

A professional sounding woman's voice greeted him. "Mr. Marks, this is Sergeant Weiss with the Beaverton Police Department. We have some information regarding your father, Andrew Marks. If you could please give us a call back, I'd appreciate it. The number here is five-zero-three—"

"Crap." He scrambled for a pen and Mona pointed to the whiteboard on the wall behind him where he found a dry erase marker and scribbled down the number the woman gave him, relieved that she repeated both it and her name at the end of the message.

"So?" asked Mona. "What's up? Who's after you?"

"A woman named Sergeant Weiss, and she didn't say much. Only that..." He hesitated. The sergeant's words hadn't sunk in immediately, and now that they had, he was more than a little leery. "It has something to do with my father." It felt strange to say it. He hadn't seen his father in years, and he rarely thought of him and never fondly. He wasn't sorry to have left that chapter of his life in the dark past where it belonged.

Mona's eyes went wide, and she nearly dropped the tray she held. "Your father? I didn't know he was in Beaverton."

"Neither did I. Hell, I didn't know he was still alive."

"So what's that rat fucker done now?" It was one of the few subjects that brought out her inner lioness. Her normally warm and fuzzy demeanor turned sharp-edged and dangerous whenever she sensed a threat to Todd, and his father was the longest-standing threat there was.

For both their sakes, he did his best to hang onto the feeling of comfort that had come over him when he'd entered the room. "Who knows? It must be something particularly heinous for them to call me. I'm not even sure how they found me. He sure as hell didn't have my contact information. I wonder if they've found my mother yet."

"I didn't know she was lost."

Todd shot Mona a wry smile, glad that she too was trying to keep cool after her initial knee-jerk response. "You know what I mean."

She smiled back. "I was just trying to ease the tension." She grew serious once more. "You aren't worried that maybe your father found her, are you?"

It was always a possibility—assuming the bastard stayed sober long enough to go looking for her. It wasn't like she'd covered her tracks when she'd remarried and moved to Arizona with her new husband. He shook his head. "Unlikely."

"But not impossible."

"Pessimist."

"And again, I have no witty, one-word comeback." She shook her head. She finished up with the cookies and loaded the empty pans into the Hobart. "I'm just trying to be realistic—as unpleasant as that may be."

"No, I know. But realistically, if he'd found Mom, it's more likely the call would have come from the Phoenix PD, not Beaverton." He took a sip of his coffee and stared at the number on the whiteboard.

"True. So. You gonna call?"

"I suppose I should."

"You'll feel better once you know what's going on."

"You hope. *I* hope."

"Do you need me to dial it for you?"

"No."

"Do you want some privacy?"

He didn't even have to think about his answer. "No. Please stay."

Mona had been there for him as the horror of his childhood had grown into the hell of his teenage years. It was to her and her parents that he and his mother had fled all those years ago. Her family had taken them in, protected them, given them a safe place to stay while the restraining order and divorce were filed and finalized. It was Mona's dad who had gone with him to clean his and his mom's stuff out of the house before it was sold off. It was Mona who'd sat around waiting for him during his after-school counseling sessions so he didn't have to walk home alone. Whatever the police had to tell him wasn't likely to be good news. He wanted Mona with him now like she'd always been with him before.

Taking a steadying breath, he dialed the number.

"Beaverton Police, is this an emergency?" came the voice through the line.

Todd was momentarily taken aback by the question. "Uh, no."

"Thank you. How may I direct your call?"

"I have a message from Sergeant Weiss. My name is Todd Marks."

"Sergeant Weiss is away from her desk. Is this about a case?"

"I really don't know."

"Did she leave a case number?"

"Oh. No. I don't think so." He mouthed "case number" at Mona, who shook her head in response.

"One moment."

Mona tilted her head, questioning, and he explained, "I'm on hold."

"Oh, for fuck's—"

Before she could finish the oath, someone picked up the line. "This is Sergeant Schwartz. Is this Todd Marks?" said a nasal male voice.

"That's right. I had a message from Sergeant Weiss."

"Yes, sir. I'm her partner. Do you know an Andrew Brian Marks?"

Despite the forewarning, Todd tensed at the sound of the name. He did his best to unclench his jaw and answered the officer's question. "He's my father. Why?"

"Yeeeeah."

Todd didn't like the hesitant way the man drew out the word. He braced himself for something nasty.

"I'm sorry to be the bearer of bad news, but I'm afraid your father is deceased."

Silence.

"Sir? Are you still there?"

"What's going on?" whispered Mona, a worried frown on her face.

The officer's voice became more urgent. "Mr. Marks?"

"I'm here," said Todd. "Did you just say that my father is deceased?" He repeated the words not only for Mona's benefit, but for his own. He wasn't sure he'd heard right. He looked at Mona who looked as shocked as he felt.

"I'm afraid so, sir."

"Can you tell me what happened?"

"Ahh..." Todd could hear him clicking on a computer

keyboard. "Drunk driving accident."

"Jesus! He didn't hurt anyone else, did he?" It would be just like his father to take an innocent down with him.

"No, sir. He and his pickup truck met with a dividing wall along the Beaverton-Tigard Freeway at about two-thirty on Monday morning."

"So no one else was involved?"

"No, sir. A trucker witnessed the collision. Said he just swerved off the road and into the wall."

"Oh my God."

"I'm sorry we didn't notify you sooner. It took us a while to track down your contact information."

"No, I understand." He hadn't deliberately made it difficult, but neither had he made it easy, just in case his father should ever get it into his head to try to find him. "Have you contacted my mother? Her name is Eliza Dougherty. She lives in Phoenix."

"I'm afraid I don't know. My partner was making the calls."

"Please tell Sergeant Weiss not to bother if she hasn't already. I'll call her myself. Is there anything you need from her or from me?" Did his father have any property or legacy? He'd probably pissed it all away—literally.

"No, sir. Your father didn't leave much behind. The truck was totaled. There's no sign of any will. His address was a trailer park outside of town. If you want to come down and go through his things—"

"No, thanks," Todd cut him off quickly. "He didn't have anything I want. Just...do whatever you do with people's stuff when they have no next of kin, okay? Donate it to charity. Auction it off. Hell, burn it to the ground for all I care." He reined in his growing anger. There was no reason to be angry, he reminded himself. His father was long gone from his and his mother's lives, and now the bastard was dead. He wouldn't be hurting anyone ever again.

"Is there anything else?" He left the question hanging.

"There's the matter of the body—"

Christ. "I don't know what to tell you."

"Perhaps your mother knows what he might have wanted done?"

"Right. I'll ask. I'm sorry."

"Not at all. It happens."

"Thanks. So… Anything else?" Todd crossed mental fingers the answer would be no. Luck was with him.

"No, sir. That's all," answered the officer.

"Okay. Thank you, Sergeant."

"Yes, sir."

Todd ended the call and, pocketing his cell phone, met Mona's stunned gaze.

"He's dead?" she asked in disbelief. "Like really most sincerely dead?"

"Drunk driving accident. Ran into a freeway divider in the middle of the night."

She looked instantly horrified, eyes wide. "He didn't—"

Todd shook his head. "Nope. Just him. Apparently he had a pickup truck. I didn't ask what kind."

They were silent for several moments as the news sank in.

The alcoholic son of a bitch, who had spent too many years beating up Todd's mother until the night seventeen-year-old Todd had snapped and taken her away, was finally dead.

A slow smile spread across Todd's face. "Get your coat," he said. "We're going out."

"Don't you have paranormal investigators coming over?"

"That's not for"—he checked his watch—"nearly seven hours."

"You should call your mom. She deserves to hear it from you if she hasn't already heard it from the cops."

"You're right. I'll call her on the way."

They left the kitchen. Todd poured his coffee into a to-go cup and capped it, then bagged and pocketed the rest of his scone while Mona changed out of her kitchen shoes and gathered her purse and coat.

"Hey!" exclaimed Lily. "Cookies?"

Mona pulled on her coat and stuffed her purple bandana in the pocket. "Sorry. They're cooling. Do you mind putting them out? I need to go."

"No problem. Where are you guys going?"

Todd looked at Mona, smiled, and then turned his smile on Lily. "Out to celebrate a happy ending."

The barista looked bemused but only shrugged. "Whatever. Have a good time!"

At the door, Todd paused and turned back. "Oh! Lily, are you opening on Tuesday, not this coming one, but next week?"

"Presumably, yeah. Why?"

"There's a delivery coming." He shot Mona a grin. "A new industrial mixer."

"Okay. See ya!"

Outside, Mona grinned back at him. "Two reasons to celebrate. Woo-hoo!"

He laughed and linked his arm in hers. "Come on. I want champagne cocktails, and I know just where to get them."

Chapter 20

SUNDAY NIGHT WAS COLD AND SO CLEAR THAT BEN COULD make out several constellations despite the ambient city light. He and the rest of his team finished loading up the PUPI van and Adam took the wheel for the drive over to Todd's house. Ben wasn't lying when he'd told Todd his request made the job easier. Now, instead of splitting their resources, they could equip three people inside the house and have one monitoring the equipment in the van at all times. It was definitely preferable to the previous plan. Hell, it was almost as good as the setup those guys on TV had.

Adam parked on the narrow street and they quickly unloaded the gear. Ben was glad when they finished getting everything inside. Now the heat could stop leaking out through the open front door and start warming up his chilled extremities. At least he'd worn his warmest gloves, but he hadn't had the balls to wear his silly hat in front of Todd. He wasn't quite ready for that. Not until they had a real first date in the books. Possibly not until they had a second.

While Frieda coordinated camera setups with Mona, Ben spoke with Todd. "You're sure you don't want a camera in the coffee shop?" he asked, just in case Todd had changed his mind again. "We could set up a single static cam aimed toward the condiment stand and the doorway to the kitchen, and we could set Danny to monitoring it." The two men stood in the kitchen, out of the others' way but nearby in case anyone had questions for either of them.

Todd shook his head. "No, thanks. At this point, missing coffee spoons are the least of my worries. Whether it was a ghost with a fetish or a bunch of high school students on some sort of scavenger hunt, at this moment, I couldn't care less. If anything happens at Midnight Jones again, I'll let you know. Right now, it's my home that needs dealing with."

"All right. I'm going to go check on the setup. You're welcome to come see what we're doing if you want to."

"I appreciate that, but I think I'll just stay out of the way until it's time to go. Good luck getting Mona to leave your team alone, though," he added with a small smile. "She's playing it cool, but she's a little starstruck by you guys."

Ben let out a bark of surprised laughter. "By *us*? Are you kidding?"

"Nope."

"Then I suppose I shouldn't laugh." He schooled his expression to something approaching seriousness, but inside he was still amused and bemused. He vaguely recalled Freida saying something similar the night they'd met Todd and Mona. He hadn't believed it then and could barely fathom it now. That anyone could be starstruck by him or the others was such an alien concept that he had trouble wrapping his mind around it. "I'm going to see how the others are doing."

Leaving Todd alone in the warm, comfortable kitchen, he went out into the front room. It took only a moment to spot Freida unwinding cords for the stationary cameras while Adam angled one to best effect in the dining room using the same end-table-plus-stack-of-books arrangement Ben and Freida had used last night.

"Where's Danny?" Ben asked.

"I sent him downstairs with Mona to set up equipment around the car," answered Frieda.

At that moment, they heard feet hurrying up from the basement, followed shortly by Mona's voice as she poked her head out the narrow doorway. "Todd, I need your car keys." They heard the jingle of keys as he tossed them to her, and then her footsteps quickly descending again.

"Sounds like they have it under control," said Frieda with a smile. She went on in a low tone. "You know, if we ever needed a fifth..." She left him to complete the sentence for himself.

He gave her a half-amused, half-cautioning look. "I don't recommend saying that around Adam." He looked around, just realizing the third member of the team was no longer in the dining room. "Where is Adam?"

"Right here." He came around the china cabinet, causing Ben to jump. "I put a camera on top of the refrigerator. It's angled to pick up the dishwasher, sink, and the silverware drawer. The real action may be out here, but we got the call because of missing spoons. Remember?" His tone held an edge of smugness that Ben did not begrudge.

"You're right. Good thinking."

A double set of footsteps rising from below announced the return of Mona and Danny. "Camera is up and running in the garage," Danny announced, rounding the corner from the kitchen to the front room. "Should I go check that the receivers are picking them up?"

"I'll do it." Adam grabbed his coat from the rack of pegs inside the front door. "Is your communicator on?" The last was for Frieda.

She checked it, pulling the little yellow walkie-talkie from where she'd hooked it on her belt. "Aye, Captain," she said in her best imitation of Scotty from *Star Trek*. "We're on channel six sub ten, correct?"

"Correct. I'll hail you when I'm in place." He was out

the door in a moment, closing it behind him to keep the chilly night air out of the warm house.

Danny spoke softly in the brief interval. "He's into *Star Trek*?"

"Fanatical about it."

He smiled broadly, his eyes alight. "He just got so damned sexy."

Frieda snorted a laugh. "I'm glad you two seem to be getting along."

A split second later, Adam's voice came through the walkie-talkie in her hand. "Away team, do you read me? Over."

"Loud and clear," Frieda responded. "What do you see? Over."

"I have camera one. Looks like it's pointed at the car's radio. Is that correct? Over."

Frieda looked at Danny, who nodded, grinning. "Affirmative. I am switching on camera two." She crossed to the dining room camera. "Are you getting the dining room? Over."

"I see it. Can you get camera three? It's the one in the kitchen. Over."

"I'll get it," said Ben. He doubted either of the other two could reach it on top of the fridge. "Got it!" he called before rejoining the others.

Frieda relayed the message as Ben moved to the fourth and final camera that was set to capture a wide shot from the entryway into the living and dining rooms, catching a small wedge of the kitchen and the door that led to the basement stairs. He wished for one more to put upstairs since Todd had mentioned a couple of encounters up there, but they'd agreed to focus on the car and on the main floor since that was where the majority of the activity thus far had taken place. Maybe after this job he'd see about getting a fifth static camera. There was bound to be a good used one available online if he just took the time to look for it.

"All four cameras reporting in," Adam announced. "I'm coming back inside. Out."

Frieda clipped the walkie-talkie back on the belt she wore with her jeans and moved on to surveying the status of the remaining equipment. As Ben watched, she sorted out the various handheld cameras.

Adam returned in a rush of cold air. Shivering, he closed the door and shrugged off his coat once again.

"Time to go dark," Ben announced. He turned to where Mona and Todd waited next to the stairs to the upper floor. "We'll give you a call when we're done here. Go get some sleep. Someone should."

"Thanks, but that's not very likely," Todd said. "Could you sleep with this going on in your house?"

"It's okay," put in Mona. "I went out and bought the whole *Lord of the Rings* trilogy—the extended versions. I wanted them anyway." Ben laughed when he saw Todd's eyes bug out slightly at her words. She grinned at her friend. "Don't worry. There's always Food Network if you get sick of Tolkien."

"That shouldn't take long," muttered Todd, and Ben chuckled. They bundled up in coats, scarves, and hats for the short walk to Mona's apartment. Picking up a small overnight bag, Todd waved a quick goodbye, and then the two headed out.

Ben clapped his hands once in anticipation. "All right. Let's do this. I'll take the first watch in the van." He donned his wool jacket and gloves and picked up a walkie-talkie from the equipment kit. "Six sub ten, right?"

"Affirmative," Adam replied.

"Okay." He headed outside as the others began switching off all the lights, saving the porch light until he was safely inside the van.

*

Frieda handed Danny a thermal imaging camera, glad to have an extra pair of hands for the night's work. "If I remember right, you know how to use one of these." It was the first piece of kit he'd identified in the PUPI offices the morning she'd brought him in to patch him up after his collision with the lamppost.

"Sure. It's been a while, but I remember."

"Good. Keep your eyes open for extremes. Cold spots. Hot spots. Also look for identifiable human shapes, full bodies, hands, arms. That sort of thing."

"Right."

She turned to Adam. "You want the video or the night vision?"

"Night vision," he said.

She handed it over. "Everyone got their flashlights and walkie-talkies?"

"Check."

Danny patted his pockets and nodded. "Got them."

Frieda thumbed on her walkie-talkie, backing away to avoid feedback from the others' while she spoke with Ben out in the van. "We're spreading out now. I'm taking the upstairs to start. See if I can't catch something up there. Adam, you take the main floor. Danny, since you set up the garage camera, you can start downstairs. Ben, you got all that? Over."

His voice was staticky but intelligible through the walkie-talkie. "I've got it. Over."

"Okay. We're moving out."

This was the grunt work of paranormal investigations—padding quietly around a house turned spooky by nothing more than darkness and the nature of the job they did. The time ticked slowly past. Occasionally someone would call with a cold spot that moved where there was no draft or breeze to explain it or an equally inexplicable EMF spike, but those were moments of excitement amidst hours of quiet tedium.

Frieda took the second watch in the van, allowing Ben time to warm up inside the house. That was when they'd also swapped floors, Danny moving to the top, Adam to the basement, and Ben to the main floor.

Eventually, they switched it up again and Adam headed out to the chilly van. Relief couldn't come too soon for Frieda. Monitoring equipment was her least favorite part of any investigation, and it was that much worse when it was so damned cold.

She headed to the basement with the thermal camera while Ben moved to the second floor and Danny took the night vision camera and manned the main floor.

"Good luck finding any cold patches in the garage," Danny whispered to Frieda, poised at the top of the basement stairs. "It's Arctic down there—and I'm from the Midwest, so I know cold."

She chuckled wryly and pulled her hat down over her ears. "Thanks." She wasn't optimistic about her chances either, to be honest. Nor about the investigation in general at that point. It was past one in the morning and still they'd gotten nothing more remarkable than the EMF spikes and cold spots, and one comment by Ben that something had poked him in the shoulder when he was heading upstairs.

Frieda yawned and stepped into the basement. The space was submerged and only partially insulated. Todd used it as a mix of laundry room and workshop. It wasn't as chilly as she'd been warned, but it wasn't exactly comfortable either. It was very dark with only two narrow windows set lengthwise at ground level, near the top of one wall. She yawned again and wondered if Todd would mind if they brewed up a pot of coffee after they'd wrapped things up.

She panned her thermal camera around the room from where she stood at the bottom of the stairs. A sudden fluctuation on the screen caused her to pause and backtrack. She focused on it, wondering if it was just cold air from the uninsulated windows. Two things happened then that put that idea to bed. Her eyes spontaneously began watering, indicating spectral activity, and the cold spot moved independent of any apparent force.

Keeping the camera trained on the moving patch of purple-blue, she pulled the walkie-talkie from her belt. She held it close to her mouth and spoke softly into it. "I have a cold spot down here in the basement. I'm following it. It seems to be moving around the edge of the room from the workbench to the garage." Wait. Where did it go? "Damn. I lost it. Hang on. Got it again. I'm entering the garage. Infrared thermometer is reading fifty-five, fifty-six. There's some decent insulation in here."

They'd shrouded the motion sensor light after setting up the camera, so the garage stayed dark as she entered it. This part of the basement had one external window on the north wall, so the blackness was nearly absolute. Only the little bleed from the room behind her and the smidgen of moonlight kept her from running into things. She wanted the tiny flashlight from her pocket, but she only had so many hands.

"Do you see anything?" It was Ben from his post upstairs in the master suite.

"Nothing. I'm going to check the camera inside the car. Hang on." She released the button on the walkie-talkie and clipped it on her belt again. Her hand now free, she dug the mini-Maglite from her jeans pocket. Moving carefully, she opened the car door and used the little light to look around. The cold spot was close. It felt like a bag of ice hovering just beyond her left ear. She shivered and dabbed at her eyes with the cuff of her sweater. When her vision was clear, she focused her light at the radio dial, and then traded her camera for her walkie-talkie.

"Danny?"

His hushed voice came through the handset. "Yeah? Right here."

"Tell me again what frequency you left the radio on."

"Ninety-one point three, give or take."

She smiled in satisfaction and knew it carried over into her voice. "Not anymore. It looks to be sitting around one-oh-four point five."

"Is that the oldies station?" Danny asked, but his question was lost in Ben's more urgent one.

"Did we catch it on camera?"

It was Adam out in the van who responded. "I'm checking." Another silence while he ran back the recording looking for the moment the dial changed. "Looks like it, but it's hard to tell on this crappy old monitor."

"Leave it for now." Ben again. "We'll check it out later back at the office."

"I hear something in the kitchen," Danny announced, sudden urgency in his hushed tone. "Checking it out."

Frieda backed out of the car and closed its door. She resettled her gear about her, ending with the thermal camera once more in hand and scanning for cold spots.

"This is Danny. I'm in the kitchen talking to the spoon ghost. I'm going to try to cut a deal to get Todd's silver back."

"On my way," said Ben immediately.

Frieda followed with a quick, "I'll be right there."

*

Ben hurried down the stairs only to stop dead in the kitchen doorway behind Danny. He peered over the smaller man's shoulder at the spoon hovering above the counter.

"Whoa," he breathed.

"I told it Todd would bring spoons for it if he could get his good stuff back in exchange," whispered Danny.

"Good thinking." He aimed the digital video camera at it and hit Record.

"Are you getting this?"

"I'm getting it," Ben assured him. "Where's Frieda? I want to get a thermal reading on this thing."

"She should be here any second. She was only in the garage." Danny reached for his walkie-talkie.

In a blink, the spoon was gone.

"What the hell?" Danny exclaimed in an excited whisper, communication with Frieda forgotten. "Where did it go? Did you see it go?" He slowly panned the night vision camera around the room.

"No." Ben moved forward, reaching a hand into the empty air. "Not even a residual cold spot where it was hanging." He pulled a walkie-talkie from his pocket and spoke softly into it. "Adam, did you get that footage on camera three?"

Adam's voice came through the device, staticky but intelligible. "Hang on." They waited. "Yeah. Whoa. Dude, that is *wild*! It just shimmered and disappeared."

"It shimmered?"

"Looks like it from here. Checking it again... Yeah. Totally shimmered and then *blip*! Gone."

"All right. Thanks." Ben looked around. "Where the hell is Frieda? She should be here." The door to the basement stairs was right there. She couldn't have slipped past him no matter how engrossed he'd been in the spoon-stealing ghost. He thumbed on the walkie-talkie again. "Frieda? It's Ben. Come in."

Silence was the only response. His stomach twisted anxiously. Not waiting any longer, Ben opened the basement door, still trying to contact her via walkie-talkie. "Frieda? Where are you? Come in."

"Watch your step," said Danny from behind him. He shined his flashlight down the stairwell since both of Ben's hands were full and followed him carefully down the narrow wooden steps.

Reaching the basement, Danny shined his light across the room. They looked around both with and without the cameras. The main room was empty of anything out of the ordinary and they turned to the door that led into the garage. Ben opened it and Danny aimed his flashlight into the small, crowded space.

Tension and worry twisted Ben's stomach and filled his voice. "Frieda? Frieda, where are you?"

There was still no answer.

Ben didn't have Frieda's sensitivity, but he couldn't help feeling there was something in the garage, and he didn't want to draw its attention. He spoke to Danny in a harsh, strained whisper. "I'll go right. You take the left."

Danny nodded, and they began circling the Beetle. The static camera they'd secured inside the car appeared untouched. Ben panned around with his video camera, looking for signs of their missing team member.

"Over here!"

Ben practically jumped out of his skin at Danny's shout. They'd been speaking in low tones and whispers for so long, the sudden yell was a shock to his ears. He spun around. Saw no one. "Where are you?"

"Passenger side," came Danny's disembodied answer. "Get the light. Frieda's down!"

"Shit!" Ben grabbed the shade off the light, which immediately came on full force. He blinked in the sudden bright flood and hurried around the side of the car.

Adam's indignant voice crackled through three walkie-talkies. "What the fuck? Camera one just blew out. Nearly blinded me!"

Ben ignored him, rushing to where Danny knelt beside Frieda. She was flat on her back with her head next to the Beetle's rear tire. Her eyes were closed, and her naturally pale face looked white as paste. The thermal imaging camera she'd brought with her was several inches away from her out-flung right hand. At a glance, it appeared to have hit the floor with her and skidded away to rest against a yard waste bin full of garden tools.

Video camera discarded on the floor beside him, Ben worked to revive her. He spoke to her, patted her cheek, and rubbed her hands. "God, she's like ice."

"What can I do?" Danny asked. Ben heard the edge of fear in his voice. "Should I call Adam? I don't know what to do."

"Let Adam know the situation. Tell him to stand by. Then check Frieda's camera. I want to know if she caught whatever took her down."

"Right." Danny set his camera on top of the car and pulled out his walkie-talkie. Ben only spared him a sliver of his attention as Danny quickly explained the situation to Adam.

"I'm coming in there!" insisted Adam when Danny took a breath.

"No, you're not!" Ben shouted, glancing over his shoulder. His eyes were on Danny, but his words were for Adam. "Stay where you are and check the damned feed! See if camera one got anything before the lights went on!" It was doubtful, but worth looking. He remembered there was a bit of the windscreen at the top of the camera's frame.

Adam's answer was frustrated but he acquiesced. "Yeah, yeah. I'll get on it. Out."

There was a quiet groan from the floor. Ben turned back, relieved to see Frieda's eyes open in a pained squint.

"Don't move," he said, one hand on her shoulder to stop her in case she tried to sit up.

"Wasn't planning to," she said. Her voice was low and groggy. Not surprising, thought Ben, considering the circumstances.

"Are you hurt? I didn't feel any broken bones."

"I don't think so. My head, though..." She reached up a hand to feel the back of her head where it had hit the cement floor. Ben heard her hissed intake of breath and saw her flinch. "Motherfucker." She looked at her hand. "No blood, though. That's better than I'd have bet on."

"Did you see what took you down?"

"Not exactly. Help me up. Slowly." Ben took her hand and steadied her as she sat up. Even so, she wavered a bit. "Whoa. Gonna be a minute here."

"Take all the time you need." Ben looked up at Danny. "Check her camera. See if she got anything."

Danny jumped. "Right! Sorry." It took him a moment to go around the car to get to the camera. Ben appreciated that Danny had the sense not to try to climb over them to get to it. The one-car garage was crowded with everything stored in it plus the three of them.

Danny picked up the camera and began searching the recording.

Ben waited, his worry over Frieda making him impatient. "Anything?"

"I'm not sure yet." Danny narrated what he saw on the little screen. "She's looking into the car. There's a moment when she must've been answering my call from upstairs. And then... Whoa!"

"What? What is it?"

"It's a hot spot. A seriously hot spot. There's a biggish red area that concentrates down to a small white center." He frowned over the screen and Ben fought the urge to snap at him to hurry up. "Looks like she moved around the car to get a better look at it. It's focused on the hood of the car."

"That's right," Frieda said. "I was there—" She pointed, wincing, to the front passenger-side corner of the Beetle.

"Hold still," Ben admonished gently.

"Yeah."

"What the hell?" exclaimed Danny.

"What? Give it here." Ben held out a hand for the camera.

Danny took a half step back. "Wait. It's changing shape. It's a hand."

"Just a hand?" Ben glanced at Frieda for explanation.

"Yeah," she said again. "It was a hand."

Danny moved back around to the front of the car to look at the hood. He gave a low whistle. "Todd is gonna be *pissed*."

"What? Damn it!" Making sure Frieda was steady enough to sit on her own without falling over, Ben rose and quickly moved to join Danny at the front of the car. There, in the shiny navy-blue finish of the Beetle's hood, was a bubbled and burned patch in the shape of a hand. "Whoa."

"Right?"

"On the upside," said Frieda in a strained voice, "we now know that the thermal camera can take a serious hit and still function. Can I get another hand here? I wanna stand up."

"Are you sure?" Ben asked, quickly returning to her side. He still wanted a crack at the thermal cam, but it could wait.

"I am *not* sitting here on this cement floor any longer. It's fucking freezing."

"Okay." He knelt and offered a strong hand to help pull her to her feet.

"Thanks." Once she'd recovered enough of her equilibrium, they joined Danny and looked over his shoulder at the handprint on the car hood.

"That's nasty," said Frieda.

"Is there more on the camera?" Ben asked.

"There should be. Danny, back it up and play the segment for us."

The three watched the screen where the red patch became white hot and morphed into the shape of a hand. Then it faded to become an indistinct wash of yellow. Finally there was a sudden flash of white as it swept toward the camera. Ben jumped and then shook his head at himself. The next part was too fast to see, especially on such a small screen. As best he could tell, the camera had caught nothing but a quick pan up the wall to the ceiling and back down the other wall to where it had hit the ground, still recording. The last images were a static shot of the cold yard waste bin and what looked like the toe of Frieda's right boot, then Danny's feet as he came around the front of the car.

It was Danny who voiced the question Ben was also thinking. "What was that?"

"That," answered Frieda, "was the ghost we need to get rid of."

Chapter 21

CONVERSATION FELL TO NOTHING WHILE BEN HELPED Frieda make her way up the narrow staircase to the main floor of the house. Danny followed closely behind them, loaded with gear. Reaching the kitchen, Frieda sat down in the dining nook while Danny unloaded the various pieces of equipment onto the table.

"Can you break down things in the basement on your own?" Ben said, his jaw and words equally tense.

"Sure." Danny headed back downstairs.

Now that he'd gotten over being frightened, Ben was furious. He turned on the light under the microwave and began hunting around the kitchen for a towel. Finding one in a drawer, he filled it with a handful of ice from the freezer and gave it to Frieda.

"Thanks," she said, gingerly placing it against the back of her head.

He pulled out his walkie-talkie and called Adam. "I'm calling it a night. We have plenty of data, and I'm not risking any more injuries. Shut down out there and come on in to help break down. Over."

"I'll be right there. Out."

"This isn't your fault," said Frieda.

"You don't think so?" He paced the long galley kitchen as they argued.

"Of course I don't. What could you have done?"

"I should have anticipated it."

"You're not clairvoyant."

"It attacked you before!"

"That was up here. I was in the garage this time. It's only ever manifested on this floor before. There was no reason to suspect it would show up down there."

"Still, I shouldn't have let you wander around this house by yourself!"

"Excuse me?" She glared at him, irritation and challenge fighting for dominance over her expression. "You shouldn't have *let* me? I don't see you *stopping* me, do you?"

He stopped pacing and spun to face her. She was right. He was behaving like an idiot. "You're right. I'm sorry."

"Accepted. Now, are you done beating yourself up?"

He sat down across the table from her and made an inarticulate noise that was neither affirmation nor denial.

She interpreted it correctly and continued to press her point. "There is nothing you could have done. I told you that spirit was pissed off, and you can't fix that."

"No, but I can't help feeling responsible for what happened either. You're my friend. You're my teammate. I should have been looking out for you."

"I am perfectly capable of looking after myself. The fucker just took me by surprise. I'll be fine." Her blue eyes were intent on him, although he could see she was fighting not to squint against what must be a killer headache. "Okay?"

Before he could answer her, Danny emerged from the basement and set more equipment on the table.

Ben was happy for the interruption. "Thanks. Do you need any help?"

"No. I've got it. Just this part left." Danny picked up a wheel for winding the power cord to the static camera and bounded downstairs once again.

"Okay?" demanded Frieda again, immediately picking up their interrupted conversation. Ben shrugged. He wasn't quite willing to let go of his guilt yet. "Gods! Will you just drop it?"

"I thought you couldn't read me as well as that." He tried to turn the conversation around on her. He should have known it wouldn't work.

"Please." Her tone was disdainful. "The guilt is rolling off you so thick you'd think you were Catholic! *Anyone* could read you like a book right now. One of those chewable children's books with enormous letters and only one word per page."

At that, Ben let out a snort of laughter.

Frieda favored him with a small half smile. "Better."

"Yeah." He met her gaze. "I'll get over it, but give me more than five minutes, okay?"

She gave a grudging nod. "Okay." Then she grew serious again. "There's something else you should know."

"About?"

"About that ghost."

"Of course."

"It's definitely hostile, but that's not all I felt."

"What do you mean?" Ben frowned. It wasn't like her to beat around the bush. When she did, it didn't bode well. He was certain he was not going to like whatever she said next. "What else?"

"It felt...familiar."

"It hit you last night. Of course it felt familiar."

She gave him a look. That wasn't what she meant, and he knew it. Yet he'd felt the need to delay the inevitable. Why did he even try?

"Okay, okay. Familiar how?"

"It felt like Todd."

Silence. He must have misunderstood. "What?"

"It felt like Todd," she said again. "I noticed it last night too. That's why I asked if he'd ever been a smoker."

Ben had forgotten about that. He shook it off and focused on tonight. "You don't know what Todd feels like when he's angry." Ben had gotten a hint of it over lunch that afternoon. Now, for the first time, he wished Frieda had been there. She'd have been able to judge it, to make a guess as to how much of it had been real and how much was residual spirit energy.

Frieda was adamant. "I'm not stupid. I know what his energy patterns feel like. I know what angry feels like. Two plus two doesn't always equal four when you're talking metaphysics, but in this case, I know I'm right. The energy was boiling in that thing tonight. You saw the thermal images. The heat it generated was insane. You saw what it did to Todd's car. Shit." Her expression changed, her eyes going wide. "If we didn't know what a furious Todd felt like before, one look at what that thing did to his Beetle, and we will." She laughed and winced. "Gods, that's not funny. Sorry. Ow. My head is killing me." She closed her eyes and shifted the bundle of ice against her head.

Taking a deep breath, Frieda opened her eyes and focused once again on Ben. He waited, stomach turning unpleasantly, for what she had to say. "I don't need empirical evidence to tell you what I felt tonight. I swear to you that spirit felt like Todd. An enraged version of Todd. Call it Todd's evil twin if that makes it easier for you."

"So, what? Do you think he's manifesting a poltergeist or—?"

Further discussion was forestalled as Danny emerged once more from below, the plastic wheel with the wound power cord in his arms. Ben rose and took it from him and followed him into the living room where they met up with a shivering Adam.

"It is *cold* out there tonight," Adam complained. "You'd think it was December, not October."

"Can you get the lights, please?" Ben asked. "Then you two can start breaking down the rest of the equipment while I box up what Danny brought up from the garage."

"Right." Adam found the nearest light switch and worked his way around the ground floor, lighting the rooms where they'd set up their cameras.

"I can help—" Frieda called from the kitchen, and then cut herself off with a wince. "Fuck that. You boys have fun. I'll be sitting here waiting when you're done."

Breaking everything down took about a third of the time that setting up had, and Ben spent every minute of it in self-recrimination. Logically, he knew Frieda was right. She was perfectly capable of looking after herself, and neither of them could have predicted the attack in the garage. They couldn't have anticipated the strength the spirit possessed or that it would manifest in such a tangible fashion in a room they had no reason to suspect it would haunt. But no logic could make him feel better about the fact that his best friend was sitting in the next room with an ice pack on her head. Hell! He hadn't even checked her for a concussion! God, he was so made of fail.

Once all the equipment was packed up, Adam and Danny began loading it into the van, giving Ben a moment to talk to Frieda again without the concern of being overheard or interrupted.

"Do you have a concussion?" he asked as he sat with her at the table. "Where's your Maglite? I packed mine already. I should check your pupils."

"My pupils are fine. Will you stop stressing already? You're giving me a headache," she muttered.

"You already have a headache. Although I admit that is my fault."

"Well you're making it worse. Knock it off. Call Todd and tell him we're done."

"You're right." He had to let it go. What was done was done. It was time to tell the client that the surveillance was also done. He pulled his cell phone from his pocket and dialed Todd's number. The other man picked up after only one ring.

"Hello?" Todd managed to make the single word sound slightly manic.

Ben couldn't keep the amusement out of his voice as he replied. "Are you that desperate to escape from Middle Earth?"

"Yes."

"You can come home any time if you want to. We're finished and we're just cleaning up our mess."

"I'll be there in five minutes."

"See you then." He hung up and pocketed the phone.

"You didn't tell him much," said Frieda.

"What did you want me to say?"

"Nothing. Sorry. You're right. That's not a discussion to have over the phone at oh dark thirty."

"We're clear." Adam came in from the living room in a wave of chilly air. Danny was right behind him. "How are you?" he asked Frieda.

"Okay, thanks. I should go out to the van, though. The client doesn't need to find me sitting here with a head injury." Frieda lowered the ice pack from her head and started to rise. Ben was at her side in a heartbeat.

"Here." He took the towel full of ice and handed it off to Danny. "Deal with that, would you?"

Danny took it without hesitation. "Got it."

Ben put a hand under Frieda's arm and helped her the rest of the way to her feet. Never taking his eyes from her, he said to the others, "I'll be right back."

Ben got Frieda bundled up and settled into the van. Glancing up, he saw Todd's long-legged form striding around the corner at the end of the block. "You okay for a few?"

"Sure. Like Adam enjoys pointing out, I'm pretty hardheaded." She chuckled grimly.

"That's not funny."

"No? I'm off my game. Must be the head injury."

"Frieda…"

"Kidding. Sorry," she said, her voice as pained as her expression. "I've got ibuprofen from the first aid kit and a bottle of water. I'm warm enough for now. Do what you need to do, but don't dawdle, okay?"

Ben nodded in sympathy. "I'll try to be quick." He closed the van door and braced himself for the inevitable.

Todd wore his glasses and was bundled up against the cold. His hands were tucked deep into the pockets of his coat. "Hey there."

Ben dredged up a smile. "Hi. Let's go inside." He let Todd lead the way into his own house where they met Adam and Danny just wrapping up the teardown. "Can you handle loading up the van?" he asked them.

"Sure," said Adam, and Danny nodded.

"Thanks." He waited until they were outside before turning back to Todd. "So." No more stalling. "Are you someone who likes the good news or the bad news first?"

"Um, I think I'll go with the good first," Todd said.

"Danny spoke to your spoon ghost."

His eyes widened. "Did it answer?"

Ben shrugged. "Not that he or I heard, but we haven't had a chance to check the recordings for EVPs. We might have caught something. Or we might not."

"So, then, what's the good news?"

"He tried to make a deal with it, like you suggested. If it worked, you should get your Norwegian silver back. You'll want to start buying thrift store spoons for it, though. To keep it appeased, so to speak."

"Okay. If the silver comes back, that is good news. Now, what's the bad?"

Ben took a deep breath and squared his shoulders. "There's something you should see downstairs."

"Okay. Lead the way."

They trooped downstairs and Ben paused at the door to the garage. "You remember last time, how Frieda said the ghost was angry?"

"Sure. Why? Was it something else this time? Or was it angrier or what?"

Ben opened the garage door with an air of doom hanging over him. He didn't think Todd was the sort to shoot the messenger, but that didn't dull his feeling of dread. Frieda's reminder that Todd might still be feeling the aftereffects of the ghost's hostility didn't help.

He stepped aside. "Maybe you can judge that for yourself."

Todd entered the garage, triggering the light, and stopped.

Ben waited in anxious silence for the hammer to fall.

"Son of a bitch!" Todd took one long stride and bent over the hood of his car. "Poor baby!" He reached out a hand and barely brushed the burned patch as if he were caressing a lover. In a way, maybe he was. Ben had never understood the whole car-fascination thing.

Ben stepped in and paused next to the open door. He hesitated to interrupt the obviously painful moment, but he had questions that needed answers—if he could get them. Frieda had said the ghost felt like Todd. They'd been interrupted before she could go into much detail, but he had a couple of ideas what she might mean, and he didn't like either of them. He crossed mental fingers and asked what he felt was the less disturbing possibility. "Is there anyone you can think of who might want to haunt you?"

Todd straightened up quickly and Ben took an involuntary step back, bumping into the doorframe.

"What do you mean?"

"Just that. This"—he pointed to the damaged car—"suggests something personal. You value your car highly. You've invested a lot of your time and energy into it. Can you think of anyone who might want to hurt you in this way?"

Tense silence filled the enclosed space, making it seem even smaller. Ben shivered and didn't know if it was the normal chill of the subgrade garage or something more. He waited.

Finally, Todd spoke.

"No. I can't think of anyone."

Ben regarded him for several moments, observing all the silent signals in Todd's body language. It didn't take Frieda's talents to see that he was hiding something, but it *would* take them to figure out what that something was. And she was in no state to make that sort of assessment tonight. "You're sure?"

"Yes."

He was lying. Ben was certain of it and hated it. Hated even more that there was nothing he could do about it. Maybe later he would find a way to win Todd's trust, but not tonight. "All right. If you think of anyone, will you call me? Please."

Todd nodded once. "I will."

With a little luck, that part was true.

Chapter 22

FRIEDA WOKE WITH A SPLITTING HEADACHE AND A feeling of dazed confusion. The first thing her addled mind sorted out was the fact that she was in Ben's guest room. Then, in a rush of painful memory, she remembered why. The how, though, escaped her.

She rolled over in the hide-a-bed and found a note pinned to the arm of the sofa.

Water and meds on the table, it said in Ben's scrawl. *Coffee downstairs when you're ready.*

Gods, was she ready. She pushed herself to a sitting position, wincing as her hip and shoulder protested painfully. Her head wasn't the only thing to have hit the garage floor hard. Ben had left bottles of Advil, Tylenol, and AC&Cs for her to choose from. Sending a silent thanks to the universe for Seattle's close proximity to Canada and easy access to codeine, she shook a couple of the AC&Cs into her palm and downed them with the entire bottle of water. She sat for a few moments just breathing until she felt ready to get out of bed.

She was dressed in one of Ben's t-shirts and a pair of sweats she had to roll up three times so she didn't trip on the hems. Vaguely, she recalled donning the clothes before crawling under the covers in the wee hours before dawn. It took her a moment to find the woolly socks she'd worn the night before and pull them on. She used the upstairs bathroom, splashed some warm water on her face, and wished for a ponytail holder to pull back her ratty morning hair. Then and only then did she attempt the stairs down to the second floor.

She said hello to Ben's cat, Demon, who was curled up in his favorite chair. The cat yawned, blinked at her, and unfolded himself. He trotted over to his empty kibble bowl and looked up at her expectantly.

"When I get my coffee, you get your kibble," she told him.

Another missive awaited her in the kitchen. A neon-pink sticky note stuck to the counter by the coffee pot. She turned on the pot and picked up the note, also in Ben's unmistakably poor penmanship, and squinted at it.

Gone to shop, reviewing data. We'll do lunch/dinner when I get home. I have your car keys.

Frieda pursed her lips in annoyance at his over-cautious ways. She was perfectly fine to drive, she thought, reaching up into the cupboard for a mug. A wave of dizziness hit her, and she clutched the mug and counter with equal urgency. Okay. Maybe not so fine to drive after all. But that wasn't going to stop her from *walking* over to the shop to see how the analysis was going. She could do that at least. She might not be able to stare at a computer screen or listen for electronic voice phenomena for hours at a time today, but that was fine with her. Analysis had never been her favorite part of the job.

The coffee pot sputtered to a finish and she poured herself a cup, then went to the fridge for something milkish to put in it. She briefly considered the bottle of Irish cream liqueur she found in the door and decided it probably wasn't the best choice, even though it was—she glanced at the clock on the microwave—past two. Still, booze and codeine? Not the smartest. She would have her coffee with ordinary milk in it, and she would have some breakfast.

"Merrow!"

"Okay. Okay." She went to the pantry where she knew Ben kept the plastic storage container of kibble and put a heaping scoop into Demon's bowl. "There you go, and don't tell Ben I gave it to you. Now." She looked over the pantry shelves. "My turn."

Ben was sure to have cereal. The apocalypse could come, and he would still have cereal. She found a box of something sugary with colors not found in nature. Maybe she could make toast. There was peanut butter and jelly in the fridge; she'd seen them when she'd gotten the milk. She dug around until she found a loaf of bread and put two slices into the toaster. "Good," she muttered. Breakfast first, then she would get dressed and walk over to the shop. She needed to talk to Ben. He needed to know what else she'd learned in her encounter with that spirit last night. The sooner that happened, the sooner they could take the information to Todd. The sooner they had Todd on board, the sooner they could get that horrible ghost out of his house.

~~*

"How can you be so sure?"

Ben usually didn't challenge her so adamantly, but she couldn't blame him this time. "I just *am*. I'm *positive*. I swear to you this isn't some sort of concussed delusion. I know what I know. That ghost is directly connected to Todd."

"Why didn't you say something last night?" asked Adam. He sat at Frieda's desk, the computer screen displaying the paused static camera image of Todd's dining room. At least she assumed it was paused. The image was unchanging, but that didn't mean anything. Still, Adam was meticulous at analysis. He would never take his eyes from the screen without pausing it first.

Frieda looked back at Ben where he sat at right angles to his own desk, his old-style wooden office chair tipped back against the wall, and let him answer Adam's question.

"She did." He focused on her again. "Although what you said yesterday isn't the same thing you're saying now."

"What *are* you saying now?" Adam looked back and forth between them, waiting, clearly annoyed to have been out of the loop until now. "And what did you say last night? And why am I only hearing about this now?" The last was a shot at Ben.

"Sorry. I had a few other things on my mind last night, remember?"

Adam backed off. "You're right. Sorry." He gave Frieda a contrite look.

Frieda tipped her head to him, silently acknowledging the apology. "Last night I said the ghost that took me down felt like Todd if he were really angry. What I'm saying now is that, whoever that ghost is, I believe Todd knows him. I think pretty personally too, like…family."

"He said he doesn't know anyone who would want to haunt him," said Ben. "I asked him."

"And yet he has two separate entities in his home and a third in his car," Frieda pointed out the obvious, irony rich in her tone. "That's more than enough to suggest to me that there is something about him that attracts the paranormal. Why is it so tough to take it a step further and assume this newest spirit has a personal connection?" She could see Ben searching his brain for a reasonable argument. He came up blank. She narrowed her eyes at him, puzzling it through. "You're sure he doesn't know of anyone?"

"He *said* he doesn't," Ben repeated.

Adam sat up straighter in his seat. "Did you ask if

anyone he knows has died recently?"

Ben shook his head and made a noise of impotent frustration. "I'm an idiot! That never even occurred to me."

"You're not an idiot," said Frieda.

"Yes, he is," deadpanned Adam.

"Funny." She shook her head at him, and then smiled at Ben, a touch teasing, a touch sympathetic. "No. He's just a little overcome by Todd's magnetism, so he's not thinking as clearly as he otherwise might."

Adam barked out a laugh as Ben exclaimed, "Oh God, you're right!" He let his head fall back against the wall with a quiet thud. "I am so not objective about this job. I hate that Todd lied to me, and that's only partly because it's impeding the investigation." He sat upright, the big spring in his chair's support structure creaking its complaint at the sudden change of angle. "All right. So spell it out for me because as you like to point out, 'Boys are slow.'"

Frieda uncrossed her arms and pushed away from the doorframe where she'd been leaning. She sat down in the comfy chair and sighed audibly. "I didn't realize how tired I was until I sat down. Damn." She took a moment before going on. "Okay. Talking strictly about the angry spirit," she began, and the men nodded confirmation. "I had an idea it might be Todd's own psychic energy poltergeisting around the place."

Ben nodded thoughtfully, frowning a little. "I wondered about that after what you said before, about it being familiar."

"You thought it was a 'geist and you said nothing to me?" said Adam, offended. "I *am* the resident expert on them, you know."

Frieda held up a placating hand. "I'm sorry. You're right. See what you think once I've filled in any blanks, okay?"

Adam nodded. "Okay. Speak."

"It's not impossible that it's Todd causing the entity to manifest, but at this point I doubt it."

"Why?"

"When that thing showed up without him there last night…"

"That doesn't mean anything," Adam said. "Poltergeist energy, if it's built up enough, doesn't need the originating person to be present."

"Can it build enough in under a week?" Ben asked. "As far as we know, that's the maximum time it's been around."

"Meh. Maybe, but it's not likely."

Frieda shrugged. "So, setting that possibility aside, what else do we know about the spirit other than that it's angry and it's new?"

"It's violent," said Ben quickly.

"It wants out. Or it wants Todd out," Adam added. "Remember the EVP?"

"Todd said he didn't know anyone who would want to haunt him," Frieda repeated thoughtfully. "Why would he say that?"

"I'm sure he was lying," said Ben, unhappy and letting it show.

"Why lie? What would he gain from it?" asked Adam.

Frieda sighed. "Good question."

They all fell silent, thinking. Ben's eyes practically glittered with the intensity of his concentration. "So what does that get us? None of this is new information."

Frieda sighed again. "You're right. I think we have to talk to Todd. Correction. I think *I* have to talk to Todd."

"You want me to make the call?"

"Go for it."

Ben used the PUPI landline on his desk to dial Todd's number. Frieda noticed that he'd already memorized it, and she smiled to herself.

There was a pause before Ben looked over and said, "Voicemail." Then another pause before he spoke again. "Todd, it's Ben. Can you give us a call back at the office number when you have a minute? We have a couple of questions for you about that spirit who…fried the hood of your car." He winced as he said it, and Frieda found herself mirroring the expression. "Frieda has an idea, but she needs to discuss it with you directly. Okay. Talk to you soon. Bye."

~~*

Todd stared at his cell phone. He should have answered it when it rang. He knew it was probably Ben. The caller ID had identified it as Presence Unknown. Instead, he'd sent the call to voicemail. Why in hell had he done that? Ben's questions rang in his memory: *Is there anyone you can think of who might want to haunt you? Can you think of anyone who might want to hurt you in this way?*

Yes and yes.

His father.

Why hadn't he said so last night? Why had he lied to Ben? Ben and his team could help him for Christ's sake! But not if he wasn't honest with them. What had kept him from speaking up, and what had kept him from answering the phone just now?

The answer was easy to guess if not easy to admit.

Fear.

Fear of what? Fear of the ghost? Fear that if he voiced his suspicions they would magically become true? Or fear that Ben would discover his secrets, his painful past, and discard him as damaged goods?

"Don't be an ass." He pulled up PUPI's number from his list of missed calls—and froze. Several seconds ticked past as he stood there in his bedroom, the late-afternoon light dying outside the windows. He closed the phone and set it on the nightstand. He would call back, just not right now. Not when someone else might answer the PUPI line. He would call Ben directly tonight.

"Tonight," he repeated aloud to make the resolution stick. "I'll call him tonight."

~~*

"Okay. Sure. We'll see you tomorrow evening, then... Right. Bye."

Ben closed the connection and slipped the phone into his coat pocket. He looked at Frieda standing next to him, waiting patiently while he'd taken the call. "We're on for tomorrow."

"Good news."

"Yeah." It was late to be out on a weeknight, especially after the weekend they'd had, but Ben didn't care. He was too keyed up to sleep anytime soon, and when Frieda had suggested a late snack and a pint, he'd leapt at it once she'd convinced him she really was all right following last night's excitement. He was still a little dubious, but when she promised that if she felt the need, she would crash at his house again, he'd relented. And he really did want to go out and talk things over, just the two of them.

So here they were, crossing Market Street, headed for Old Town Ballard and their favorite pub. They walked in silence through the chilly night air, and eventually turned the corner down Ballard Avenue. Soon, the signboard for their destination came into view.

The Basement was just that. Underneath one of the stone buildings, with a narrow cement staircase and iron railing leading to its door, it was the converted basement of some old business, long since forgotten and replaced by an outdoor store and a picture-framing place. It was easy to miss if you didn't know where to look, and that was one of the things Ben and Frieda both liked about it.

They entered the cheery space, all golden wood paneling and heavily varnished slab wood tables, and found an empty spot along the wall. Caleb, the bartender, nodded hello and indicated he'd be with them shortly. He was tall, skinny, blond, and disappointingly straight. Ben had had a fanciful crush on him for years.

They unbundled themselves, and Ben took both coats and Frieda's scarf and tucked them into the corner of the bench where he sat.

Caleb approached them. "The usual for you tonight?"

"Actually, what's your seasonal beer?" asked Frieda.

"I've got an Oktoberfest on tap, and bottled I have a pumpkin ale."

Frieda's eyes lit up. "Oo! I'll take a pumpkin ale, please."

"I'll have a Red Menace," said Ben.

"I'll be right back with those." Caleb left them to return to the little bar in the corner.

"So," Ben said softly, even though there was no one within hearing distance. "Do you have any idea about what you want to ask him?" He didn't need to specify which *him* he meant.

Frieda shot him a wry look. "What do *you* think?"

He let out a chuckle that was as low in volume as it was on humor. "Pretty much what I asked him before, I suppose."

"Basically. Those and some that Adam suggested, and some of my own."

"And unlike me, you'll be able to tell if he's being honest."

"Don't be so hard on yourself. You said you knew when he was lying."

Ben shrugged. "Knowing it didn't give me any answers."

"Yeah, well. Whatever. We'll talk to him tomorrow, and we'll get the answers then. Together."

Chapter 23

"So," said Frieda. "Who do you know who's recently deceased?"

"I'm sorry?" The question, and her blatant challenge, took Todd completely by surprise. He looked at her across his kitchen table and knew there would be no hiding the truth from her or Ben this time.

"You'll have to forgive Frieda," said Ben, sending her a warning look. "She wouldn't know subtle if it kicked her in the head."

"That wouldn't *be* subtle," she pointed out. The two had a brief staring match, which ended in stalemate. Then she turned back to Todd. "Forgive my indelicacy, but who just died?"

Todd racked his brain for an explanation. Who would have told her? Not Mona. She would never have shared that news with people they'd only recently met, not even ones she admired as much as the PUPI team. The only other person he'd told was Shell, and there was no reason she would volunteer anything to Presence Unknown on the unlikely chance they had contacted her. So...

"How did you know?"

"So there *is* someone in your life who's transitioned lately."

"Transitioned?" he echoed her word with a hint of irony. "Interesting word choice."

"I find it's more comprehensive." Her expression

softened, but that wasn't saying much, considering how hard it had started out. "Listen, I'm sorry for your loss, but I'm serious about the question. Who is newly dead?"

He snorted derisively, startling both his guests. There was no getting around the direct question, which she had now asked in three different ways, and he wasn't going to pretend to be upset about his answer. He hoped Ben would understand. That he wouldn't see Todd as cold and bitter and decide he wasn't worth the effort.

Todd took a cleansing breath, let it out, wrapped his hands around the mug of tea on the table before him, and explained. "I'm *not* sorry, and it's not a loss. I got word Sunday. After we had lunch," he added to Ben. Bad enough he'd lied to Ben, but he couldn't bear to have the other man believing he'd been keeping the secret any longer than he had. "My father died in a car crash early last week."

"Oh my God," said Ben softly.

"It's okay. Honestly. I hadn't seen him in over twenty years. Not since he and my mom divorced my senior year of high school. I knew he'd moved out of state, but there wasn't any reason to keep track of him, so I didn't. Frankly, I'd have been perfectly happy never to hear a word about him again. But the police tracked me down in order to give me the news. It turns out he was living in Oregon. He got drunk one night, as usual, and drove into a freeway divider someplace outside Beaverton. I'm only glad he didn't involve anyone else." He chose not to mention that he and Mona had promptly gone out to celebrate his father's demise over champagne cocktails. He was already pushing it with Ben. He didn't want to put him off any further with what would undoubtedly seem like terrible callousness. It wasn't anything the other man was likely to understand without historical context, which Todd had no intention of providing anytime soon. Better to tell them both only what they needed to know and keep his mouth shut about the rest of it.

Unfortunately, that turned out to be tougher than he expected.

"We're missing something," Frieda said. Her eyes narrowed as she scrutinized him, and it was all he could do not to squirm under her penetrating gaze. She was worse than the nuns from his elementary school days. "Why would he come after you like this?"

Todd gritted his teeth. "Because he never did when he was alive."

"Because...?" she echoed, prompting.

"He kept that special attention for my mom."

She inhaled slowly and nodded, at last understanding. "I'm so sorry."

What could he say to that? To his relief, Ben rescued him from the awkward moment.

"Early last week." Ben looked at Frieda and then at Todd. "You said early last week."

Todd huffed out a breath. "Yeah. Monday around two-thirty a.m., the police said."

"And the first time you encountered that angry spirit in the dining room was Friday night?"

"That's right." Todd gave Ben a puzzled frown. "So?"

Ben turned his penetrating gaze on Frieda. "Are you thinking what I'm thinking?" It took only a moment before her eyes widened in understanding.

"I think so, Brain," she said in a cartoony British accent. "But does that make me the Gate Keeper or the Key Master?"

All right, now it was Todd who was missing something. "What are you two getting at?"

Ben shook his head at Frieda in mild reproach. "*Our client* would like to know what's going on," he said pointedly.

Frieda pulled herself together, and this time her

expression was genuinely apologetic. "My bad. I shouldn't mix my pop culture references like that. What we're getting at," she went on in a businesslike tone, "is that the malevolent ghost who attacked you and me, and who did the fry job on your car, is likely to be your father."

Todd almost laughed. It was too absurd. Too coincidental to be plausible. Sure, the notion had crossed his mind. Sunday night when he'd looked at his car and Ben had asked who would want to hurt him, his father was the one person who had leapt to mind. It hadn't taken much effort to convince himself the idea was absurd. Now, though, he had fresh doubts.

"What..." He took a moment and forced himself to speak professionally. "What brings you to that conclusion?"

"You think so too," Frieda said instead of answering.

He gave up any pretense. "It crossed my mind, yeah. But I dismissed it immediately. I thought I was being ridiculous. How could it be him?"

"Your father may not have known where you were before he died, but the spiritual planes are different. Physical distance and location are irrelevant. Whether you like it or not, your father had—*has*—a strong connection to you. And he found you once his spirit was free of his body. The fact that you're a sensitive just made it that much easier for him to home in on you."

Todd was confused before, but that was nothing to what he felt now. "A what? What do you mean?" The first part of her argument made sense in a weird, spooky sort of way, although it would've made more sense to him if his father had chosen to haunt his mom. He thanked God for small favors on that score. But that last bit? "What the hell is a sensitive?"

Frieda was matter of fact. "You are. It's pretty passive in you, but it's there. How else do you explain three separate spiritual beings all haunting you at the same time?"

"You call three ghosts passive?"

"Not them. You."

"Oh." Todd didn't quite know how to take that.

"Most people are sensitive to varying degrees," Ben put in quickly, rescuing him once again. "Generally it's in one specific area, so specific they don't recognize it for what it is. Like people who never get stuck at red lights or people who always manage to get in line at the store right before the crowd hits."

It was starting to sink in. "Like how Lily, my lead barista, always knows when Mona needs to make extra pastries or when to make a fresh pot of drip before a rush happens?" Todd suggested.

"Exactly."

"Huh. I never put that together before."

"There's no reason you should when you're not in the paranormal business." Frieda briefly took up the narrative. "There are more active examples too. Like people who can see auras or fairies."

"It's perfectly normal. I'm sensitive to the weather," said Ben. "I know with absolute certainty it's going to rain buckets tomorrow, then be warm and sunny for the next two days."

"Doppler radar could tell me that much," said Todd. It came out sharper than he'd intended, and he winced internally, hoping Ben didn't take offense. That was just what he needed on top of everything else. To upset the man he not only wanted to get to know more intimately, but who had also just revealed personal information in an attempt to help him. Jesus, he was fucking up his chances in all sorts of ways. "Sorry. That really rude."

"No, you're right. Doppler radar *can* tell you that much. But it can't tell you that two weeks from today we'll get a cold snap that will dump unseasonal snow that'll then get melted off by rain before the weather falls back into its usual autumn pattern."

Todd stared at him. He could be making it up. He might be counting on Todd forgetting before the day arrived. But why would he do that? There was no reason for him to lie about it when, two weeks from today, he could unequivocally be proved wrong. "Seriously?"

"Seriously."

"So, then, what am I sensitive to? Ghosts?"

Frieda nodded. "For starters. There may be other things, but right now it's the ghosts that matter."

"So what do I do?" He looked from Frieda to Ben, back to Frieda, and then back to Ben again. Would rescue come a third time from him? Jesus, he hoped so. Saying that this was outside his comfort zone was a gross understatement.

Ben and Frieda exchanged another one of those looks that made Todd feel like he was missing some sort of psychic communication. Hell, maybe he was. It wouldn't be any weirder than anything else they'd discussed tonight. He didn't find the thought at all pleasant or encouraging and felt an urgent need to interrupt them.

"Well? You're the paranormal investigators. Tell me what the next step is."

Ben turned to him, his expression unreadable. "We need to finish going over all the data we collected."

"Okay."

"That's going to take a few days. We have a lot of hours of footage to cover."

"When do you think you'll be done?" Todd was getting snippy and short tempered. All this beating around the bush was starting to wear thin. He took a deep breath and tried to rein in his rising temper. He had a moment of fear that it might not be *his* temper. He shuddered.

"Are you all right?" asked Frieda, frowning.

"Not quite."

Ben stiffened and spoke warily. "With a little luck, we'll be ready to meet again on Thursday."

Todd took another calming breath that had marginal effect. "Good. Come over here Thursday evening with whatever you've got, done or not. I want to know exactly what the hell's going on in my house, and then I want my father gone. Can you do that?"

Another look, a quicker one, between Ben and Frieda. This time Todd held his tongue.

It was Frieda who answered him. "We can try."

Chapter 24

ON TELEVISION THEY CALLED IT "THE REVEAL." TODD HAD learned that much from Mona. She was so excited about the whole process that he invited her for what, according to her, would normally be the last stage of the job. The fact that he had his father's malevolent spirit in the house meant that there had to be at least one more stage after this. No way was he going to let Presence Unknown off the hook yet if there was even the slightest chance they could get rid of his father's ghost. He wondered what an exorcism cost nowadays, and then felt more than a little ridiculous. He was glad he hadn't put voice to his musings.

"They're that sure it's your dad?" Mona spoke quietly. She and Todd sat in his living room while Ben and Frieda set up their equipment on the kitchen table where they would all be able to sit and view the footage from the investigation. It wasn't as spacious as the formal dining room, but they had all agreed it was a better choice.

"They're convinced it is."

"What about you?"

"It makes enough sense that, well...yeah... Don't you think so?"

She shrugged and said nothing.

Todd couldn't blame her. He didn't want to believe it either, but he could see no other realistic alternative.

"Honestly, when you think about it, I'd be surprised if they turned out to be wrong. I mean, between the timing of the ghost's arrival and the fact that, apparently, I'm some sort of ghost magnet. Sure. Why wouldn't my abusive, alcoholic, dead father come back to haunt me?"

"Gods."

"You said it."

They fell silent. Todd could hear the two in the kitchen muttering technical jargon at each other. The few words he caught flashed him back to his years in the dot-com industry, reminding him how much he didn't miss it. He didn't even manage the website for his own coffeehouse. He left that job in Shell's more than capable hands.

"They really said you're a ghost magnet?" said Mona, breaking the short silence.

"Not exactly. They said I was 'a sensitive.' I'm still not completely convinced. It sounds ridiculous."

Mona made a noncommittal noise, but before he could ask what she was thinking, Frieda poked her head into the living room. "We're ready if you are."

They rose and went into the kitchen. On the table were a laptop computer and a large, external monitor. Ben sat where he could run the computer and the others arranged themselves to best advantage to view the monitor.

"We have a lot to discuss tonight," Ben began. "First, we'll talk about the car, since that's what's been haunted the longest as far as your experience goes." He directed their attention to the screen. "You'll recall that we placed a static camera inside the Beetle and aimed it at the radio dial. We got an interesting result at about two and half hours into the investigation." He played the clip and there, clear as day, they saw the dial rotate of its own accord, moving the tuner bar.

"Wow!" Mona leaned forward, eyes wide. "Can you

play that again?" Ben did and she exclaimed again, "Wow! That is insane!"

Frieda spoke up. "That's only half of it."

Mona looked at her. "What do you mean?"

"The station it's on isn't the local oldies station."

Todd sat up straight. Was Ben challenging what Todd knew for a fact to be real? Other people had witnessed it. Mona had witnessed it. She would back him up if necessary. "What? But it's *always* playing oldies music."

"No one's disputing that," said Ben. "However, the local oldies station is down around ninety-seven. If you look closely, the radio has been set at about one-oh-four. It's difficult to be precise with those old-style car radios, and the picture isn't as clear as I would like."

Todd's eyes narrowed. "So, what are you saying?"

Instead of answering directly, Ben said, "You gave us the name of the person you bought the car from, so we did a bit of digging. Before the previous owner, the car had two original co-owners. A man named Alfred Torgeson and his son Bobby, the latter of whom died in a car accident in 1965."

"My car hasn't been in any major collisions. I may not have researched its owners, but I did check on that."

"The only newspaper article that we found about the accident said that Bobby Torgeson was a passenger. There was no mention of a '63 Beetle."

"Our best guess," said Frieda, "is that Torgeson bought the car as a gift for his son. He was a pretty big business-owner back in the 1950s and '60s. We think that when Bobby's spirit and body were separated, Bobby gravitated back to the car as the thing he most connected to on this plane."

"So Bobby's the one changing the radio dial?" asked Mona. Todd looked at her. Her eyes were huge and her face was a portrait of fascination. She'd always loved the whole "there are other worlds in and around this world" thing.

"More than that. He's not simply changing the station. We did some research on that too. Or rather, Adam did some research. You know how the FM band is numbered on the bottom and the AM is on the top on these old radios?"

Todd nodded as Mona said, "Sure."

Ben picked up the narrative. "One-oh-four FM roughly corresponds to fifteen hundred on the AM dial. According to the data Adam dug up, fifteen-ten was the frequency of station KHIP back in the late fifties and early sixties. He couldn't find much more except that, aside from their musical programming, they had a contract with the San Francisco Giants to broadcast their home games. At the time, that was the closest major league team."

"You haven't happened to catch any baseball, have you?" asked Frieda.

"No," answered Todd warily. He suspected he knew what they were driving at, and just as strongly suspected that he didn't want to hear it. His week had been crazy enough already.

"Or any advertisements, or DJ chatter?" she persisted.

"No," Todd confirmed again, even more tense as he realized just how odd that was all on its own. "It's always on music, and I usually change the station before whatever song is on is done."

Ben went on and Todd wished he hadn't. "The ghost isn't tuning into FM, or any current local radio. Bobby is tuning your radio not just to the AM band, not just to the station he would have listened to, but to 1963 itself."

Todd could only stare. He didn't want to hear this. Even with everything he'd personally experienced, he couldn't, *wouldn't*, wrap his head around Ben's revelation. He looked at Mona to see if she was managing any better, only to find her just as dumbfounded as he. The idea that his radio was picking up broadcasts that were over half a century old was... He shook his head and turned back to Ben and Frieda. "I have to think about that."

Ben nodded. "I'm not surprised. We couldn't believe it either, to be honest. We can do some more checking on it later if you want. If you don't mind one of us riding around with you the next time you're running errands."

There was a note in his voice that made Todd sit up a little straighter and look at him a little closer, but Ben had already turned away and was loading another clip onto the computer screen. Maybe he'd imagined it. It might have been a product of wishful thinking. But he couldn't help feeling that Ben had been volunteering, that Ben wanted the excuse to spend more time with him.

Yeah. Wishful thinking. Had to be. And yet maybe...

"That's fine," he said, directing the words toward Ben. "You'd be welcome to come with me any time."

Ben shot him a quick smile. The moment was brief, but there was definitely interest in his eyes. Todd fought back a grin. This was neither the time nor the place. Ben must have thought the same thing because he promptly turned his attention back to the computer.

Mona gave him an encouraging smile. "At least you got a name for the ghost, though, right?" she said, and Todd got the feeling she was fishing for something that would help him deal with the strangeness of it all. It was a valiant attempt and doomed to failure.

He mustered up a weak smile for her efforts. "Yeah. Good point. At least now I can call him by name when I talk to him, right?"

"Right."

Ben pulled up a new piece of video footage. "This is night vision footage that Danny got here in the kitchen," he explained. "We also caught it on the static camera we set up on top of your refrigerator, and on the digital video camera I was using at the time."

Todd studied the screen. It showed varying shades of greens and grays that bled into deep black in some areas. Despite the odd coloration, it was immediately recognizable as his kitchen. He could see the window over the sink, the countertop, the silverware drawer that was partly open and... He leaned in for a closer look. "It's a floating spoon."

"It's a floating spoon," confirmed Ben. He switched to another shot of the kitchen. This one from a higher angle and in more familiar black and white low-light images. There was the spoon again, and there was half of Danny at the edge of the frame. "This is the video footage from the static camera we positioned on top of the fridge. Adam synched it up with the voice recorder Danny had on at the time. He tried to engage the entity verbally and got an interesting result."

They watched and listened as Danny asked questions of the spoon.

"Hello?" Todd saw the spoon freeze in midair. *"It's okay. I'm not here to stop you. Can you tell me your name?"*

Silence.

"Did you used to live in this house?"

Silence.

"Did you... did you die in this house?"

Silence.

Movement.

Todd couldn't repress a shiver as he watched the spoon slowly drift downward to rest on the countertop. Beside him, he heard Mona whisper, "Whoa."

Just as Todd had suggested and Ben had told him, Danny tried to cut a deal. As he talked, the spoon seemed to move in response to what he said.

"So, uh, what's up with the spoons? Todd said he doesn't mind so much you taking the spoons from in here

but, uh, he'd really like to have his good silver back. He said he'd trade you some others if you want. Special ones. He said he'd buy ones just for you. Only he needs the good silver back. Please. He said to say please."

The spoon moved again, sliding this time along the counter as the drawer rolled open of its own accord. *"No, no. You can have that one."*

The spoon rose into the air again and hovered there.

Ben paused the clips, clicking a few keys and speaking at the same time. "This is the simultaneous footage I got on the digital video camera when I came into the kitchen." Ben clicked a few more keys and the monitor showed a split screen of the static cam on the left and Ben's video footage on the right. The opposing angles were hard on Todd's brain, but he watched intently nevertheless. The sound quality improved as their voices were picked up by the camera mic instead of the muffled voice recorder.

They heard Danny speaking first: *"Are you getting this?"*

And Ben's reply: *"I'm getting it. Where's Frieda? I want to get a thermal reading on this thing."*

Danny again: *"She should be here any second. She was only in the garage."*

Then, without warning, the spoon vanished from both of the images at once.

"I know it looks like a simple trick of editing," said Frieda. "But we can assure you that this footage has in no way been tampered with. What you're seeing is exactly what we caught."

Mona grinned from ear to ear. "That is so freaking cool!"

Frieda smiled back at her. "Isn't it?"

They watched it a few more times just because it was, indeed, so freaking cool.

"Did you get any audio of the ghost?" asked Mona,

finally tearing her eyes from the screen. "Did it answer any of Danny's questions?"

Frieda shook her head. "I'm afraid not. We were hoping for a name, of course. That would have been ideal."

Todd turned to Ben once more. "Okay. So what do we do now?"

Ben answered his question with another of his own. "Has any of the missing silver you told us about reappeared?"

"I don't know. I haven't checked. I keep the silver in the china cabinet in the dining room. Should we go take a look?"

"Let's wait until we're done in here. There's not much more to see."

"As if what you've shown us already isn't enough," said Mona, still obviously astounded and delighted by the whole thing.

"But there's still the issue of…" Todd couldn't help but hesitate. "My father."

Mona's face fell. "Oh yeah. I'd almost managed to forget about that rat bastard of a ghost."

Ben and Frieda exchanged a quick look of surprise. Todd couldn't blame them. It was the one area where Mona's natural cheerfulness was utterly absent. She didn't make any effort to moderate her expression of her opinion of his dad.

Ben spoke up. "We didn't get anything in the dining room, which was disappointing. However, Frieda did manage to catch quite a bit on the thermal camera she had in the garage." He called up yet another clip. Along the right side of the image was the color gauge. White at the top, descending from pink to red down through the spectrum to the colder blues and black. "This is the thermal imaging footage I told you about," he said to Todd.

It was physically painful to watch. Even though he'd seen the result, had been driving around with it for several days now, watching it happen on the screen made him sick to his stomach. So, instead of focusing on the way the handprint melted the finish on his beloved Bug, he focused on trying to see the entity itself. He didn't have much luck. A sudden flare of white made him jump in his seat, and then the image froze.

"Shit," breathed Mona. "Your poor car." She'd seen it already but apparently felt as uncomfortable as he did watching it in action.

Despite everything, he said, "Play it again." Ben did as he asked, and this time Todd was more successful in divorcing his emotions from his mind while he watched it. That was definitely a cold human form in purple-blue, and then the red hand descending on the hood, turning white hot on the thermal image. No living hand could be that hot without turning itself to ash. This time he was ready for the flash when it came and only blinked in response. He turned again to Ben. "And you think that was my father's ghost?"

"It makes sense. Frieda says it's the same ghost that you've both experienced in the dining room."

Frieda nodded in confirmation. "It felt familiar," she said, explaining more for Mona's sake than Todd's. He'd already heard much of it the other day. "Not just because it hit me once before. The spirit felt like Todd, only not exactly. If you know what I mean."

Mona nodded slowly. "I get it. Like how someone can physically resemble their parents. You're saying that their, what, energy patterns are similar?"

Frieda smiled, looking pleasantly surprised. "Yeah. That's exactly what I mean. Which, frankly, answers a lot of questions and makes me feel better about everything."

Todd remained intent on the still image on the screen.

Enough ghostly chit-chat. He wanted to see more. "What happened next?"

His question was met with silence. He looked up to see Ben and Frieda avoiding his eyes. He pinned them both with a stare. "What. Happened. Next?"

It was Frieda who replied. "Nothing spectrally significant. We shut down observations shortly after that."

She wasn't telling him everything. He could sense it. "Do you have the static camera footage from the garage?"

"Not on this box," Ben said, and Todd was certain that they were both concealing something. "The camera was inside the car. It picked up some shadowy movement through the windshield but only at the very top of the image, so slight it could have been an anomaly. It wasn't anything we could use, so there was no point loading it onto this hard drive."

"Nothing you could use," Todd echoed. "But there was something. Wasn't there?"

"Todd?" Mona put a hand on his arm. "What are you doing?"

He didn't take his eyes from Ben. "They're hiding something. I want to know what and why."

Ben met his gaze with cool blue eyes. "We've told you everything we know about the spirits haunting you."

Again, there was a subtle deception in his words. Cold anger built in Todd's belly. He didn't like them keeping secrets from him. He found himself echoing the other man again. "About the spirits, huh? Okay. So that means whatever you're hiding is something else."

"Todd!" Mona looked at him, appalled. "What's gotten into you?"

"Nothing," he snapped. "I just want to know what they're not telling me. You're hiding something. Why? What is it?"

"It really is nothing," insisted Frieda, trying to

appease him. "Your father's ghost knocked me down before he took off. That's all."

"He *what?*"

"I'm fine," she said in lieu of a direct answer. "It's a bit unusual for a spirit to manifest that strongly. I mean, I'm little, but I'm no pushover." Her attempt at lightening the mood was met with stony silence. She licked her lips nervously and tried another tack. "The important part is that he didn't notice me until *after* he'd done the damage to your car. That's how I managed to get it all on the thermal cam. And when he hit me, that's when I was able to confirm what I'd felt the first time I encountered him in the dining room. It was definitely the same spirit. And it was definitely familiar. And once you told us about your father's recent passing, everything fell into place."

"Jesus!" swore Todd. That was the white flash that had so startled him. It must have been. That white heat flaring as it swept toward the camera. "Are you all right? You didn't get burned, did you?"

"Not at all! Heat is difficult to manifest. Physical manifestations of any kind are pretty tough, actually. He couldn't have burned me and knocked me over at the same time. He's not strong enough for that."

"You must have gotten the shot of him coming at you. Did you?"

She made a face, obviously reluctant to admit it. "Yes."

He couldn't have explained why, but he needed to see it. "Do you have the rest of the thermal footage on this computer?"

Ben shook his head. "I didn't see the point. That's not the relevant part of the footage."

"Not the relevant part?" Why couldn't he stop repeating everything Ben said? It was annoying even to himself. Todd turned sharply to Frieda. "Are you all right?"

"I told you, I'm fine. No burns. The important part is that now that we know who we're dealing with it should be easier to make contact and, hopefully, make him leave."

Todd cut her off angrily. "You're *fine*? You'll excuse me if I don't believe that. Even if you didn't get burned, you still got knocked down by a disembodied spirit. That's got to freak even you out. The fact that it was my father... I know what he can do. I've seen it. No one is 'fine' after he's done with them."

"Please, take it easy," Frieda said. "I swear to you there's no lasting damage. Adam will tell you how hardheaded I can be." She gave a little chuckle that was obviously meant to mollify him, but failed utterly.

"You hit your head? Where? On the car? On the *cement floor*?"

"I really don't see—"

"He could have killed you!" Todd was livid. The fact that she'd been injured during an investigation that he'd sanctioned was enough to turn his stomach. He couldn't help feeling responsible. She wouldn't have been in that position the other night if he hadn't asked them to be here. He never would have asked either if he'd thought there was any real danger in it. And worse than that, her casual dismissal of what she'd gone through made him furious. His father had hurt her, and she was trying to pass it off as nothing. Images of his mother flashed through his mind: smearing aloe gel on a fresh cigarette burn, wincing as she dabbed hydrogen peroxide onto a cut on her scalp, crying silently over the sink when she thought Todd wasn't watching. And now, even from the grave, his father was beating up on women. In Todd's basement! His own home! Todd was so angry he couldn't even speak. He struggled for air, his wrath choking the words that might have otherwise escaped his throat. He could feel it welling up like fire, turning his vision red—

"*Todd!*"

Mona's shout was like cold water dashing his face, calming the burning rage that threatened to engulf him.

She grabbed him by the shoulders and shook him. Shifted her grip to the sides of his face. Shouted at him from inches away. "Todd! Snap the fuck out of it!"

Todd shuddered and gasped in a huge breath. He still couldn't speak, but he felt his racing heart begin to slow, and the red that clouded his vision receded. Finally, he sighed out, "Whoa."

Mona didn't release him yet. She shot an accusing glare over her shoulder at the pair from Presence Unknown. "What. The *fuck*. Was *that?*"

From the corner of his eye, Todd saw Ben looking concerned and more than a little disturbed. More directly, Frieda's worried frown met his gaze. She answered Mona without taking her eyes from him. "Residual energy from his father's attacks. He's affected you more than I realized. You need a cleansing even worse than your house does."

Mona finally released her iron hold on him, and he could move his head again. He fought back a wave of baseless irritation at Frieda's new-agey talk. The idea that his emotions were being skewed by the residue of his father's ghost was yet another thing he did not want to think about.

"Fan-fucking-tastic." As suddenly as it had built, the fury was gone, leaving him weary and battered. He let out a mirthless laugh. "You know, I've spent way too much of my life being afraid I'd turn into my father. I'm not going to let him do this to me now that he's dead and hopefully toasting on Satan's backyard barbecue grill."

Mona looked positively stricken. Her voice was soft and full of anguish. "You never told me that. Oh, buddy." She took him by the shoulders again, this time with tenderness. "You are not and never will be your father."

He looked deep into Mona's green eyes and saw her worry, her pain, her love. Her thinly veiled anger. A tiny smile curled up the corner of his mouth. "You can put your pissed off face away. He's dead, and we're going to get rid of him for good."

Shaking her head, she dropped her arms but kept her gaze trained on him. "You know, when I hid the spoons at the coffeehouse, I never thought it would ever come to this." She pursed her lips and raised an eyebrow at him like a perturbed Vulcan. "Especially since you still wouldn't have called PUPI if I hadn't dialed the number for you."

"You—?" It took several seconds for him to process what she'd said. "*You* took the spoons from the coffeehouse?"

"Yep."

He was astonished. Speechless. Unable to find words, he merely sputtered. He couldn't help it. He knew Ben and Frieda were sitting there, watching him stare at her in blank amazement, gaping like a fish out of water, and there was nothing he could do about it. What had she been thinking? What would cause her to do such a random and bizarre thing? He finally managed to spit out, *"Why?"*

Mona shrugged but had the decency to look chagrined. "I wanted you to think, well, what you thought. That your ghost was spreading its wings."

"Why would you want me to think that?"

"Because even if you're content to talk to a nameless entity all the time, I wanted to know who was in your car, and I knew you'd never ask on your own!"

Todd had thought he'd hit his limit for stunned stupefaction in one night. He didn't enjoy finding out he'd been mistaken. "But..." Too many words clogged his brain. *It's not your car. Why do you care? You don't even drive it! It's a harmless ghost, who cares what its name is?* What finally came out was, "You didn't know about the spoon thing here! You said you didn't know!"

"I didn't! I swear to you I didn't. That was just...a really fortunate coincidence."

"But why *spoons*?" he practically shouted.

She matched his volume. "*I don't know!* Because they're funny? Because they're less likely to poke holes in a plastic bag in your purse when you smuggle them out? Because our customers use them less than the other utensils? Because Cartoon Network did a weekend marathon of *The Tick*? Take your pick!"

They stared at one another for countless suspended moments before they both burst out laughing. Mona hugged him hard and tears mingled with his mirth.

"You're completely insane. You realize that," he said through his laughter. "Manipulative and utterly mad."

"You're the one who needed a supernatural kick in the ass just to get your head out of it," she countered easily.

"Bitch."

"Coward."

He felt suddenly tired and was glad for her strong arms encircling him, holding him up. The reality of it all—the ghosts, his inter-dimensional car radio, his father's death, Mona's admission, *everything*—landed like a bucket of bricks that spilled its contents all over him. What a mess. "Jesus. How the hell did we get to this moment in our lives?"

"Beats the hell out of me." She sat back, holding him at arm's length and staring him down. "But I'm not letting it happen again."

Before he could form any sort of response, she looked across the table at Ben and Frieda. "So," she asked them, "what do we do now?"

Chapter 25

As Frieda answered Mona's question, Ben watched Todd's emotions play across his face, wanting all the while to reach out and lay a hand over the other man's as a sign of support and sympathy. But it wasn't his place. Todd had his best friend for that sort of thing, and she was sitting right next to him. That didn't stop Ben from wishing, though. He understood only a small part of what Todd was going through. It was challenging enough being haunted, but the multiplicity and variety of entities involved in this case had to be overwhelming. To have Frieda making the offer she was making on top of everything else would be a lot for any normal, sane person to deal with.

Todd found his voice and asked, "You want to hold a what?"

"A transition ceremony," Frieda repeated. "It's pretty straightforward, really. Especially since we now know exactly who the spirit is who needs to transition. That will make it easier to connect with him and guide him along his path out of this realm and into the next."

Todd glanced at Ben who gave him the most encouraging look he could muster. It seemed woefully inadequate under the circumstances. Ben was only vaguely familiar with what Frieda was talking about. She'd performed two transition ceremonies since PUPI's inception, and Ben had been present for neither of them.

In truth, which he'd kept to himself but had no doubt she knew, he'd deliberately found excuses to be elsewhere both times. This time was different. If Todd decided to do this, Ben would be there for him. Assuming Todd wanted him.

Unlike Todd, Mona was digging every moment of the discussion. She leaned both elbows on the kitchen table, hands wrapped around a mug of tea. She'd insisted on making a pot for everyone although she was the only one drinking any. Her eyes were wide, and she was listening in such an active fashion that Ben wondered if she didn't hear everyone's hearts beating.

He took a deep breath and tried to exhale it without it sounding like a weary sigh. He thought he might have succeeded.

Todd glanced at him, and then turned back to Frieda. "A transition ceremony. What does that entail? Just give me the CliffsNotes version. I don't think I'm ready for the whole smash just yet."

"Right. Well, basically, we make contact with your father's spirit, we open a door for him to move on, and we help him through it."

"You make it sound so simple." His tone dripped with sarcasm, and Ben couldn't blame him. She made it sound way too easy.

"You did ask for the short version," Frieda said.

"I did. Okay. So what do you need from me, and when do you want to do this?"

She answered without hesitation. "Saturday night. If you can stand waiting the couple of days."

"What's special about Saturday?" asked Mona excitedly. "Is it a full moon or something?"

"Not as far as I know. But there are a couple of reasons. First, we have another job tomorrow night. A haunted barn out in Sammamish."

"Snohomish," Ben said.

"Snohomish. Whatever. Second, it's..." Frieda looked slightly chagrined but then sat up and spoke firmly. "The Mariners have an early day game in Toronto before flying home Saturday, and Sunday is an off day for the AL playoffs. I don't want to miss the game, and it'd be nice to have all of Sunday to sleep in and regather my energies after the ceremony."

Todd laughed, sounding genuinely amused. It was a nice sound. Encouraging and hopeful.

"It was a good game this afternoon, wasn't it?" Todd said.

Frieda perked up at his question. "Good? It totally kicked ass! I mean, seven to one? That's the way to start a playoff series! And how glad am I that they're playing Toronto for the ALCS and not Anaheim? I hate the Angels!"

"Jesus, so do I! They're just so damned good you have to hate them."

"Oh, I know! I'm only sorry they didn't get swept by the Blue Jays in round one. That would have been so satisfying. Still, I'm happy. It's all good. We just need to win this series, and all will continue to be well."

"If I might interrupt?" Ben was amused more than anything, but he made certain his tone meant business. "I know baseball is life—Frieda's made sure I understand that much about the sport at least—but we need to wrap up here and plan for Saturday."

"You're right! Okay. The transition ceremony," said Frieda, as if it were the most common thing in the world to assist someone's disembodied spirit on to the next plane of reality. She looked at Todd and her whole demeanor grew professional. "You can be here or not, although I would recommend you participate, it being your house, your father, and your haunting. We can even do a cleansing as part of it. Two birds, one stone, and all that."

Ben saw Todd's suddenly overwhelmed expression and did his best to ground Frieda's witchy words in something more familiar. "Remember at lunch when I told you about the whole spiritual cleansing thing? It will help you get rid of that unusual anger you've been feeling." It took a moment for Todd to nod his understanding. Ben didn't need Frieda's talents to recognize a man struggling to grasp too many new and strange concepts in a short span of time. Frieda's knack for switching topics faster than one could blink didn't help. In a heartbeat, she'd shifted from talking about baseball playoffs to planning the Wiccan equivalent of an exorcism. That was a bit of a jolt even for Ben, and he was used to it.

Todd rallied with admirable quickness. "Right. So, we open the door to the next realm and usher the ghost through it. Is that right?"

"Essentially, yes," answered Frieda.

"And then you do something else that will...scrub away anything leftover and sort of...lock the door behind him?"

She smiled. "Right!"

"And you've done this before?"

"I do cleansings pretty often. After every job we do and at other times just for my own peace of mind and soul."

"And the transition ceremony?"

"Only twice. But both times were very successful."

Ben looked at her intently. She was holding back, and he wanted full disclosure, but he wasn't going to challenge her in front of their client. He should have known he wouldn't need to.

"We did have an advantage on both of those occasions, though," she went on.

"What kind of advantage?"

She hesitated, glanced at Ben, and looked back at Todd. "In those cases, the entity wanted to move on. In your case..." She shrugged. "I don't see your father being eager to cooperate."

Mona surprised them all by speaking up. "Oh, he'll be willing. I am not letting that bastard, disembodied or not, spend one minute more than he already has hurting Todd." She raised her voice, turned her head toward the dining room. "You hear that, you drunken fuckwad?"

"Mona," Todd said before she could go on. The expression she turned on him was a mix of protectiveness and challenge. "I hate him too, but let's try not to antagonize him until we're ready to deal with the consequences, okay? I still have to live here until the ceremony."

"You could stay with me."

"Mona..."

Her reluctance was clear in her narrowed eyes and pursed lips. Her whole body was wired with tension. She was ready to take it to the ghost right then and there. Ben was glad Todd was thinking more practically. After a moment of hesitation, Mona nodded, and everyone relaxed. Somewhat.

Todd heaved a small, relieved sigh. He turned back to Ben and Frieda. "How safe is this ceremony going to be? Will we be in any danger?"

"That's a very good question," Frieda equivocated.

Ben wanted to reach out and smack her on the arm, but it wouldn't have been professional. Why was she acting like this? She needed to get to the damned point. He contented himself with a tight-lipped glare in her direction.

Todd was no more pleased than Ben, judging by his expression. "That's not an answer."

Ben spoke for her, whether she liked it or not. "We will do everything in our power to make sure everyone involved is safe."

Frieda and Todd looked at him in equal surprise.

"We?" they said as one.

Todd shot a look at her and then back at Ben. Frieda managed to hold her tongue while Todd asked, "Will you be participating?"

Ben imagined Todd looked hopeful. Like he wanted Ben there to support him through the strange, unfamiliar ceremony, through the passing of his father's spirit. Or Ben might be projecting his own desires. Again. He'd always sucked at telling the difference. Still, he was optimistic by nature and had no intention of changing.

There was a moment of silence before Ben answered. "Yes. I'll be there."

Todd smiled and Ben felt suddenly warm inside. It wasn't just his imagination or wishful thinking or projecting. He was sure of it. Todd wanted him there.

"What about the rest of your team? Will they be involved?" Todd asked.

"No. It's not Adam's thing, and Danny"—Frieda's lips pressed together as she sought the right words—"isn't necessary for *this* ceremony."

Ben puzzled over her choice of words: This *ceremony*? As opposed to...? But now wasn't the time to ask.

Todd took a deep breath. "So, it's just the three of us, then?"

"Four," said Mona quickly. "There's no way in hell you're leaving me out of this." The stern expression she gave Todd turned softer as she shifted her focus to Frieda. "I'm not much of a practitioner these days, but I know some Wiccan traditions from when I was better than I am now. I want to help."

"That would be great," Frieda said with a smile.

"Okay." Todd took a deep breath, let it out in a long stream, and visibly steeled himself. "So, what do you need us to do to be ready for Saturday night?"

~~*

With the computer and other gear packed up and stowed in the trunk of Frieda's car, and she and Mona off on a spontaneous trip to the herbalist shop over on Fifteenth, Todd and Ben were alone in the house. Well, alone except for the two ghosts, plus the third one hanging out in Todd's car in the garage. Todd still couldn't fully wrap his mind around it all. Everything that had occurred in the past two weeks was just too much crazy coincidence, and he said as much to Ben.

"Frieda is a big believer in coincidence," Ben replied.

"Is that right?"

"Oh yeah. You should have seen her when Danny showed up unexpectedly the day after he delivered a package to the bookstore. Then discovering that he knew you and knew about your haunted car?" He shook his head as if he could barely believe it himself. "Huge, *huge* believer in coincidence."

Todd couldn't help but see her point of view. "With evidence like that staring her in the face, why wouldn't she be?"

"Exactly."

There was a brief silence between them while Todd tried to think of something clever to say.

He failed.

"So," said Ben, a hint of a wry smile on his lips, "do you really believe that Frieda *just had* to go to the herbalist shop *right now?*"

Todd chuckled. "And that Mona *just had* to go with her to show her around and point out the *best essential oils?* No." He was glad to see he wasn't the only one who'd noticed their friends' lack of subtlety. The pair's exit was obviously contrived to give the men some quiet time alone together.

"I hope you don't mind. Along with her more positive traits, Frieda also has the bad habit of being a bit of a matchmaker."

"It's okay. Mona's no better. And, honestly, I don't mind." He gave Ben a tentative smile and found it mirrored on the other man's face. Yeah. Frieda or Mona or both could play matchmaker between him and Ben as much as they wanted.

"And yet they, themselves, remain single," joked Ben.

"You noticed that too?" Todd chuckled again. "It hasn't always been that way. Both Mona and I used to have long-time partners."

"What happened? If you don't mind sharing. You mentioned your ex at lunch the other day."

Ben's gaze once again held that glittering interest Todd had noticed the first time they'd met. Instead of feeling intimidating, this time it felt inviting. But was this really the sort of conversation he wanted to get into right now? Discussing his biggest romantic failure with the man with whom he'd like to achieve success? And this on top of the revelations about his family's past? Then again, if they couldn't discuss the important things, then what was there to build a relationship on?

He cheated and started off easy. "Mona's partner went nuts, basically. She hit an early midlife crisis and moved to Bangalore."

Ben's expression altered to include incredulity. "Bangalore, India?"

Todd nodded. "I know. Crazy, right? Never been there before. Didn't have roots in the country. Just up and left. She said she needed to 'find herself.'"

Incredulity became irony. "I didn't know people still tried to find themselves by going somewhere they've never been. Frieda would say she was being retro in all the wrong ways."

Todd chuckled at that. "She'd be right."

Irony became quiet curiosity. "So, what about you?"

Jesus, Ben had an expressive face. How did he do

that? Go from one emotion to the next so seamlessly and genuinely? It was all Todd could do not to stare. He was certain he could spend hours just watching Ben's expressions change and never get bored.

He gave himself a mental shake. Time to answer the pretty man's questions.

"My ex didn't like sharing my time with...well, anything really. Or anyone. I admit he was a bit of a car widow while I was restoring the Bug, but we made it work. He wasn't happy when I bought this house and started remodeling and updating it. It wasn't until I opened Midnight Jones that he cracked, though. Maybe I shouldn't have tried doing both things at once."

Ben shrugged. "You do what you have to do. You can't take all the blame on yourself."

"I don't. He had his...quirks too."

"Starting your own business is a lot of work. It takes time and energy."

Of course Ben understood. He co-owned both a bookshop and Presence Unknown. Todd should have expected it. "You know exactly what I mean."

"Mostly. But I had Frieda to help. We opened Hole-in-the-Wall Books together. If you don't have a partner who'll back you up... I'm impressed you did it all on your own. I don't think I could have done it alone."

Todd had never been great at accepting compliments. Even implied ones tended to make him uncomfortable. "I wasn't really on my own. Mona worked with the contractor to get the kitchen design the way she wanted it, and I had Shell working to staff the place so we'd be ready when it came to opening."

"But you did the bulk of the work otherwise. Didn't you?" It wasn't really a question. Ben understood.

"It was a lot of phone calls and consultations with contractors, electricians, interior designers. And I had to get in a restaurant design specialist." Todd could only hedge so far. "Yeah. It was a lot of work."

"And your partner couldn't handle it?"

Todd gave a small snort. "That would be putting it mildly."

"I'm sorry."

"There's no need to be. I figure if it wasn't meant to be, it wasn't meant to be, and that's fine. It took me a while to accept that, but I got there." He leaned back against the bench seat and gestured expansively, encompassing not just the kitchen but the whole house, the whole world. "I'm happy. I have a good home, a great business, an awesome car, and amazing friends. What more does a guy need?" He smiled and met Ben's gaze and knew he wasn't fooling either of them. He let his arms fall to the tabletop where he laced his fingers together to keep from fidgeting. "Yeah. Well. There's that whole happily-ever-after thing, but who gets that? I mean, realistically?"

"I think more people than we might expect."

Ben's choice of phrasing caught Todd's ear. More than *we* might expect. Interesting. He decided it was time to deflect the conversation from himself. Give and take. It was only fair. "Your turn."

To his surprise, Ben laughed. Not a chuckle or an ironic snort of mirth, but an actual laugh. "Oh my God! You so don't want to know!"

Todd found himself smiling back, half-bemused. "No, I do. In fact, now I *really* do."

"You want the short version or the gory details?"

Uncertain if he was serious or cracking a very dry joke, Todd said, "How about a bulleted list of the highlights?"

Ben laughed again. "Oh. Well. That's a pretty short list. And 'highlights' is a misnomer." He sat back and crossed one ankle over the opposite knee. "High school boyfriend was experimenting."

Todd nodded in empathy. Who hadn't been there,

right? Whether it was high school or college or even later in life. He doubted there was a gay man out there who didn't have at least one of those in his past.

"Two boyfriends when I was in college. The first one started a punk band that, last I heard, was touring the Maritime Provinces and doing quite well. The second one used his chemistry degree to pursue the more lucrative hobby of meth making. I think he's doing prison time in Illinois."

"Shit."

"Total shit. Should I go on?"

"Are you kidding? It's just getting good." Todd smiled to show he was joking. Ben quirked a smile back at him.

"Since then it's been a few second dates and not a lot more. Decent guys who just didn't click."

"Been there, done that."

"And of course, there is the requisite ex-lover who can't let go."

"Is that really requisite? Because I don't have one of those, and honestly, I'd like to keep it that way."

Ben sat forward again and rested his elbows on the table. "Oh my God. Be glad. I ended it with him years ago, and we weren't together long, but he still keeps turning up like the proverbial bad penny. If I'm lucky, Frieda's magic will keep him away long enough for him to find a new hobby."

Todd couldn't keep from showing his surprise. "You're serious? About the magic thing, I mean."

"Absolutely. She did a protective spell the other day. Or she said she would, so I presume she did."

"But, *you're* not—?" What was the appropriate term? Wiccan? Pagan? Neo-pagan?

"A witch? That's the term Frieda prefers. No. I'm not. I was raised Episcopalian, actually. Not that it matters."

"Recovering Catholic," offered Todd, pointing a thumb at himself.

"My condolences."

"Thanks." Todd held back any further comment. There was no need to get into his family's nasty history any more than they had already. An abusive and alcoholic father was plenty for one evening. Ben didn't need to hear about all the unanswered prayers and wasted votive candles that had finally driven Todd away from religion and everything connected to it.

He shifted in his seat, willing the awkwardness he felt to pass. A change of subject was in order, and he was curious. "So, this magic of Frieda's—"

Mona's voice sounded from the front room. "Hey, guys! We're back!"

Before the moment could be lost, he caught Ben's eye, silently urging an answer. It was too important, too much was riding on Frieda's magic for him simply to take it on faith. He needed someone's reassurance. He needed Ben's.

Ben shrugged, and his eyes glittered again in the incandescent kitchen light. "It may not be my mythology, but I'm not about to discount it."

Chapter 26

SATURDAY NIGHT FELL LIKE A SHROUD, AND TODD couldn't help second-guessing the wisdom of their plan. Technically, it was more like eighty-seventh guessing, but he'd not bothered to count every single time he'd had doubts since Thursday night's meeting. Ben's outsider's faith in Frieda and her abilities could only buoy his own confidence so far. He couldn't help feeling that this transition ceremony was a bit too much like an exorcism, and what was an exorcism really but some seriously intense praying? Okay, so it was more *active* praying than he'd grown up with, but that didn't change how he felt about it. Lighting candles and saying prayers hadn't made the bad things go away when he was a child, and flinging holy water at them struck him as patently ridiculous. He hoped Frieda had more in mind than that.

He kept his feelings and doubts to himself. Mona was so excited about the whole thing and so convinced it would work that he didn't want to taint her enthusiasm. The last thing she or the others needed was him spreading his negativity. And of course there was still the possibility that his negativity wasn't really his but residue from his father's angry spirit. He didn't tell any of them that he'd briefly encountered the ghost yet again last night. He was smart enough to recognize a fight he couldn't win on his own and had walked away when he'd seen the spectral shadow in the dining room. If Mona had been surprised by his sudden arrival at her door with a bag of Indian take-out at nearly ten at night, she'd given no indication of it.

He crossed his arms over his chest and leaned a shoulder against the doorframe between his living room and dining room. The picture from the far end of the room had been removed to the relative safety of the living room sofa. The china cabinet had been pulled out from the wall, wrapped with shrink-wrap like movers used, and slid back into place. They'd all been glad of the Teflon treads on the bottom when Ben had told him Frieda wanted to wrap the cabinet. It saved wear on both them and the hardwood floor.

"Ghosts often like to slam doors and pull drawers out. This should prevent damage if your father tries that," Frieda had explained. He hadn't bothered to ask if ghosts also liked to break glass. There was nothing much they could do about the bay window or the chandelier whatever the answer was.

Currently, Frieda was turning his dining table into an altar. As he, Ben, and Mona looked on, she unpacked a bizarre collection of arcane items Todd suspected would have sent his Catholic mother's brain spinning. Or would it? Frankly, some of the stuff wasn't that different from what he remembered from Sunday mass. The incense was one very familiar item, although he hoped it wasn't the same scent the priests had used. He'd never liked the smell of it even before he went off religion.

Next, there were candles, of course. Was there a faith on Earth that *didn't* use candles? Maybe, but he'd never heard of one.

"Do you have a photograph of your father?" Frieda asked out of the silence.

"No. I deliberately purged them all a long time ago. It never occurred to me that I might need one for an exorcism," he answered sardonically. "I could Google him if you want. There's bound to be a mugshot online somewhere."

He was relieved when Frieda shook her head. "That won't be necessary. We can manage without it."

She drew something wrapped in a scarf from the box she'd brought with her. She unwrapped it to reveal a sheathed knife with a jeweled hilt. "Athame," she explained to Todd.

Todd nodded as if he had the slightest clue what the hell she was talking about. He glanced at Ben, who stood in the corner between the living room wall and the china cabinet, hoping to see that he wasn't the only one out of his depth here. He couldn't make the slightest guess as to what the other man was thinking. Before long, he had to give up his scrutiny or risk being caught staring.

Todd felt certain that even once he'd unraveled the mystery of Ben—if he ever could—he would never get bored. The little glimpses he'd gotten over lunch and while they were alone the other evening were enough to convince him of that. He'd seriously contemplated asking Ben to stay that night. Then he'd thought about all the reasons it was a bad idea, and he'd kept his mouth shut.

Idiot.

"May I?" Mona pointed to the knife. Frieda put it into her hand. The hilt sparkled with cut stones, and Mona examined them, naming each one. "Obsidian, amethyst, rose quartz, azurite. Wow. Is that a zircon or a real diamond?" She pointed at the small, brilliant stone at the end of the hilt.

Frieda answered, a hint of vexation in her voice. "It's real. It so sucks to have diamond as your birthstone when you're trying to personalize your kit, you know?"

"It could be worse," said Mona, always the optimist. "You could have an affinity for platinum or alexandrite." She handed the knife back reverently.

Frieda took it and placed it on the table. Her tone was

wry when she replied. "Yeah. Or *both*."

By the time she finished unpacking everything from the battered wooden box she'd brought, Todd's table looked more like Brother Cadfael's apothecary than the Chippendale antique it was. He began to wish he'd thought to put two tablecloths over it instead of just one to protect the surface. Even the large and fairly thick woven scarf Frieda laid out wasn't enough to allay his fears. *Let it go,* he silently ordered. *If it gets rid of the ghost, it'll be worth a few little scratches.*

Frieda smiled at him. "Don't worry. We'll be careful. It's a beautiful table."

"How did you—? Never mind."

Along with the athame, the candles, and the incense cones, there were copious branches of sage, several bound sticks of herbs, a pot of water, a jar full of pins and nails, a short broom with a very bizarre face carved into the end of the handle, and a small, cast iron pot that he could only think of as a cauldron. At least she'd brought a thick silicone pad to set that on. Scratches were one thing if it got the angry spirit out of his house, but heat scarring of his antique, mahogany dining table was more than he was willing to accept. He already had to fix heat damage to his car. He did not want to add his table to the list of repairs.

"Mona, would you scatter the sage branches?" Frieda asked.

Mona jumped in surprise and then smiled, pleased to be asked to help. "Sure. Where?"

"The window and both doorways, please."

"Sure," she said again.

While Frieda arranged everything to her satisfaction atop the scarf, Mona began scattering the sage.

Todd sidled over to Ben as much to be close to the other man as to get out of Mona's way. "Do you know what any of this is for?" He watched the whole process in wary fascination.

Ben shook his head. "Only a little. Like I told you, Frieda handles this sort of thing. But I know a few things. I can explain if you want. I'm sure she'll correct me when I get something wrong."

"I always do." She shot him a playful smile.

"Thanks." He pointed to each item in turn. "The athame is a ritual blade for all big workings." He looked at her for confirmation.

"Go on," she said.

"The saltwater and sage are for purification. What's the incense?"

Frieda continued to organize, not looking up as she spoke. "Frankincense. It's for protection."

"I think the broom is for sweeping away old, negative energy patterns."

"Correct. You *do* listen to me," she teased.

"I don't know about the scarf or the candles or the jar of nails. Like I said, this isn't my mythology." Ben's tone was apologetic.

"That's okay," said Todd. "Right now, I'm for whatever mythology gets my life back to normal."

Finally satisfied, Frieda turned to Todd and Ben. "The scarf is my altar cover and therefore holy ground, so to speak. The jar of pointy things is to trap and shred negative energies in order to clear the path for the transitioning spirit."

"I like the idea of shredding that fucker's eternal spirit," said Mona, her expression grim.

"That's not exactly what I meant."

Todd shot his friend a cautionary and somewhat worried look. "Mona, did you catch some residual negativity from him when you stayed over? I know you despise him, but you've been especially vicious about it lately."

She met his gaze across the room. "I don't think so. I

just know that I've spent way too much of my own energy hating your father on your behalf. I know you never asked me to, but I could never help it. I want to see him well and truly gone from this world."

There was a charged silence while the two stared at each other across the room. Finally, Todd nodded once. "Me too."

Mona broke the tension with a grin. "Afterwards, I can get back to my usual light-bringing self."

Todd laughed. "I'd like that."

"Okay. Moving on," said Frieda. Todd and Mona both focused back on her.

"Sorry," he said. "Go ahead."

She picked up a tightly bound bundle of fresh and dried herbs and continued her explanations. "This is a smudge stick. It's got more sage, some cedar, lavender, and mugwort in it for purification. It's also good for freeing and releasing anything from a grudge to trapped spirits. It's gonna smell a little like pot, but there's no cannabis in it."

Todd wasn't sure if she was serious or pulling his leg, so he made no comment. He would almost have felt better if there were marijuana in the thing. At least then he could blame the drug for whatever weird shit went down tonight. Sort of, "Yeah, it was freaky, but we were stoned so it probably wasn't as weird as I thought it was." Instead, he was facing this exorcism completely sober. Deep down, he knew it would be better that way despite his uneasiness.

Frieda completed a few final adjustments, and Todd looked at everything as a whole for the first time. His table had gone from antique to apothecary to altar in a few short minutes. He almost laughed. Really. What *would* his mother say if she could see him now?

Despite his uncertainty about this whole endeavor, he had to ask one more question. He knew whatever

Frieda's answer was, it wouldn't change his mind about what had to happen. He just needed to know. "You're sure none of this is going to disturb the other ghosts in the house? I mean, I don't mind the spoon thing so much or the car radio."

Frieda gave him an encouraging smile, although her expression was tinged with doubt. "Honestly? I can't say with absolute certainty this won't affect them. We are very much focusing on your father's spirit, though, so the others shouldn't be too bothered by it. They might even appreciate having him gone."

"Theoretically."

"Theoretically," she echoed with a small nod.

Todd considered it and nodded. "Okay. I'll take the chance."

"If everyone will come fully into the room," Frieda said, "we can start." They all shifted so they were standing around the table, Ben and Todd in between the table and the china cabinet, Mona with her back to the bay window, and Frieda at the end of the table nearest the living room and the switch for the chandelier. "All right, we're ready to go dark."

Ben handed her a box of matches, and with her free hand she reached out and shut off the lights. She began lighting candles that had been placed at five points, with a sixth one in the center.

"October is the dying time. Worlds separated by invisible barriers bend close to one another as Samhain and the New Year approach. Death by its nature must lead us to rebirth. There is no ending in Earth's cycles, only a changing of season from winter to spring, summer to fall. We sow and we reap so that we may feast and sow again. Thus it is with the spirit as it is with the flesh. That which has fallen must continue on its path, turning in cycle to the next stage of existence."

Candles alight, she lit the incense, letting it burn for a

moment before blowing out the flame to allow it to smolder fragrantly in the cauldron. Next, she lifted the bowl of saltwater and the unsheathed athame, using the blade to stir the water three times counterclockwise. She returned the athame to the altar.

Dipping her fingers into the saltwater, she dashed some at each of them and then proceeded to do the same to the doorways and the window. The others stood where they were while she circled the room, once again in a counterclockwise direction, and returned to her place at the end of the table. She set down the bowl and reached for the smudge stick. Lighting it from the center candle, she allowed it to flame before blowing it out as she had the incense. She waved the bundle gently, spreading the purifying smoke throughout the room.

She was right. It did smell like pot. *Pot and lavender,* thought Todd. It was strange and at the same time calming.

Frieda spoke again, raising the smudge stick aloft like a torch. "We seek to open a door to allow a traveler to continue on his way in life's eternal cycle. We seek contact with the traveler that we may aid him in his journey. Andrew Brian Marks. Andrew Brian Marks. Andrew Brian Marks. We summon you."

The triple repetition of his father's name caused Todd to shiver. A mix of fear, anticipation, and disgust twisted his guts. He felt a large, warm, reassuring hand slip into his own, and he gave Ben a grateful look he hoped the other man could make out in the candlelight.

Frieda was silent for several seconds. The tension in the air was as palpable as the mingled scents of incense and herbs as they waited for something to happen.

"Andrew Brian Marks, come forth. Make your presence known."

Another long minute ticked past.

"Andrew Brian Marks," Frieda said again more firmly.

"Come forth!"

It was Mona's gasp that alerted them. Todd shot her a quick look and then followed her wide-eyed stare to the far end of the table. The place there was no longer empty. A shadow filled it. Not seated but seeming to stand in the same space as the chair. The anger rolling off it was stifling, like an overheated room with no ventilation.

Todd glanced at Ben whose expression was as closed as he'd ever seen it, and then to Frieda who, inexplicably, was smiling.

"Welcome," she said.

That wouldn't have been Todd's greeting of choice. His first thought was to hurl a curse at his father's eternal soul. That was one of the many reasons why he wasn't running things tonight.

"Andrew, this is no longer your world. It's time for you to move on. We wish to aid you in your journey."

The temperature in the room dropped to a chilling degree. Even the candles seemed to burn cold. No warmth emanated from their glowing flames. Todd shivered again and he saw Mona wrap her arms around herself, rubbing her hands briskly up and down the sleeves of her cotton cardigan.

Frieda appeared unfazed, but Todd realized she had come prepared. He'd wondered about her choice of a heavy wool sweater on what had been as warm a day as Ben had predicted. Now he understood.

"Is there anything you wish of us as you depart?"

Why had she asked him that? Couldn't she feel the malevolence spewing out at them? Todd seethed with it, his free hand balling into a fist at his side. His heart raced as irritation and anger spread through him. His breathing deepened and increased in speed. The stink of bottom-shelf gin and cheap cigarettes filled his nostrils, cloying and clinging to the back of his throat.

Frieda continued to try communicating with his

father's spirit. Her words became meaningless to him as the rage inside him grew. Jesus fucking Christ! Why couldn't she just shut the hell up and get on with it? All her pointless chatter was infuriating! What the fuck was she waiting for? How could she stand there talking to it like that? Why didn't she just open this goddamned door she kept going on about and kick his father's ethereal ass through it?

She didn't understand how dangerous he was, how much he hated women. She should know better, damn it! He'd attacked her twice already! What made her think she could reason with him? You *couldn't* reason with him! He wouldn't listen. He would only strike out again and again and again! She had to stop talking! Todd wanted to reach out and grab her and shake some sense into her.

A squeeze of Ben's warm hand in his own startled him from his roiling and raging thoughts. He looked to his right to see Ben staring at him, eyes glittering, and this time his gaze was open and unguarded, offering stability and sanity in the morass of fury that threatened to overwhelm him.

Then, as if they weren't in the middle of an exorcism, as if Todd wasn't being emotionally poisoned by his father's spirit, as if it were the most natural thing in the world to do, Ben leaned in and placed a soft kiss on Todd's lips.

Like a tub with the plug suddenly pulled, the anger drained out of him, washed away by the tenderness of Ben's kiss. Todd was floating on opalescent clouds, buoyed by gentle strength and an inner peace he knew was no more his own than was the fury it replaced. But that didn't stop him grabbing it and hanging on for all he was worth.

Frieda's voice came to him as if from a great distance. Her words made sense once again.

"Andrew Brian Marks, your time on this plane has ended."

Ben released Todd from the kiss, but its effects remained through the connection of their clasped hands. Todd smiled at him, grateful, and returned his attention to the ceremony.

"The door is open to the next realm. Pass through and find peace."

Blue candle flames flickered in a sudden gust of icy wind that emanated from everywhere and nowhere.

The shadow at the head of the table remained unmoving and malevolent.

"Pass through and find peace!" repeated Frieda, kind yet firm.

The wind picked up, sending smoke from the incense and smudge stick swirling thickly about them.

"Pass through and find peace!"

As the wind increased, whipping at their hair and tugging at their clothes, Frieda's volume rose. "Pass through and find peace!" She looked at the others, urging them to join her.

Mona was the first of them to shout it. "Pass through and find peace!" Todd could practically hear the unspoken epithet he knew she wanted to hurl after it.

Behind him, Todd felt as much as heard the china cabinet rattling and prayed it and its contents would remain intact.

Ben was next to join in Frieda's chant, then finally Todd. They were all shouting it, overlapping and out of synch. Shouting at the specter like a bunch of lunatics.

Swirling with the smoke, the thing finally rose, spiraling up to hover like a storm cloud around the chandelier, causing the fixture to sway and shake. Todd had a moment of terror that the ghost might tear it down, sending it crashing onto the table, shattering light bulbs and glass shades and sending shrapnel flying to tear through mortal flesh. His heart raced again, this time with fear. His breath was short and shallow. Was the air in the room being sucked out? He had a sudden flashback to his childhood, riding in his father's car down the freeway, his head out the window like a dog, his breath being torn from him by the speed at which they drove. Wild-eyed, he looked around to find that Ben and Mona were in the same predicament, gasping for air. Only Frieda seemed to be able to catch a decent breath to keep shouting. The rest of them were forced to choking silence.

"Pass through and find peace!"

Faster and faster the dark shadow spun. The candles went out as one, robbed of oxygen or blown out, Todd couldn't guess which. And still Frieda continued her mantra.

"Pass through and find peace! Pass through and find peace!"

A sound like the crash of thunder, waves against a stone cliff, trees being ripped from the earth, a landslide, and an avalanche all at once echoed through the room. It beat against their senses, deafening them, making them cringe and wince and cover their ears.

"Pass through and find peace!"

All at once there was nothing. Silence and stillness. The heavy hush was almost as painful as the noise that preceded it.

For several moments, Todd wondered if he had been struck deaf. Did your ears ring if you were deaf?

And then Frieda spoke. Her voice was tired and ragged, but he could hear her clearly through the ringing. "So mote it be." She picked up the jar of pins and nails and screwed on its lid. She relit the candles, which burned warmly once again. When the center one was burning well, she used it to drip hot wax around the rim of the jar, sealing it securely. Placing the candle back where it belonged, she said, "October is the dying time. A time for quiet reflection and preparation. The seasons change, ever circling. Life and death and life again." She picked up the broom and handed it to Todd.

"What do I do?" he asked as he took it from her. His voice sounded unnaturally loud even though he knew he was whispering.

"Sweep all around the doorways and the window. It's okay if you disturb the sage branches."

Feeling foolish despite everything they'd just been through, he did as she directed. She spoke while he swept.

"Old energy is swept away. Negative patterns are banished." She raised the smudge stick again and waved it about, swirling fragrant smoke as she had when they began.

Todd finished sweeping around the big bay window. Before he could retake his place, Frieda said, "Open the window, please. We need to release the smoke so it can take any residual negative energy away."

He handed the broom to Mona. "Would you?" She took it with a silent nod. "Thanks." Todd threw open the windows, and they all shivered as the night air swept in. The candles flickered again but this time remained lit. Todd retook his place with the others at the table. Without thinking, he reached out to Ben and grasped his hand once more.

Frieda continued as the stuffy dining room was refreshed by cool, clean, autumnal air. "This space is cleansed as are we all. May our positive energy fill us and all we encounter. Merry meet, and merry part, and merry meet again. So mote it be."

"So mote it be," echoed Mona.

Todd muttered an instinctive, "Amen."

Frieda put the still smoldering smudge stick in the

cauldron with the incense and placed the heavy lid on the cast iron pot. She snuffed the candles in the reverse order from which she had lit them. They all stood in the quiet darkness for several moments, no one inclined to move or speak.

Todd could feel the peace and calm that filled both him and the house. It felt lighter. *He* felt lighter. A weight had been lifted from his chest. He no longer felt the bitterness and guilt that had become such constant, quiet companions in his heart and mind that he'd all but forgotten they were there. He almost laughed with relief. Was this what his mother had meant all those times she'd spoken to him about forgiveness?

"I'm going to turn the lights on," Frieda said in a near whisper. "Mona, would you close the window?"

While Mona went to shut and lock the bay window, Frieda raised the light level in the room slowly. Todd was glad for the dimmer switch he'd installed. It allowed everyone's eyes to adjust gradually to the change.

He reluctantly released his grip on Ben's hand as the lights came up, unsure how Ben would feel if the others noticed their small yet intimate physical connection. Ben gave his fingers a reassuring squeeze before letting go.

It occurred to Todd that he was being silly. He was worried about holding hands now when their friends had seen the two of them kiss just a few minutes ago. Or maybe they hadn't seen. There'd been a lot going on at the time.

Frieda smiled at him. "How do you feel?"

"Better. Definitely better," Todd answered with equal parts relief, surprise, and exhaustion. The tension that had held them all, the power of the ritual that had connected them, broke. As one they relaxed, smiling at each other. Mona spontaneously hugged Frieda, who looked briefly stunned before hugging her back.

"That was amazing!" she exclaimed with a breathless laugh. Todd couldn't help but echo it.

Frieda grinned at them all. "I fucking *love* October!"

Chapter 27

IT HAD BEEN A BLESSEDLY ORDINARY WEEK SINCE THE transition ceremony with only a few pleasant exceptions. Mona's new industrial mixer had been delivered on Tuesday, much to her delight, and she'd promptly inaugurated it by making Todd's favorite whole wheat cinnamon rolls—without raisins, just as they should be. On Wednesday evening, Todd discovered the return of his good Norwegian silver spoons. As a reward to the ghost responsible, on Thursday he brought home two old-fashioned collectible spoons he'd found at Goodwill. One had Mount Rushmore on it, the other a picture of Shakespeare. They had disappeared before he'd even had time to clean the tarnish off them. Now if he could just learn the name of that particular ghost, he would be content. As long as they stayed on friendly terms, he didn't mind the company of disembodied spirits.

To top off the good week, the Mariners had won the American League Championship. Todd was still on cloud nine over it. He hadn't stopped grinning for three days. For the first time in its history, his team was going to the World Series!

It was about fucking time.

He stared at the two tickets in his hand. They were for game one of the Series. Ready cash and some old business connections had scored him the coveted seats. They weren't behind home plate or anything as glamorous as that, but they *were* on the 200 level of the ballpark, where people came to your seat to take your order for Ivar Dogs and overpriced beer, and then brought the food to you. You could even watch the game from inside when it got too cold, which in late October was likely, especially when the day was as clear as today. When it came down to it though, he'd have been happy with nose-bleed or bleacher seats. The game itself and the person joining him for it were more important than where he sat.

But he was still glad to have such fantastic seats.

"Todd!"

He looked up from where he leaned against the big bronze mitt sculpture outside the ballpark, and his face split into a grin. He waved at Ben through the thick crowd of baseball fanatics. The two of them were crazy early for the first pitch, but so was everyone else. Historic occasions did that to people.

He stood up straight as Ben wound his way through the throng.

"Hey there!" Todd greeted him with a smile.

"Hi! Wow!" Ben looked around him in awe. "I've never been down here on game day before. This is *nuts!*"

"You've *never* been to a game?" Todd could hardly believe it.

"No."

"Not even back when they played in the Kingdome?"

Ben shook his head and buried his hands in the pockets of his wool jacket.

"I thought you grew up here."

"That doesn't make me an automatic fan. The only sport my folks watched was golf."

"Why does anyone watch golf?"

"I have no idea." Ben gave the giant bronze mitt a closer look. "This is cool!"

"Wait until you get inside the park. I admit I voted

against the taxes to build it, but at least they did a good job with it. And now that the Mariners have made it to the World Series, in my opinion as a taxpayer, the team's earned it."

"And how many years did that take?"

Todd laughed. He could laugh about such things now that they were in the past. "Too damned many. Come on." They got into one of the many long lines entering through the large, left field gates, and Todd handed Ben a ticket. They made it through security and the press of people relatively quickly and climbed the steps up to the main concourse.

"Hey, you should know, we haven't had any luck identifying your spoon ghost," said Ben. "She could be a previous owner of the house or someone completely random who came in through you. Frieda says it may take a séance to figure it out."

"Maybe after the holiday season. I'm not in that much of a hurry to know." The idea of working more magic in his house right away did not appeal. He refocused on what really mattered today: baseball and Ben.

"You want a tour before we find our seats? There's an amazing glass sculpture in the home plate rotunda." He should calm down. Play it cool. He didn't want to come across as pushy or overeager. But then again, it was the freakin' *World Series*, and he was there with *Ben Chalfie* on a *real date*! He took a breath and let it out, trying to pull himself together without looking like he was trying to pull himself together. "Or we could grab a bite to eat if you're hungry. We might be early enough to score a table at the Hit It Here Café if we go straight there. Or the tacos at Edgar's Cantina are excellent. Or there's always the sushi. I love the Ichi-rolls they make." Jesus. Why didn't he just shut up?

Ben glanced at him with an amused and inquisitive look. "Sushi? With baseball? What happened to hotdogs and Cracker Jack?"

"This is Seattle."

Ben burst out laughing. That particular hearty and joyful laugh Todd had only heard him use once before in relation to something Frieda had done or said. Happy butterflies flitted around his stomach at the discovery that he too could elicit such a reaction.

"You're right!" Ben linked his arm with Todd's, surprising him. Ben grinned. "I'm not hungry yet, though. Let's get beers, then we can drink them while you show me around."

Todd wasn't sure wandering through the crazy pregame crowd carrying open containers of liquid was the best idea in the world, but he wasn't about to say no to anything Ben suggested tonight, no matter how long the night lasted.

They got a couple of microbrews, and Todd set out to show Ben all his favorite things about the park, from the enormous and elegant glass sculpture hanging over the inlaid terrazzo compass rose, to the life-sized statue of the late, great Dave Niehaus, to the team logos "quilts" made of pop cans, old license plates, and found metal items.

Ben looked at the quilts with wide eyes. He opened his mouth and closed it again without speaking. Todd wondered if the look was awestruck or appalled. He couldn't quite tell, and he had to know.

"What do you think?"

Ben glanced at him and looked back at the quilts. "I love this! It's industrial and rustic at the same time. I think they're fantastic!"

"Good. I love them too, but they're not everyone's thing."

"But they're brilliant! Show me more!" Ben linked their arms again and with his other hand raised his beer and took a drink.

"You know," said Todd as he continued to play tour guide, leading Ben to the escalator. "I can't thank you enough for what you and Frieda did for me."

"It was mostly Frieda," said Ben dismissively.

The escalator dumped them off on the 300 level and Todd took the opportunity to guide Ben over to the railing, out of the way of the growing crowds and potentially prying ears. They stood side by side and leaned on the rail, sipping their diminishing beers and looking out over the city. The urban skyline was laid out before them—a clear, pale blue sky over dark water and orange dock cranes; the architectural mishmash of buildings, some more picturesque than others; and the ever-present traffic. Still, it was his city, and he found it especially beautiful tonight.

It was colder and windier up here, but that only enhanced the feeling of privacy as they huddled close to one another. Wind whipped at Ben's short hair, and Todd thought he might surprise him later and buy him a logo knit cap to keep him warm. Todd hoped Ben had brought some gloves since it was likely to get seriously chilly. But of course, he realized, Ben knew better than anyone what the weather was going to do. So why hadn't he worn a hat? The sun hadn't quite set yet, but it was cool enough that Todd was almost ready to pull his own knit hat from his pocket and put it on.

He forced himself to set aside trivial thoughts about chilly ears and cold fingers and returned to the subject that had been on his mind since Saturday night's ceremony.

"No, it wasn't." At Ben's inquisitive glance, Todd went on. "I know Frieda ran the ceremony. I wouldn't be free of my father's ghost without her help, but..." He took a steadying breath, trying to control a feeling of gratitude so heartfelt he suspected Ben would be made uncomfortable by it. But Todd needed to say what was in his heart.

His voice was low, and he looked into his half-finished beer. "I was starting to lose control of myself. I've always fought my own short temper, and the addition of my father's anger was dragging me into a very dark place. I couldn't get out of it on my own." He turned to see Ben watching him with attention free of anticipation. As though whatever Todd might say, Ben would hear it through without judgment.

"I don't know what would have happened if you hadn't been there for me." Todd lowered his voice again, although no one was near to overhear him. "If you hadn't kissed me, I don't think I'd have survived. I don't think I would have died. I just mean... I don't know exactly, but I think I wouldn't be here if it weren't for you. Thank you." It was wholly inadequate, but how could you ever repay someone for saving you from a paranormal abyss of violence and rage?

Ben smiled, and the warmth of it lit his eyes, making them glitter like royal-cut sapphires. "You're welcome. I'd do it again without hesitation." Now his smile grew slightly sly and he leaned in a little closer. "Next time I kiss you, though, I'd rather there weren't so many distractions."

Todd's heart did a happy little leap, and he smiled back with a hint of the same wry humor. "That's going to be a problem as long as we're here." He made a show of looking around the busy concourse with its fans and food vendors, closed-circuit televisions, and souvenir stands. "Way too many distractions."

"I hope I'm not going to have to wait until the whole World Series is over."

"I promise you, I can't wait that long."

"They don't have a kiss cam here, do they?" Ben was only half joking.

"No."

"That's a shame."

"Of course, if we win tonight's game, all bets are off, kiss cam or not."

"All the more reason to root for the home team."

"You'd better!"

Ben laughed his wonderful laugh again. "I will. I promise!"

"We should find our seats. Are you hungry yet?"

"No."

"Okay. This way. Back down to the 200 level."

Most of the pregame festivities had concluded by the time they reached their seats. They both spent a few minutes simply admiring the view of the field while the players were announced. The roof was retracted, revealing another view of the city skyline and the setting sun in a nearly cloudless sky.

Todd quoted one of his favorite catch phrases. "It's a beautiful night out for baseball."

Ben nodded and took another drink of his beer. "It will be all week."

Todd was about to say more when the PA announcer interrupted. He had to wait while everyone stood up and listened or sang along while the octet from the Seattle Choral Company sang the National Anthem.

In the shuffle of everyone sitting down, Todd said uncertainly, "So, I was thinking about my season tickets for next year. They have a sixteen-game package I usually get. I know you're not a huge baseball fan, but I was wondering... What if I got two?"

Ben's reply was gratifying in its swiftness. "I'd love it!"

"Great! You're sure Frieda won't be too jealous?"

"She'll get over it if you take her to a game against the Yankees."

"I can do that."

A cheer rocked the ballpark, matching Todd's mood perfectly. They rose to their feet with everyone else and looked around.

"What happened?" Ben shouted over the noise.

It took Todd only a moment to sort out what was going on. "One pitch, one out! Sweet! That's how you start the World Series!"

Ben laughed. "If this is what it sounds like when the game is just beginning, I'm a little scared of what will happen if we win."

"*When* we win," Todd corrected him as they retook their seats. "You have to keep a positive mindset. Think good thoughts for the outcome." He looked into Ben's eyes, and their gazes locked. For that one moment, they could have been anywhere in the world with no one around and nothing to distract them. "I, for one, can't wait to find out what happens next."

Mona's Whole Wheat Cherry Almond Scones

3/4 cup whole wheat flour
3/4 cup all-purpose flour
1-1/2 tsp baking powder
1/4 tsp kosher salt
1/4 cup granulated sugar, plus extra for sprinkling
1/4 cup unsweetened dried Bing cherries, roughly chopped
1/4 cup (~1 ounce) toasted slivered almonds
3 Tbs chilled unsalted butter
2/3 cup cold milk, plus extra for brushing
1/4 tsp almond extract

Pre-heat oven to 350F. Line baking sheet with parchment paper.

Mix flours, baking powder, salt, and sugar. Cut in butter.* Rub cherries with a bit of flour. Add them and the almonds. Add extracts to milk. Mix in milk a little at a time until dough comes together to form a ball. (You might have a little leftover. That's okay.) Turn out onto floured board and knead 3 or 4 times. Shape into a rough ball, flatten to roughly 1-1/2 inches thick, and cut into 6 or 8 wedges. Transfer wedges to parchment-lined baking sheet.

Optional: Brush tops of scones with a bit of milk and sprinkle with sugar.

Bake 18 to 20 minutes, turning pan halfway through to ensure even baking.

*Mona's tips:
Use a cheese grater to grate in chilled butter for more even distribution. If grating in the butter, add the cherries and almonds to the flour mixture first.

Midnight Jones Soundtrack

Music plays a significant role in the PUPI universe. These are the songs mentioned in this book. I recommend listening to them all wherever you like to stream your tunes and purchasing the ones you love from your preferred music retailer.

Lennon, John / McCartney, Paul. *Please Please Me.* London: Parlophone, 1963. The Beatles.

Hewson, Paul David / Clayton, Adam / Evans, Dave / Mullen, Larry. *Sunday Bloody Sunday.* Dublin: Island Records, 1983. U2.

Gluck Jr., John / Gold, Wally / Wiener, Herbert / Gottlieb, Seymour. *It's My Party.* Manhattan: Mercury Records, 1963. Lesley Gore.

Lewis, Edna / Ross, Beverly. *Judy's Turn to Cry.* Manhattan: Mercury Records, 1963. Lesley Gore.

Wilson, Brian Douglas / Christian, Roger. *Little Deuce Coupe.* Hollywood: Capitol Records, 1963. The Beach Boys.

Gore, Martin. *Waiting for the Night.* Milan, Gjerlev, London, New York: Mute, 1990. Depeche Mode.

Brel, Jacques / McKuen, Rod. *Seasons in the Sun.* San Francisco: Capitol Records, 1963. The Kingston Trio.

Edwards, Michael. *Right Here, Right Now.* London: Food, 1991. Jesus Jones.

Author's Notes and Acknowledgements

It's been a long road for this book from its origins as my third NaNoWriMo novel, written primarily in November of 2008. In many ways, Seattle and the world have changed significantly; for one round of edits I had to replace all the flip-phones, and IM is a thing of the past. In other ways, things remain stubbornly the same; the Mariners still haven't been back to the postseason, and traffic in town is terrible.

Many friends have stepped up over the years to act as alpha- and beta-readers, and I'd be remiss if I didn't thank them. So, thank you, **Susan**, for standing behind this book, and series, from page one. After me, you're probably the person who's read it the most. I wouldn't be here without you. Thanks, **Janet**, for your knowledge of classic VW Beetles and your offer to join you in front of your big-screen TV whenever the Ms finally reach the World Series. (Someday, someday...) Thank you, **Kati**, for being the best critique partner a chick could ask for even when I switch genres on you. Thanks, **Jenny**, for your multifaceted feedback—writerly, witchy, and bakery. Finally, thank you, **Dave**, for your enthusiastic support of the story and particularly of Danny's character. We <3 Danny!

I originally wrote *Midnight Jones* as a love letter to Seattle. A lot of that was lost over the course of edits, but I hope at least a little of my love for my flawed and beautiful city still comes through.

About the Author

Maia Strong lives in Seattle, WA, where she enjoys acting, aerial circus, bellydancing, and baking. When she's not writing, she works in local theatre, watches lots of sci-fi TV shows and police procedurals, and hangs out with her husband and cat. She loves men's baseball, women's basketball, daffodils, grey skies, Shakespeare, travel, and a damned fine cup of coffee.

Also by Maia Strong

The Ballad of Jimothy Redwing
Client Privileges
Compass Hearts
Rose & Thorn

False Dawn

Gearheart

You can find her online on at
www.maiastrong.com
Instagram: @maiastrong01
Twitter: @maiastrong01
Facebook: https://www.facebook.com/MaiaStrong/

Made in the USA
Columbia, SC
08 February 2025

52873348R00186